To Lindsay
Thank ~~you for your~~
on going Support ...
All the best
Jim

What if you had a secret that could change the world forever…

[signature] 2022

Other Books by Jim Ody

The Place That Never Existed
A Cold Retreat
Beneath The Whispers
…Just South of Heaven
Noah's Lament
Mr Watcher
The Revenge of Lisa Lipstick

Lost Connections

?
Question Mark Press

All rights reserved. No part of this publication may be reproduced, distributed or transmitted in any form or by any means, without prior written permission.

First published in 2015 by Hambrook Press
Second edition in 2016 by Hambrook Press
Third edition in 2017 by Zombie Cupcake Press
Fourth edition in 2018 by Crazy Ink
This edition published in 2019 by Question Mark Press

Copyright © 2019 by Jim Ody

?
Question Mark Press

This is a work of fiction. Names, characters, places, and incidents are a product of the author's imagination. Locales and public names are sometimes used for atmospheric purposes. Any resemblance to actual people, living or dead, or to businesses, companies, events, institutions, or locales is completely coincidental.

Lost Connections Jim Ody. – 5th edition
ISBN: 9781713414421
Cover design by: Emmy Ellis @ Studioenp

For Kara, Leena, Jessie & Rocky, the inspiration behind these words.

Prologue

Diagonal rays of light cut through the room, emitting dancing sprites of dust from the window to the wooden floorboards. The air was thick with nostalgia— a mix of smells, each projecting an abundance of memories for me in a house that had been in my family for nearly two hundred years.

I had procrastinated long enough that now there were financial implications to hanging onto my childhood house in the Wiltshire countryside. I admit, whilst the thought of living here filled me with dread, there was also something darkly magical about it— an unshakable folly deeply rooted in my past that I had trouble letting go from my life. But clarity can be born of time, and with recent events it had become wise to close up this chapter and bury it away forever.

My thirteen-year-old daughter Daisy was sweeping the path from the front door leading out towards the long driveway. I am incredibly lucky to have her, and despite entering into her teenage years, she is of little bother to me. Placid and bright, she shines amongst the clouds of life quite spectacularly, existing in a world full of joy, almost dismissive of any negativity. Considering the stormy relationship between her mother and me, this is quite remarkable.

I was busy searching high and low for the key to my father's study. I had officially owned this house now for a couple of years, but had never opened up this important room. Of late, everything led me to believe that there was something important behind this old study door. I wanted it to remain as I remembered and longed for it not to be relevant in my future. The past should remain just that, but I was only beginning to take my first steps into letting it go.

My father was a complex man, and therefore it is of no surprise to me that the simple task of unlocking an old door has now become likened to searching for the Holy Grail.

I looked again at the handful of papers left for me that hinted at clues. Again, I wondered why a simple key-press was not sufficient in this instance like normal people would've decided upon. I had been hard at it for an hour, and had succeeded in finding four clues, each which should lead to the next. I cannot relay my disappointment in the fact my father, after compiling this elaborate key-finding treasure hunt, would not be confident in my code-cracking capabilities. The pity in me evident as I glance over a 'hint-sheet' devised especially for me. It may as well have the words: "An Idiot's Guide To Finding This Easy Treasure For My Stupid Son" on the cover.

It took me ten more frustrating minutes before I was thumbing through the aforementioned guide trying to decipher just what the Hell he was going on about. His eccentricities bypassed me, and whilst they appear charming to some, for me they're the root of much annoyance. *Here's an idea old man,* I pondered*: One key for one lock. And no bloody puzzles!*

Just what the heck was he hiding back there?

I was busy tentatively pushing the floorboards of the lounge floor down, where according to the manual, one was to pop back up or release some sort of mechanism. So immersed was I in an amateur Indiana Jones fantasy that I hardly even registered the sound of a vehicle pulling up outside. It was only when I heard voices that I made my way out to see who it was.

As a father, one thing you recognise instantly is that feeling that something just isn't right. There was something in the way that Daisy was standing there that told me she was uncomfortable. She is normally fearless, brimming with confidence, but here she stood rigid, wringing her hands together in a nervous manner that I'd only seen a handful of times previously.

"I don't know what you are talking about," my daughter was saying to a guy sat in a slightly battered white Ford Transit van. The man had opened his door and was walking around the side with a cold-hard stare as he replied, "Don't mess around with us." At which point he noticed me.

"Can I help you?" I asked, although just the very nature of the scene in front of me made me want to attack him. To protect my daughter in any which may deem necessary. Then I saw another guy with dark glasses on was also in the van. He was watching my every step whilst putting something in his ears.

The stocky driver with his short-cropped hair and a flabby jawline said, "Eddie! I'm a friend of your father's. He has something of mine that I need back." This came out as one long rhetorical statement, and all I could think about was how they were both closer to my daughter than I was.

"My father is dead," I replied. "So unless it's buried with him, then I don't see how I can help."

The driver smiled, but there was little or no amusement in it. He pulled on some sunglasses with wraparound elastic instead of arms, and replied, "Okay, let's not piss about now. We both know your father's coffin is empty – in fact there is no coffin under the plot, am I right?"

"What's your point?" I asked and threw a glance to Daisy. She turned to me as the driver also placed something in his ears. Just as I was about to shout to Daisy, the driver rolled something small, black, and solid along the ground towards me. Before I could register it, my whole world exploded into a brilliant white light.

For approximately five long seconds, I was lost in a white world with no sound. I felt a burning sensation on my leg and on my right side, and my breathing was heavy with panic. Stunned on the ground, I laid facedown, and through bleary eyes I turned and saw the van leaving in a cloud of smoke.

My daughter was nowhere to be seen.

Still deaf, the bottom dropped out of my world.

Chapter One

Friday: The Day Before

The late afternoon sun still shines brightly, giving off a heat that's in equal parts impressive and oppressive. The British summer has an awkward tendency of switching between thunderous humidity, utopian blue skies, and sporadic heavy rainfall, posing some to wistfully question whether a higher power is rolling a meteorological dice.

A welcome breeze dances playfully over my arms. Any goosebumps are well hidden under sleeves of bright tattoos, and whilst their appearance will have tongues tripping over many derogatory words quite unapologetically, I like to think of myself as a one-man crusade, knocking down the stereotypical walls, proving that tattoos, crime, and thuggery are not synonymous with each other.

It is at this time the school kids meander home in the contrary fashion of youth. Laughing at inconsequential observations, whilst the older teens are either stone-faced and self-absorbed, or happy and carefree– some plotting unspoken acts that will have parents nursing migraines and stomach ulcers until the end of time.

The slightly haunting echo of Tammy Wynette can be heard bouncing over the invisible airwaves as she suggests we all '*Stand by your man,*' which itself is slightly comical as the owner of the said musical graffiti is my neighbour Miss Chambers, a deaf old spinster that to my knowledge has not stood by a man for any length of time since we had a King in charge of the monarchy. Any man since has understood immediately with sixth sense capabilities that his longevity in life may very well rapidly decrease if he does not turn on clicked heels and run for the proverbial hills forthwith. It is possible that at some period of time, she was a Hell-Raiser, (there is a playful meanness in her eyes) and I hold this hope dear to my heart, but I have no doubt she is a woman not to be crossed. My guess is that whilst she is certainly old, the cantankerous old maid would most likely scare the Grim Reaper into leaving her be for a little while longer. Bizarrely, she says I'm a Nazi because of my inked skin, and once told me that if she'd known the future would hold the likes of me in it, then she wouldn't have bothered to help win the war. These flippant comments would have you believe that she won the war single-handedly, when I could believe it is more likely that she barked orders to army sergeants with more influence than Winston Churchill himself.

I'm certainly no expert, but I would think she enjoys our verbal duelling; it's what keeps her alive. Thinking up insults which she executes with a grin and could be construed as playful banter. I'm like the wayward grandson she never had, but takes upon herself to scold and ridicule with much aplomb.

Some days we both sit out on our weather-beaten porches staring at each other. Possibly sharing a bond of being the only two buildings of un-British house design sat at the end of a cul-de-sac that boasts other larger, if not slightly more boring homes. Our natural shabby-chic could also be construed as quirky, rundown, and tired against the well-maintained facades of the rest of the street.

When I'm feeling slightly spiteful, I'll raise a hand and wiggle my fingers in a camp wave and then flex my levator labii superioris muscle that turns a lop-sided smile on my face into a crazed sneer. Some days she's been known (quite un-lady-like, I might add) to give me the finger, and I'd suggest American television has a lot to answer for.

I also remember the time that she threw dog poo over the hedge at me, saying aggressively that I could have it back. I don't own a dog, and neither does she, so God knows where she got a fist-full of canine faeces from. However, today she is nowhere to be seen, and I wonder whether she has spied me out here trying to enjoy a moment's tranquillity and thus taken it upon herself to turn the speakers to her record-player up as loud as they will go so as I too can endure Ms Wynette's powerful lungs in all of their glory. I'd wager that whilst Miss Chambers may agree with the 'First Lady of Country Music' that it is indeed sometimes hard to be a woman, I am certainly not the man in question that she would stand by.

I take a deep breath and try to ignore the Mississippi-born singer.

Like most fathers, I swell with pride when I see my daughter skipping up the road towards me. Daisy is thirteen and the proverbial apple-of-my-eye, even with the local preacher in tow as a chaperone. I was expecting my estranged ex-girlfriend to be returning my daughter to me after she'd taken her out for one of her few and far between visits. Even if this was just to pick her up early from school and grab a milkshake. I was geared up for a couple of rounds of verbal sparring which I'd most likely later regret, so to have the local preacher instead was neither a worry nor a relief. Part of me might even go as far as saying that the two were polar opposites. Miss Chambers is fond of the preacher, which I use as my own entertainment. Right in front of me I can see the forces of good and evil battling with each other.

"Hey, Pops," Daisy smiles as she always does with her cheeky slice of irony. "Why are you looking so sad?"

"Your mother seems to have morphed into a preacher. I don't remember her being that ugly. Has she finally filed away her horns and sawn up her forked tongue?"

"You're silly, Dad," she giggles. "Jean was late for some meeting some place."

Whilst I try not to show any anger towards my ex, Jean, I let a glance up to heaven escape. "Why didn't she ring me then? I could've picked you up."

Daisy shrugged like it wasn't anything to worry about. However, any father of a young girl will tell you, his daughter walking anywhere on her own is a grave cause for concern. She lovingly touches my shoulder and heads into the house, whistling to Tammy bloody Wynette, whilst I'm faced with the cold-hard stare from Father Dugan. He's a man of large stature with a clipped white beard and a voice that's a gentle but forceful whisper. I've known him for as long as I could remember. "Evening, Ed," he says succinctly, raising a hand just in case I'm deaf as well as dumb.

"Evening, Father," I reply, looking up like a child awaiting a scolding from a parent or school master. However, the truth of the matter is we dance this masquerade in perfect time. We've a relationship that others would look upon as strange. Father Dugan had been my grandad's best friend. Although they argued and appeared to hate each other, they hid the fact they had a deep and mutual respect. When the sands of my grandad's life suddenly emptied through a large hole made by cancer a couple of years ago, Father Dugan started helping me look after Daisy, and whilst the two of us bickered, he's my best babysitter by a long shot. He actually fully understands me and knows I need the arguments and friction in our relationship so as to keep us from being too close. He's astute enough to know that I hold him in high regard and have a fondness of his company and, like my granddad, a deep respect I will never fully show or outwardly admit to. Perhaps some of this is rooted in him knowing my family and the truth I've so long tried to bury– the skeletons he's helped to close the closet doors on.

"You should really come by some time, you know?" And I probably would if he was talking about his home and not that of the man upstairs.

He puts a hand on his hip that seemingly takes the load off. His waistline seems to be expanding more these days. I guess servants of the Lord eat well.

"The next time I have a free slot in my busy social calendar, I might just do that."

"I would bet your calendar is slightly more social than you, my boy."

"And I would bet you're not allowed to bet, Harry."

"I'm a new breed of Vicar. I have an iPod, an XBOX, and a Kindle, you know."

"You don't have an XBOX."

"I have a broken plastic thing with XBOX written on it."

"That's my old XBOX, you were going to fix."

"Possession is nine-tenths of the law and all that," he grins, fending off the comment with his hand. "That thing is past repairing."

I scratch my chin and before I can help myself, I turn into an arse, as I reply, "I was just wondering: has God got a Twitter account? Wouldn't that be a good way to get His message across?"

"Every time you mock me, it tells me more about your insecurities and your worries about life's offerings, as it does your need to be a smart-arse. You do realise that, huh?"

"Hashtag Passive-Aggressive," I mutter.

He grins, "LOL XD!"

I'm confused. "What does that mean?"

He chuckles, and shrugs. "I've no idea. I've heard Daisy say it!"

I smile at that. He knows me well. Once I again, I have no idea why I feel the need to say the things I did to him.

"You still going out tonight?" he asks in babysitter mode, which instantly put me at ease.

"That's the plan, Father. I have to warn you, I will be partaking in copious amounts of the Devil's Water tonight. I may be in need of a confessional tomorrow."

"Son, as sure as I have hair on my backside, you'll stumble in and tell me exactly what you think of the world – exactly the same as you do each and every time you drink."

"There is nothing wrong with a predictable drunk."

"That there isn't."

"And don't you be sneaking off next door to see your fancy lady," I add, but as soon as I say it, I wish I hadn't. Once again.

He smiles defeated, and just when I think he's going to say no more, adds, "She's a sweet lady." And then as an afterthought, "Although her musical taste is interesting."

When I've composed myself again, I say, "See you tonight Father."

"Good bye," he replies, raises a hand, and strides off.

Chapter Two

I took another gulp of the strong Columbian Suarez coffee. There were sweet caramel and chocolate undertones that lingered between mouthfuls. It was my preferred coffee. I'd picked up a new bag from Rave Coffee - an excellent specialist roaster a few miles away. This was a special time for me. Daisy was safe home from school and likes to have half an hour to 'de-student' herself (her phrase not mine), and so I enjoy a coffee and watch the world go by, collecting my thoughts and thinking about upcoming designs for my job.

I'm a tattooist by trade. My role is to talk, and be talked to, in order to relax a client. Some people are happy to blabber on to me for a couple of hours. Their nervous energy peaking whilst I unleash my creative juices over their skin. It is my job to transform their human canvass to something of either beauty, or some horrid idea of theirs into something mildly palatable on the eye. My expertise lies in bright colours and abstract interpretation on cartoonish reality. The style is called New School, and is known for thick black outlines, and bold bright colours that make the tattoo pop. I try to take even the most boring of objects and magic it into a fresh, artistic piece of fun.

I should've relocated to London years ago, but I love the fact that people make the effort to come all the way from the lengths and breadths of the country to collect my work on their person, and whilst I've won awards for my work, I prefer to base myself where I grew up. And do you know what? I'm just a country boy at heart.

Thornhill is a beautiful town in North Wiltshire a few miles from Royal Wootton Bassett and the city-like town of Swindon. Part of me enjoys the familiarity and daily habits of my life, but there is also another part that doesn't want to turn its back on my past, nor would I want to take Daisy away from here. To me, here is safe. It scares me when I think about my daughter and me living in a huge city. It just isn't happening.

I own the tattoo shop I work in, and jointly own a small but modest music venue with my friend, Jason. It's nothing fancy, but it draws the occasional known small band and gathers together potential clients. More importantly, it means I no longer work the hours I used to, but still make enough money to live off of. In some ways I've been lucky, but I guess even your wants and desires can become mundane when turned into routine. It doesn't mean you no longer enjoy them, but that you sometimes need the adrenaline rush of unpredictability to keep you on your toes, and let us be candid here – to keep you young.

Today, something extremely strange happened– something that has left me speechless and unsure of what to do.

I received in the post a short letter from my father.

My father has been missing for 10 years.

Officially, my he is dead, although his body was never found. His car was abandoned by the cliffs overlooking a small Cornish cove. Everything pointed to an accident rather than a suicide, but then unofficially– and seven years later officially– the verdict was 'death by misadventure,' and I inherited 'Caulfield Hall,' an elaborate large house that sits over the other side of Whitehorse Lake, a mile from where I now live.

Throughout my childhood, my father was an obsessed man. I didn't always know or, indeed, understand what held his attention so strongly, but he worked away in his study with an enthusiasm I've not seen in anyone since.

Most people think that he was an artist and somewhat of an inventor on the side. However, I knew him to be quite the opposite. His art was peddled out with little or no care – a safe style and medium that was popular and earned him more than a substantial wage to live on; however, this was not what he got up for at 5am. Nor was it what kept him locked away in his study until past midnight some days.

He produced no new painting when he missed my ninth birthday party, nor was he covered in paint when I found him asleep one Christmas morning. He was working on something, and this was the thing that was his biggest secret. I still wonder to this day whether it was this secret that was his downfall.

I was never close to my father, as he was caught up in his work, and I was an annoying distraction to him reaching his final goal. I never resented that, and even was jealous of his stubborn will to finish his work no matter what else in life got in the way. His work had no limits. But I never knew whether or not he reached his goal, and I suspected that one day he had an unrequited epiphany that perhaps he would never finish his work to the point that he so strived. I believe this was what drove him to the Cornish cove, and he threw in the towel for good. Without his work, what did he truly have? His family were no longer familiar to him– strangers under the same roof.

I believed he was dead. Or rather, I did, up until I received this letter.

My mother suffered the neglect of my father, and as a result started getting involved in groups and friends away from the family. She resented me and the burdened anchor that I'd become. I was a small needy human who kept her away from the fun she lost out on thanks to my father's neglect. Sometimes I was left to fend for myself whilst my mother left for weeks at a time, and my dad was locked up in his study like a hermit. After one particular disappearance, my mother decided not to return home at all. It wasn't long before my grandfather came and took me away to his house to live. Last I heard, my mother was in France living with a painter that actually enjoyed painting, and of course being showered with love and affection. I have no place in her heart anymore, nor she in mine. Just distant painful memories.

I thought about the authenticity of the letter from beyond the grave and wondered how this was so. Staring off to the larger houses either side of me, I had no definitive answer, just a whole bunch of theories and ideas.

I had to also consider the fact that my father may well be very much alive.

Chapter Three

Life is all about judgement, and today my timing and luck were not on the same team. I try not to stay out on the porch for too long for one big reason: my neighbour Jez.

He pulls up in his black company-leased Volvo V50 estate. He's waving so hard he's unable to turn the steering wheel properly and proceeds to clip his plastic recycling bin. This sending it rolling down the drive like some large cumbersome dice. Unperturbed by this, he's smiling so widely that I'm wondering whether I should pretend my phone is ringing and escape.

Jez is an over-excited person, with a wife with whom he doesn't get on most of the time, and somehow tries to live his excitement through me. Of all of the people in the entire world to be his hero, he has in a rather deluded way chosen me. He has the ability to see the brighter side of life like a naïve child. He's cheerfully innocent of my emotions, seeming not to take in the words I speak, or re-arranging them into a sentence better suited to what he thinks I might be saying. It probably doesn't help that I don't take him seriously. How can I? He looks like he's somehow fallen out of a cartoon and landed right next-door to me.

He's tall, and doesn't so much walk as lope from one foot to the other, with his long neck bent over as if trying to crouch apologetically from his six-foot-five frame towards me. His eyes permanently look tired, and he has a nose that's slightly too large for the rest of his face. He tries to hide his receding hairline by growing his hair a little longer and more floppy than suits him. He's best described as somewhat gawky, and with his dark plain suits, looks like a cross between an accountant and an undertaker.

Whilst I never encourage interaction between us, and even go as far as being as distant as I can, he maintains a lost puppy routine with me like I am some sort of Master and he a willing, apt pupil.

"Eddie, my man! How the Hell are you?" he says like he hasn't seen me in a month. He's forty-two, but speaks to me like we're college fraternity buddies, high-five-ing and belching out manly quotes and quips, recycled from movies that were amusing and palatable in youth, but in later years, slightly juvenile. He still thinks he's twenty, and is hanging on with dear life to anything that remotely resembles his teen years. Last week, he mentioned that he thought he could still get on an 18-30's holiday, and that we should book it. There are so many reasons why the suggestion is wrong that my brain has been overloaded with the inability to say only one reply. I'd love for him and a film crew to go ahead, book it, and show the world more reality-car-crash television.

I raise my mug, which is as much enthusiasm as I dare muster so as to keep things as brief as humanly possible, and this, to me, should speak volumes, but subtlety went AWOL on the day Jez queued up for it and he took an extra helping of regret that he tries to sugar-coat into it being a 'funny story' instead. "I'm drinking earlier each day, my friend." And whilst I know I am consuming coffee., Jez would assume it's generously laced with hard liquor. I am his comic-book hero, of course.

Jez works in IT for a large financial corporation in Swindon, and thinks that living next door to a tattooist somehow makes him cool. Next month he wants me to do his first tattoo. He said this to me last month. And the month before. And each month over the past three years, but of course next month never arrives. Jez loves to think that he is going to get a tattoo, which to him is halfway between being a blank (someone without a tattoo) and being inked (someone with a tattoo). There is something so innocent about Jez that you end up always feeling sorry for him, and I think that this is what I despise the most about him.

The problem is he tries to be nice, but it always ends up costing me. He's like my unlucky charm that will insist on following me around. He cooked me some burgers once, and I was so violently sick that I was sure Daisy would become an orphan. Another time, he said he could fix my TV aerial, and ended up slipping on the roof and pulling my guttering down. He was fine, which is more than can be said for the window that he put the ladder through. He had also dented my car, lost my phone, and given me an electric shock.

His house is slightly larger and certainly sturdier than mine, and he clearly had the third little pig as the chief architect, whereas mine is smaller and made of wood. You could say that I've had the metaphoric wolf trying to blow down my house for years. However, whilst it has twitched and creaked, so far the house has stood fast and has yet to fall down.

I take a deep breath of frustration, which of course will be construed as some Clint Eastwood aloofness, and look out at the houses in front of me filled with people getting on with their mundane lives, and for a second I feel a pang of jealousy.

"Life looks good on you, my friend," Jez states, embarrassing me with his fake social ass-kissing. We both know I look like shit. Even my daughter has started to comment. She asked me whether Tramp-chic was what I was aiming for only yesterday. I've no idea where she gets her quick-mouth from.

My neighbour and I couldn't be on further wavelengths if I was to move to Mars. Jez nods at my mug again. "Yeah," he sneered. "Have another of those hot dates with Ruby!" He finishes with a wink. He's a winker, you see— a nudger, a finger-pistol-drawer, a back-slapper, an arm-puncher, all of that, but mostly he's a winker. He also has a habitual misunderstanding of my melancholy. I feel like I carry the weight of the world on my shoulders, and yet all he sees is a silent debonair thoughtfulness he considers cool and unable to pull off himself. He has very limited feelings, and I assume this is why his wife thinks he's an arse.

I swallow another slug down, wishing I'd indeed laced my coffee with hard-liquor. "I can't say I will," I ponder, looking into the mug, fantasising on some level that it would swallow me up. "What with the fact that we're just friends. So unless I've drastically misread the signs, our 'hot dates,' as you refer to them, consist of two friends talking about *her* love life and our mutual love of music and tattoos." This was the truth. Ruby works in my studio and is a great friend who has the ability to choose the wrong man on increasing regularity, but I'm her safe male that wants nothing more than old-fashioned friendship. Jez can't understand why I'd want a female as a friend and not be constantly thinking up ways to take things further.

"Seems like a waste of time to me. Nice girl like that needs more than words!" He winked again. The day I look to Jez for advice will be the day I bathe in lighter fluid and dry myself off with candles.

"I'll keep that in mind."

I guess on some level, Jez and I are friends– the same level of friendship as the one I have with my dentist or the tax-man. Despite the fact he is a handful of years older than me, some days I feel like he's my stepson, and we've been thrown together threw situation. He's not someone I can fully shape and mould, but someone that I have to guide through life, a human-burden I have no recollection of requesting.

"I guess I'll see you later tonight, huh?" he said flashing teeth and dimples, which is his way of telling me he's going to gatecrash my night out. He loves turning up at the club, winking, finger pointing, and generally looking uncomfortable. In turn, and despite my best efforts, I end up either embarrassed or with him ruining my night. On occasion both.

"Really? You've been unleashed and allowed out on the prowl tonight then."

"Indeed I am. Gareth, Sonia, and a couple of others are meeting us for drinks. Should be a good night."

Gareth is Jez's mate from work who has the inability to smile and talks with an intensity that suggests either some conspiracy is happening around him, or he's about to end your life. The guy makes Jez look normal. Then there is poor Sonia, who gets dragged out on these strange escapades by the weird twins in a daft attempt to show the world that another woman can interact with them too. Sonia, however, is a naïve twenty-year-old that sees them as safe older-brother types. She is oblivious to any drunken advances that include pawing with sloppy-hugs or smelling of her blonde hair, assuming it to be part of their ways. The reference to 'a couple of others' actually means that there is no one else, but Jez assumes he will see at least one or two other people he knows, and so it may on some level of vagueness appear they're all together. Jez uses a logic that has no rules of normality.

"How's your wife?" I said, which usually shuts him up and sends him home. Instantly I paid for it as he jogged closer, presumably to be out of the hearing range of his spouse, and moved into my personal space. I hate that.

"Some days I'm the luckiest man alive, and then most days I wonder what the fuck I did wrong to end up with that moody bitch!" He half smiled, trying to conceal the serious undertone. He added, "You don't know how good you've got it, is all I'm saying."

I rubbed my chin, and felt like smashing his face into the wooden pillar. "Yep, I'm Mr Lucky," I corrected with little or no feeling. I don't mean to be mean, but it's not only Jez's wife that thinks he's an arse, and if you don't mind me being a little more candid, I'd go so far as saying he was a fucking idiot.

"Better to have lost in love and all of that stuff!" He fired a shot from his finger-pistol, and I have to wonder whether he has a license for that thing. I'm calm in the knowledge the safety is more than likely on. His hyper mood has returned now, although a strange look suddenly contorts his face as he looks behind me. The reason for this look is all too apparent as the strong voice of my other neighbour, Miss Chambers, starts up.

"Had some chaps looking for you," she said squinting with accusation. "Very rude, they were. I assumed they were family."

"Beautiful day, Miss Chambers. Did you get a name?"

"What? I'm your secretary now, am I?" She frowned dramatically. "They were asking about your father, no less, then about that fancy house of yours."

"I assume there were no contact details left?"

"You assume correctly." Blunt again.

"Did you give them my mobile number?" I said as straight faced as I could.

She straightened her blouse as she replied, "I don't know your mobile telephone number." This was her tell-tale sign of a lie.

"What about the time you texted me with the words, 'You are a Nazi?'"

She looked over my shoulder at Jez, who is convinced that at any moment she is going to turn him into a frog. She then tried to wave off the comment, "Oh, that. I'm a good judge of character."

And at that point, Jez pipes up with, "Nah, you like that German band Rammstein, don't you, Ed?" He is not someone I would ever turn to as a character witness.

"Ah ha!" She claps her hands louder than I'd ever have thought possible for an OAP and disappears, apparently victorious.

"That didn't help," I said to the dust left behind and shook my head.

He half smiled, a little embarrassed, when he agreed, "Yeah, as soon as I said it, I sorta realised. I don't think they're Nazi's are they? I get them and Germans mixed up."

"Have you ever been to Gemany?"

He looked thoughtful. I assumed it was an easy question. "I don't think so."

"Don't," I replied, but then added. "On second thoughts, maybe you should."

He frowned. "I'm confused." I let it drop. Silence filled up the space around us.

"Well, then..." I said trying to wrap things up and edging towards my door.

"Yep, better get in and see the little lady!" He clicks his heels and shoots off with a small cloud of dust. "Until tonight..." I throw up a hand, which is about as much as I can muster. Jez is like a gentle Tasmanian devil. He is quick in body but slow in the head. He entertains me psychologically in times of need when my desires coerce me into wandering off to dark places.

I got out the letter from my father that I have folded away in my pocket and scanned it again, my eyes coming to rest on the last line.

I've got something really exciting to show you. Don't show this to anyone. I will see you soon. Dad.

There's a small part deep down that feels some excitement, but a larger part that thinks: *but will you, Dad, or is this just another empty promise?*

Chapter Four

"How's your mum?" I asked Daisy as I walked into the house. She'd come down to choose which frozen pizza she wanted to eat, and I could hear the Punk band, *Alkaline Trio* rocking out of her stereo from her bedroom. The singer was telling us about being held hostage and having his fingers cut off one-by-one. In my day, Adam Ant gave me an historical lesson on highwaymen. I guess even crime in songs had evolved over the years too.

"You know her," she said with a shrug of youth, "Talks about herself a lot. Sort of distracted. Doesn't listen to me."

I nodded, and I'm not sure that Daisy realises just how often I choose not to answer with what I'm really thinking. You could say I bite my tongue so often I'm beginning to get a liking for the taste.

"She means well," I say mechanically, leaving out the silent '*the selfish bitch*'.

Daisy turns to me and pulls the hair from her eyes— a trait that she's had since before she could talk. "You don't mean that, Dad." But there was no conviction behind these words. Her mother and I remain amicable due to Daisy, and all concerned knows that without her we'd be nothing more than another lost connection.

I walk towards Daisy and pull her close to me. She's growing up so fast and is already well over five-foot. "I know, but I like to believe that she does."

"Well, her new boyfriend is a dick." I pull away to look at her.

"Don't say that," I say, although I'm amused, not so much with her crude choice of words, but more within the context that it's used.

"He's always going on about what he's got, or what he's going to get – *Like I really care!*"

I wink at her. "He's probably just trying to impress you. You don't see them that often, do you? So don't worry about it." Jean sees Daisy sporadically and seemingly on a whim, and I have to wonder whether this is tied into the times she has remembered to see her therapist. I'm not overly worried at her dislike of Jean's new boyfriend, and I think it's more a healthy jealousy over another father figure. Give it a few months and there will be another father figure, and then another after that. Since we split up, she'd installed a revolving door directly to her bedroom.

I don't know what it is with my life, but after a failed relationship, I have this magnetic attraction to people with similar traits to the person that I left. Jean, on some level, is trying to find another version of me, but one she can manipulate a little better than I'd allow. And of course, I am no different. I search for a woman who is 70% Jean, but I'm unsure of what I want in the other 30%. No one quite matches up. I know how this sounds, and I would never go back to Jean, but I also struggle moving on too. Forever measuring people up with unrealistic expectations.

Daisy grabbed her chosen pizza and wrestled it out of its packaging before slipping it in the oven for her dinner. She knows I'll have half of whatever she chooses. When she closed the oven door, she turned, and I knew that there was something on her mind. "Are we selling Caulfield Hall?" I like the way she says 'we' and not 'you;' it's like we're a team.

"I'm not sure. I wanted to do it up and maybe get a better price for it, but the fact of the matter is the place is costing us money. I don't know whether the cost of repairs is worth it." I stopped myself before I went in to too much detail. She was only thirteen, words like joists and cladding would mean much to her.

"Is it our house or granddad's?" she asked.

I couldn't quite make out whether her childhood naivety was hoping something that I didn't think was possible, even after the letter that I received— that my father was still very much alive.

"You know he's missing, right? And there's the likelihood he'll never return?"

She nods, and then adds with a grin, "All I know is that he owes me a lot of birthday and Christmas presents."

My mouth twitched slightly with that. Daisy was wise beyond her years and her humour was very open, not as dry as mine. "Well, we have to believe he's not coming back. Legally, the house is ours, and even in a court of law, your granddad is considered dead. The house could make us some money though."

"Does that mean we're rich now?" she said flatly with a dripping of sarcasm. I followed suit:

"We have– and always will have– each other, and therefore are as rich as ever could be possible."

"That may be," she winks. "But love doesn't keep me in new shoes and cool clothes, Pops." She walks to the side, picks up a Diet Coke, and takes a swig. "What's the bottom line? I feel some sort of doom looming?"

"Doom looming, huh? Is that from Harry Potter?" She rolls her eyes and slowly shakes her head in mock disgust. "No, it may just mean that whilst we look for a buyer, things might be a little stretched financially here. That place is a money-pit."

"Have I still got to become a stripper when I turn eighteen?" She lives to shock me I'm sure.

"I was thinking a rock star or an actress. Then you'd become famous and keep me in the lifestyle to which I have become accustomed."

"What, poverty?"

"Wealth is subjective."

"That's what Jean says."

"Really," I reply, but I don't care to talk about her mother. I truly believe if you've nothing nice to say about someone, then you shouldn't say anything at all.

It would be a fair assumption that I don't talk about Jean very much.

I do find it sweet that Daisy calls me Dad, but her mother by her Christian name.

"She says that with money, life is an endless supply of possibilities."

"Ah-ha." I remembered a time she'd said the same thing to me about love. I guess having a string of rich boyfriends changed her outlook on life.

The Kinks were frantically proclaiming that, '*You Really Got Me Now*' when Daisy kissed me lightly on the cheek and jogged off to her room. *Oh, the sprightliness of youth*, I mused whilst left thinking whether or not I should bother changing my clothes before I went out, or whether a quick spray of some overpriced aftershave would suffice.

An hour later, and Father Dugan was sitting in my lounge watching the madcap antics of a bunch of Northern pensioners in *Last of the Summer Wine*. Personally, it always reminded me of Sunday evenings as a child and therefore the deep feelings of anxiety of having to go to school the next day. The theme tune still haunts me to this day. However now as an adult, I take some comfort in the evidence, however contrived and set up, of still being juvenile and immature even when losing your hair and your teeth.

"Thanks again, Father," I say as I pull on a checked shirt over my t-shirt in an effort to look slightly 'dressy.' In some glossy magazines, this move might be referred to as accessorising, but I think most of us realists would admit it's actually laziness. Some days I still sport a slightly more contemporary variation to the 90's 'grunge' fashion that can border on American-Sit-Com-Dad. I'm not proud of this, but in all honesty, I'm not too bothered either.

He raises a hand, though not taking his eyes off of the TV screen whereby two of the old boys were sitting in some sort of homemade Go-Cart and looked to be hurtling out of control down a country lane. One looked positively scared, and the other looked to be having the time of his life. And for some strange fleeting moment, I could picture Father Dugan and Miss Chambers re-enacting this down the lane towards the vicarage – both having the time of their lives.

"Bye, Dad!" Daisy says coming in clutching the *Twilight* movie. *Poor Father Dugan*, I smile to myself.

"Be good." I then turn and leave the house, not as full of enthusiasm as I should be.

I hadn't got ten feet from my front door when an old female voice piped up. "Off to raise Hell, are you?" she said. "Drinking and womanising, no doubt."

"Klan meeting actually," I replied and stomped off. She really does get my goat sometimes.

Chapter Five

The hustling hysteria of a Friday night was already in motion as I walked into the main street of Thornhill. Some days I've been known to drive, but the evening was warm, and tonight I wanted to indulge in a period of solitude, and– dare-I-say– over-indulge in the Devil's water.

For some, idle chit-chat will suffice when it comes to taking stock of life; sharing your feelings, hopes and beliefs whilst enjoying some titbit of gossip to help you feel better about yourself. However, I like to have moments when I can think and almost tidy up my thoughts and experiences of the day into their correct places within my mind.

The sound of *The Ramones* inside my pocket singing a muffled version of '*Sheena Is a Punk Rocker*' tells me that my mobile is ringing. The screen says 'unknown' as I press the button to answer.

"Hello?" I say, but am met by a strange sound of static. I repeat myself, but the signal seems weak. I look at the bars on the screen, which tell me the signal should be fine with all available bars there for the world to see. Between the static, I can make out a voice, and I'm sure at one point I hear my name. The line is a thick cacophonic noise, and before long all I hear is silence. I glare at my phone, even though I know it's done the best it could, and thrust it back into my pocket.

A couple of the bars already had an overspill of teens and twenty-something's segregated into many small groups. Like small tribes, they were throwing drunken glances around and portraying to those within the vicinity that their group was having the most fun. If you cocked an ear, you were instantly able to pick up the sound of glass bottles clinking, false male laughter, a female squeal, the thumping of a bassline to some dance track, and the constant loud chatter of socialisation. I paid these groups no mind as I walked by, glancing only to return the odd nod of acknowledgement from a customer or vague acquaintance before heading into my own club called, '*Capers.*'

"And here he is," the loud voice of Jez booms across from one of the booths in the American Diner part of the bar. I try not to outwardly cringe in the knowledge I've not made it five feet into the place before being spotted.

Set out now in a large building, '*Capers*' was originally two buildings: a ballroom and a pub. Some of the walls of the pub were knocked down to open it up, so even in the American Diner you could hear the music, but you could still sit and talk with your mates. My addition was a head phone jack that you could plug in and hear nothing but the live music, and recently, we'd started playing music through these in the day, as a few regulars started to frequent on their own, embracing the American idea of using their laptops or reading whilst sipping coffee and stuffing themselves with waffles, pancakes, and French toast.

This is how we did well. In the day, we were like a large coffee shop, minus the chain-franchise -standardisation and with a huge side order of community spirit. We had become a meeting place for friends, a neutral first date venue, or a place of friendly gossip and banter. And then at night, whilst things weren't always so friendly, we had one of the best local music venues outside of Bristol and Oxford. The diner still sold food, but it was within the bar side that we then made the profit with a cocktail selection that was one of the best in Wiltshire. We realised early on that beer and lager will make you money, but cocktails will make you rich.

Jez is still beaming, seemingly waiting for some sort of acknowledgment, and wearing a t-shirt that says, "My Mum's Wonder Woman!" I'm no woman, but I'm wondering what it says about a guy in his forties wearing a superhero slogan t-shirt so proudly.

I also have a horrible feeling he's been talking about me for some time. Sonia is looking at me, smiling broadly whilst twisting her hair, and I instantly feel uncomfortable. With a vest-top that is a size too small and bright red lipstick, I am not sure whether she is hoping I will save her from Jez, or whether she is in some way flirting with me. I imagine that my sudden confused look will do nothing for my desirability, but then that would depend on how much alcohol Sonia has drunk.

If this were a movie, then some low, sombre piano keys would ring out in a sinister tune as Gareth appears, pushing past people with three bottles of beer and staring at me like I may have just burnt his first edition of 'The Hobbit.' I can count the number of people on one finger that Gareth warms to, and I am not that one person.

"Jez," I say with that upward nod that you feel the need to raise your eyebrows, which I guess is a slightly warmer greeting than I'd meant. "Hi, Sonia. Er, Gareth."

"Hi, Ed," Sonia says sitting up straight. "Are you joining us?"

"Maybe later," I lie, but then sometimes you just never know how an evening is going to turn out. When I allow alcohol to flow over my lips, I become more tolerant of people.

"Ed is too busy to be bothered by us," Gareth states, not taking his eyes from mine, but clearly not talking to me. I picture him holding aloft the voodoo doll of me and saying to it, "How do you like *these needles*, Mr Tattoo-man!" I'm no expert, but if Gareth didn't have a history of animal cruelty and/or bed wetting, then I for one, would be shocked.

"Beer," Gareth states, slamming the bottles down.

"What about my cocktail?" Sonia asked.

"What about it?"

"Where is it? 'Caper's Shenanigan,' the one in the skull glass."

Gareth slowly shook his head. "Yeah, you're going to have to get that yourself."

"I'll get it for you in a minute," Jez says, scooting closer to Sonia. "Oh, Ed, mate, your girlfriend is smooching some guy out there. Hard luck, pal."

I ignored him as I replied, "Have a good night, folks." I carried on into the main room where I see a young band are just finishing up their set to a polite ripple of claps, and an already-drunk girl is infatuated with the lead singer. She's trying desperately to whistle, but only succeeding in showering a guy in front with her alcohol-laced saliva. Middle-aged, balding, and thirty-pounds over-weight, he turns and smiles at her, thinking this may be a mating ritual currently being used by the young. She oblivious to him, and is still transfixed on the stringy lad speaking into the microphone, and sporting a scruffy look and the self-confidence of someone better at singing than he was. This little situation is played out every week in many bars across the country, and it will continue that way until the end of time.

Looking around, I saw the bright red dyed hair of Ruby as she danced closely with a guy dressed all in black. He was scanning the room and seemed not half as interested in her as she is in him. I actually feel myself sigh, *Oh, Ruby, another night and another guy.* I long for some guy to come and sweep her up with flowers, moonlight walks, and weekends away, but it was hard to see her break this cycle.

"Edward!" the deep, enthusiastic voice of my best friend Jason says, patting me on the back and handing me a whisky. "Good to see you out, my friend!"

Jason has a shaggy blonde hairdo which portrays exactly what you'd expect of him. Permanently tousled, the thin locks look neat, even though they've not been combed since his mum was allowed near his Barnet in his childhood.

He's of average build with a slight pouch from beer, but dressed in a smart shirt over brown cords. Having come from a rich family, Jason has been allowed to live out his slacker lifestyle on a very long leash. However, what you wouldn't know is that he's a hard worker, and keeps this club not only ticking over, but pulling in a major profit. He has the ability to either find good local music talent that soon build up a following (and buy food and alcohol too), or manages to get bigger and more established bands to play, either as part of the tour, or as a secret gig, or a tour warm-up gig, thus gaining exposure through features in the music press, the likes of *Melody Maker* and *Kerrang!* Or even in the sleeve notes of bands' CD's.

A long time ago— not quite as far back as the birth of Jesus, but a similarly momentous occasion nonetheless— Jason and I got some cash together (mostly him), and I financed the renovations to join the pub and ballroom together into a diner/bar and music venue/bar. Jason had managed a bar in Spain for two years and a music venue in London for a year, so I had no qualms about him being up for the job of manager here. For the first few years, I was around the bar more, but as my family fell apart, the realisation hit me that I didn't need to be there, and Daisy needed me home with her. It has been nearly 13 years now, and '*Capers*' is stronger than ever.

"Jase, how are you," I reply as a greeting rather than a question. He nods, and opens his arms out in a way that shows how proud he is of the place.

"Guess who I've just managed to book?" he asked, already looking proud of himself, and pointing to his phone like that was complete proof.

"God knows," I replied. Jason could be full of surprises, so really, it could be anyone from *Madonna* to *The Cheeky Girls*.

"Main Man Mardini!" He grinned. This was an act surrounded in secrecy. It is believed that Triple M (as he's also known) is a single guy, although he's accompanied by a female singer, and a full band. Wearing a mask, no one knows what he looks like. A few recent hits from downloads have made him an overnight sensation.

"Wow! How did you manage that?"

He shrugged, clearly happy with himself. "It's what I do."

"Wait until I tell Jez."

Jason then looked worried. "The guy will make that strange sound again. Do us a favour and tell him away from the club."

I smiled at that. "It's not going to be long before Daisy wants to come here too, you know?"

"Well, encourage her to come. That way we can keep an eye on her."

"You know that's the exact reason why she won't come here." I took a sip and felt the liquid fire burn down my throat. "She'll be in one of those bars out there." I pointed in the general direction of the main street. A slight undertone of distaste creeping in. Those would be days I wish would not come.

We make no apologies for the American theme running throughout the venue. Jason should've been born and raised in America. He loves it and everything about it. That's probably why he dresses like a California surfer. All the other pubs and clubs were either trying to be overly British, Irish, or trying to emulate some Mediterranean 18-30's nightclub. We hit eBay hard and got loads of cheap imported trinkets Americans probably think of as dime-a-dozen trash, and lined the place in our own way.

We sauntered over to one of the tables in the corner, where another of my friends, Billy, sat with his girlfriend, Toni.

I've known Billy since school, where he was slightly nerdish. Keeping to himself, with a strange love of knitted tank-tops, he was extremely intelligent, and this is probably why he detests football and all sports in general. To him sports serve no real purpose other than to let off steam and keep fit. Exercise and stress relief– nothing more and nothing less.

Billy is a problem solver, and can often see life as questions and answers or problems and solutions. Whilst he may indulge us in a hypothesis, or flippantly explore alternative thoughts and processes, he will already know the most common or highly probable outcome of whatever we are debating. Billy is a man for whom the colour grey is not an option. It is black, or it is white.

If you were to start a sentence with, "What if-," then he would quickly conclude with, "Yes, but the fact of the matter is-," or "In a recent study (add number) percent proved-."

So take a young Bill Gates, stick him in a gym with a low-carb diet, shave his head, and you will have Billy− a financial analyst with an underrated sense-of-humour, but someone who enjoys life.

Toni is Billy's wife, and these two are completely suited in the nerd-turned-into-cool stakes. As a child, Toni had puffy chubby cheeks, a red complexion that made her look like she permanently had hives, and a body that could be best described as non-descript. Somewhere along the line and a few years later, she grew tall, lost the chubby cheeks, talked her mum out of doing her hair, and found make-up.

At some point in history, Jason and Billy worked together and became mates. I guess they're best mates, whereas I've never got close enough to be on that level, so whilst we are all great mates, there is an unspoken knowledge that I am just slightly down the line from them. That is fine by me. I don't have the ability to be there for someone else other than Daisy.

"Hey, guys!" I said as they smiled and clinked glasses with me. A large Texas flag is mounted on the wall above them. I really wished I could do this more often, but then again, as soon as I agreed to take on Daisy, I had to forgo these nights and limit them to special occasions. I was getting too old for this sort of socialising anyway. Forty was only just around the corner, and people kept telling me that it was only downhill from there. Bullshit. Physically it had been downhill from thirty.

"Congratulations on the award, mate!" Billy said, his arm lost behind Toni. Whilst he didn't always understand my line of work, he appreciated an award, which was a mark of success in a certain field by virtue that you'd fulfilled the criteria and proved worthy of acknowledgment at beating your peers.

The couple had been together for nearly ten years, and they still seemed to be as much in love now as they were back when they first met. Around here, this outward showing of affection was in the minority, but I was happy for them—slightly sickened, but happy nevertheless.

"Yeah, well done, buddy," Jason added as we all clinked glasses again in celebration of my winning of *'Best Full Colour Piece of the Day'* at the recent London Tattoo Convention. It also meant a small write up and future interview piece in *'Skin Deep,'* the UK's leading tattoo magazine. So this was all helping me to be almost at the peak of my profession.

"And how's the shop?" Billy asked.

"Business is good. I'm booked up six months in advance, so I can't complain," I replied.

Jason nudged me. "He doesn't charge enough though," he said, and he was probably right.

"I charge a standard amount. People want value for money."

"People don't come to you for standard work, so with your above standard work, charge them above standard prices." He took a sip of his whisky before finishing. "Simple economics, mate." He was right, and that's why whilst we are joint owners of '*Capers,*' he's the manager, and I'm purely there for my joint injection of cash.

"I hear Ruby is doing well too," Jason then added, nodding over to where she was still swaying back and forth with the same guy. She seemed lost in his embrace, and I wondered whether she just longed to be held safe by anyone. He, on the other hand, was trying to relieve some tension in her Gluteus Maximus muscles whilst winking at a girl with blonde hair extensions and a witch's nose.

"Yeah, she's doing great. She's built up quite a client list now and is charging quite a bit more than she was a year back."

Jason gave a false cough. "So, she can raise her costs, but you can't?"

"Well, firstly, she's still learning, and therefore is getting better and better all of the time, and then of course as owner of the shop I get a percentage, so technically, as she does well, then so do I."

"D'you think she may leave at some point? Maybe start up her own shop?"

"You never can tell in this game. Some artists like to travel around. But I don't always consider all tattoo shops as being in competition with each other. Each artist has their own speciality, and collectors don't always stick to the same artist."

"Collectors?" Toni asks.

Billy turns to her and replies with a smile. "People who get tattoos from different people."

"Yeah, although a real collector is someone that researches and seeks out a specific artist so they have one of their pieces on their skin. They're almost giving their skin over to be a gallery showcasing the tattooist's work."

"Seems weird when you put it like that!"

I smile. Some people don't get tattoos, and that's fine. "Well, it's not so much different from when you get your hair done. The hairdresser is showcasing their skills on you, albeit for the period between coming out of the hairdressers to going back in there again."

She shrugged, although I wasn't sure she got the point. "I suppose so." Jason was the only one who was really into the tattoos. He sported a tribal piece on his arm around his bicep and a large back-piece of a 1973 Plymouth Barracuda car that I did many moons ago. However, one of my many issues with Jason is that he is a scratcher. By that, I mean he's an amateur tattooist. This may not seem like much to you, but to me as a professional tattoo artist, it is not a great thing. When I started out, I was an apprentice for a guy called Big Jake, a friend of Harry's. I put in two years of voluntary work before he started to pay me to clean up and take appointments. Within that time though, he had me drawing daily and showed me how to tattoo a single straight line, which is not as easy as it looks. After three years, I tattooed my first person, and it was six months after that before I was able to charge customers. However, my good-buddy, Jase, isn't interested in it like that and buys himself a tattoo machine online, and every now and then decides to ruin somebody for life by scratching some sort of picture onto their body. So not only does it belittle all of the hard-work and training that I've put into this, but it also puts out there some God-awful tattoos that give us a bad name, not to mention the fact that what he does is illegal and possibly unhygienic. Outside of tattooing, it more than likely sounds like I am just being sensitive and picky, but this is beginning to be a real problem.

A tattoo machine does not make you a tattooist.

Billy turned into Toni, and as he kissed her neck, I downed my drink and looked over the dance floor. Jason was hand-signalling the sound-guys in a gesture that was meant to mean something, and I found myself looking around and for some reason expecting to see Jean dancing in the long polka-dot dress that I remember from another lifetime and smiling to herself as she was lost in the music. A time before things fell apart. And my crazy old man was still around. Some nights, happiness and melancholy fight the right to dominate my emotions, and whisky is not a good referee.

It wasn't long before we were stacking up the empty shot glasses on the table. Jason was wandering off to sort out some problem that he couldn't leave to our friend, Neil, who is the club's assistant manager, because Jason likes to be in control. Billy had been spewing out facts and figures about things you wouldn't even believe, before Toni politely told him that he needn't talk anymore.

Within a few more minutes, Billy and Toni were dancing to a female singer-songwriter, who– along with her acoustic guitar, a guy about ten years older than herself on an upright bass, and a nerdy guy on drums– was producing some beautiful country-folk songs. The sort you just couldn't help but sway or tap your feet to.

And like a scene from a comedy, I looked over at the other three stooges that had now joined us: Jez, Gareth, and Sonia.

"The singer is cute," Jez was slurring, although I wasn't convinced that he could still see that far anymore.

"And half your age," I added.

"Age is but a number," he replied.

"But considered important in the eyes of the law," Gareth said in a sinister flat way that could have been seen as a resigned fact.

"Age is actually a three-lettered word," I stated. The alcohol formed the words for me. Jez suddenly giggled at this like it was an amusing joke and not the fact that I meant it to be.

"So," Sonia said in a way that people do to just say something. "D'you want to dance, Ed?"

"Sorry, Sonia," I said as gently as I could. "I'm no dancer. My skills are in my hands, not my feet." It is a sign of getting old when a girl in her early twenties feels too young for you. "Why don't you take Gareth here for a bit of two-step action?"

Gareth cut me off with, "I would rather drink my own urine through my nostrils."

"Thanks, guys," she said, genuinely looking hurt. And that is when the living drunken mannequin that is called Jez came to life like Dr. Frankenstein's monster from a bolt of lightning and said, "Let's hit the floor, lady!"

Sonia rolled her eyes, and as she got up, muttered, "Bugger me, it's Patrick Swayze." Jez took her hand, took two steps, and fell smack down on his face, punch-drunk.

I helped him slowly to his feet and sat him down.

"I guess my dance is off," Sonia conceded.

Gareth huffed, and unexpectedly muttered, "I'll get the knob-head some water."

Just as I thought things may get awkward between myself and Sonia, Jason returned. "Some guy has been asking for you," he said. "Not sure what he wants, but he's asked a few people."

"I'm not being funny," I said, "But if he's asked a few people, and I've been sitting here all night, then how come he's not found me yet?"

"Maybe he doesn't follow directions very well," Jason replied, shrugging.

"Typical man," Sonia added into her drink.

"What's wrong with her?" he said.

"She wants to dance with you."

Jason made a show of looking at his wrist, even though he wasn't wearing a watch. Sonia looked like she might suddenly burst into tears when Jason said, "Okay, just the one." And off they went.

"I'm good with computers!" Jez suddenly exclaimed, again drunkenly coming to life.

"Indeed, you are," I added. *Here we go*, I thought. As usual, Jez had drunk himself stupid, which of course is no great feat when you are pretty stupid to begin with, and I'm the one left to deal with his drunken babble. I would love to just walk off, but everyone else is otherwise occupied– well, apart from Gareth, who has just slammed some lukewarm water onto the table, and was looking at me like he was trying to guess the best way of skinning me alive before eating me for his supper.

"I have needs," Jez then said in a pathetic voice, which only made the whole pantomime worse. I looked around and hoped no one else had heard.

"Uh-huh," I replied by way of a conversational acknowledgement, and not an encouragement to further this line of discussion.

It was then that Gareth pulled a very strange face, jiggled on his seat, then fumbled in his pocket for his phone. Two clicks of a button, a gruff, "It's on," and he got up and left. Gareth: the only person in the whole of the world who can make Jez seem moderately normal.

Thankfully, the band quickened the pace with a real foot-tapper, and after a few minutes, Billy and Toni, having just shared a joke, came back, grinning from ear to ear.

"Great band," Toni said. "I must tell Jase."

Jez was now led half over the table with his head in his hands. "What's going on here?" Billy asked, his grin now having sly undertones. He was used to Jez's strange ways, and him ending up with us when we went out. He had calculated that other than reputation, Jez was of little harm.

"Alcoholic meltdown, I'm afraid," I said, shaking my head. "Standard part of an evening out really."

"Everything alright, honey?" Toni said, patting Jez on the shoulder. She once described him as a large, simple bear that just needs to be pointed into the right direction in life once in a while. I can't argue with that. The train-tracks are over there, Yogi....

"You guys have it all. You two have your smoochy-ness-" Billy looked over to me and mouthed, "smoochy-ness," so he couldn't see. "Jason has this club, and now is dancing with a pretty girl. Ed, you have a great job and a wonderful daughter. Gareth has his, er, his whatever-it-is-that-he-does. And what do I have?"

"A wife? And a good job?" Billy said rather unsympathetically.

"A wife? That woman hates everything about me."

"Honey," Toni said sweetly. "Why do you stay with her then?"

"Because!" he spat and then regained his composure. "Because I cannot leave her."

It was then that we heard the theme tune to the cartoon Popeye, and Jez was fumbling for his mobile. "Speak of the devil," he said with disdain, "she's outside. Want a lift, Ed?" I certainly did not want to be in between either an argument or a drive of awkward silence.

"Thanks, but I'll hang around here a bit longer, Jez."

"Figures," he said, looking over at Ruby who was now sitting on her own. And off he went like a man awaiting the death squad.

Chapter Six

Sonia and Jason came back from their dance, and judging by their shared smiles and stolen looks, both seemed to have enjoyed themselves. However, glancing at us, Jason appeared to be suddenly self-conscious. He doesn't normally show an embarrassed side when it comes to his drunken exploits with the fairer sex. Tonight, though he'd not hit the liquor like he normally does, I guess this explained why he'd not already attached himself via his lips to a woman of questionable morals. I was sure Sonia was not one of those. I'm no expert, but Jason wants a wife and a family, but he's led this hedonistic lifestyle for so long that he is not sure how to break the repetition. He buries his head in the nearest free chest and indulges in meaningless flings instead. I get the feeling he's starting to look at his outlook on life a little differently. Again, this is the perfect example showing that at the age of forty, he now sees a number of attractive women that have suddenly appeared in a group he can no longer go for. This revelation has hit him hard.

I was about to go over and speak to Ruby – *nothing more than a quick 'hello'. However, just as I was looking to get up, another guy appeared and placed a drink in front of her. She's never left thirsty at a bar. Nor lonely. Many men are happy to keep her company.

When I see her face light up with a smile, I turn back to my friends and think about making a move to go home. I've a lot to do tomorrow.

"Is that true?" Sonia is asking me, and I'm about to agree, even though I know not of what it is that I am admitting to.

"Is what true?" I say instead.

"That you saved Jason from a beating!" *Here we go*, I thought.

"Eddie is our hero, Sonia. Our regular superhero!" Billy said, and although I like the guy, there's often an undertone of sarcasm running through most things he says. I think this is the brains against brawn battle.

And so, between Jason and Billy, and the odd conversational injection from Toni, the worn-out story was retold, beefed up with poetic licence and enhanced embellishment. I wasn't around to hear it. I'd said my goodbyes, told Jason to make sure that Sonia got home safely and was off walking out of the building. I heard about it later, but by then, I had more pressing things on my mind.

I stopped by the office to see if the band's details were hanging around so I could thank them, and also to pick up any messages or bills that needed my attention. I folded up a handwritten letter and walked wearily out of the backdoor – a perk of owning a share of the business.

I'm not one to get all spiritual, especially after more than a handful of whiskeys, but I had the sudden feeling that I was being watched. Call it a sixth sense, or call it alcohol-induced paranoia, but had I been a dog, my hackles would've been up.

Something was off.

I turned quickly and was met by a fist glancing off of the side of my cheek. The force spun me, but years of amateur boxing gave me good balance and kept me on my feet. As I straightened up, I saw another punch coming for me, but this time I moved to the left as the right arm extended with force past me. I countered quickly with my right elbow to the back of the guy's head as I also swept his feet from under him. It was a defensive move that I'd learnt from Father Dugan back in the days when he didn't quite forgive in the same way as he does today.

Adrenaline was pumping through my veins, and I was wishing that I was sober. The problem with alcohol is that it slowed my reactions, and in a split second, I was grabbed from behind by someone else. Instinctively, I jumped backwards, throwing back my head and as soon as I felt the release, I knew that I'd made contact with his nose. I spun and hit him twice in the kidneys, noticing the blood was already starting to flow from his broken nose. In that second, I couldn't place the face as anyone that I remembered having seen before. The scrambling noise behind told me that the first guy was still feeling hopeful, but I turned and blocked another swing before smashing my open palm into his nose. This move can disable an opponent, momentarily watering their eyes and giving a flash of pain without doing very much damage. However, this does mean you can then land a solid punch wherever you see fit. I hit him hard with a left jab to the eye, before unleashing a right jab that sent him to the ground.

I looked behind me, but the second guy was already gingerly walking off. Then I saw the first guy getting up with his hands out in an okay-I-give-up pose. His legs were like rubber, and I had to wonder just what my boxing career could've been like if I hadn't had to give it up for tattooing. The reason was all too apparent as I looked at the way my right hand was already beginning to swell. It looked like I would be cancelling the next few days of appointments. There was no way I'd be able to sit holding a tattoo machine for any long period of time.

I thought back to the uppercut opening that I would've taken if I had been in a ring with gloves on, but thankfully, I had stopped, knowing that my power would've broken my fingers on one of the guy's thick jawline. It is not a move worth using in bare-knuckle boxing, and that is not a version of boxing that I would ever be willingly doing again.

As the adrenaline wore off, I felt the pain in my cheek and hands more. Then I had the shaking after effects of mild shock. It didn't seem like a mugging gone wrong. Were they the guys asking after me tonight? To be fair, I didn't ask them anything, but then, holding a conversation with someone looking to knock you into next week is a challenging task.

The ten minute walk home with a slight nip of cool air helped me gather my thoughts, and I knew that come tomorrow, I'd be back at the club checking out the security cameras for clues as to who these chancers were.

As I walked up to my porch, a bright torch beam suddenly intruded on my thoughts.

"Ah-ha!" exclaimed the voice of Miss Chambers. "And what in the world have you been up to?"

"Do you ever sleep?" I muttered.

"No point if I'm to be woken up by drunks."

"I've just been with my friends."

"You have some sort of disagreement with them too? They finally figured you out for an idiot?"

"What are you talking about?" I wasn't in the mood. Any more of her button-pushing, and I might be forced to hit the old bag.

"I see you there— a man who has been fighting. Thugs fight; real men walk away."

It was hard not to hold my throbbing hand, but I did glance down at it. "It's a gracious and wonderful world you live in, Miss C."

"Mocking an old lady makes you feel special, does it? Wonderful world, indeed. Wonder-fool more like: as in, you're the fool that I wonder about. Good night!" And off she went.

"Night!" I called a little louder than I should've.

Father Dugan didn't ask about my evening, but he knew by my shifty-ness that I wasn't looking to talk tonight. Some nights I will bend his ear off, and others – like tonight – I want to be left alone.

He bid me farewell, although I noticed that he had clocked my hand, and slipped off to leave me with the white-noise pounding in my head and a hand that— if this were a cartoon— would be over-exaggeratedly swollen red and pulsating.

And as if I hadn't already had enough, I liberated a half-drunk bottle of whisky from its dark cupboard prison whilst I dived into a sea of contemplation.

I found myself pressured by the memories of my childhood that slowly wrapped itself around me, and like an invisible weighted blanket, slowly started smothering me. I was idly flicking through photo albums, caught up in a cycle of regret and sadness of a past that could never be changed, then of people long gone that were sorely missed, and this inevitably lead to guilt over these feelings when I had a gorgeous daughter whom I loved more than anyone or anything on this earth. Then I sunk back into the photos, and so it carried on until at some point, I fell asleep on the sofa, either through tiredness, or through exhaustion from the emotion and loss of tears. When I woke up in the dead of the night, I found that I had an empty whisky bottle resting on my lap, and I was clutching a photo of myself, Daisy, and her mother.

As I pulled myself to my feet, knowing that in the morning my head would be throbbing, I saw the little note: *I love you more than you realise, Daddy.*

The simple words had been written by my little girl whilst I was passed out drunk. Maybe it was this that gave me the kick up the arse I needed. Or maybe it was that deep down I knew that nothing in my life would ever be the same again.

If only I'd known how true these words would be in the hours ahead.

Chapter Seven

As I strained to open my eyes, the piercing and pulsating pain in my head told me in no uncertain terms the reason why I shouldn't drink to excess anymore. My face and hands were bruised and bloated from the fight, and whilst I knew it was unprovoked, part of me thought I'd taken it too far. Playing back my memories of the scuffle suggested that whilst I'd managed to dodge the first punch, from there I should've either run back into the club to get security or even just run away. There was a machismo part of me that wouldn't run, but wanted to inflict pain on someone. I guess when you train for years as a fighter, it's hard to shake that feeling.

I have always been an early riser, so even with the late night, I was ready to face the world by eight a.m. I'd just successfully navigated my battered body downstairs when Daisy appeared with that spring of youth about her – she, too, was an early riser.

"And he lives!" She grinned, her hair pulled back in a pony-tail – a sign she couldn't be bothered to spend much time on self-grooming today.

I smiled, but I was a little ashamed that she had seen me in the state that I was in. "I'm sorry,

Daze," I said. "You shouldn't have to see me like that."

She rolled her eyes as she replied, "Don't worry, Pops. You should hear what Jade's mum gets up to most weekends!"

"I can only imagine," I said, putting two heaped tablespoonfuls of Papua New Guinea coffee into the coffee machine and adding a cup full of cold water.

"Some days, she's laid out naked on the lounge floor," she grinned. The mere thought of Jade's mum sprawled out with the flabby belly rolls, and her over-sized breasts led under each armpit like they were hiding from one another, was enough to make me feel more than a bit queasy again. I still have reoccurring nightmares from the time that she picked Jade up from a play date here a few months back. I'd opened the door to a five-foot woman of forty wearing enough gold to be traded in at a pawn-brokers for the price of a trip to Hawaii. She'd winked expectantly when I'd said the girls had popped out, and without invitation, forced her way in, thrusting out her chest in a way I thought was the first time I had ever felt threatened by a woman's breasts.

"It's hot in here?" she had said flashing her ample belly up to her bra. "Cooler in the garden," I'd added, quickly ushering her outside. Within a few minutes, she was huddled in a lawn chair, and her body temperature, like her attitude towards me had both cooled to frosty.

Since then, I'd dropped Jade back home every time.

Daisy walked over with concern on her face. "What happened to your face?"

"Age, my dear, and my boyish good looks took a beating with a daughter to constantly worry about!"

"Seriously, Dad?" she scolded.

"It was just some misunderstanding at the club. Someone was drunk, and I was trying to get them out of the way, and they accidentally caught me with a flailing arm."

"And your hand?" she added suspiciously in a tone straight from her mother's mouth, and there was also something in her eyes that flashed me back to Jean.

"Okay," I said, holding up my hands, which under the circumstances was probably not the best idea as it emphasised the bruising and swelling around my knuckles. "The guy swung at me, which I blocked with my head, and in return, I hit him back. Daisy, under no circumstances should you ever hit someone. It was wrong of me, and I'm sorry. It seems last night has not shown me as the best father in the world."

"Dad, I know you. If you hit someone, then there would be a very good reason for it. Inside that artist-slash-teacher exterior lies a man with good morals and a large heart!" She winked and went to get in the milk from outside.

I was still going over those words and allowing myself to feel a little bit proud, when I heard her shout, "Dad!"

"What's up?" I said, coming to the door.

Daisy was smiling from ear-to-ear. "The milkman has made a strange delivery this morning!"

I looked out, and above where the two large bottles of milk sat, left on the bench on the porch was Ruby. She was fast asleep with a coat laid on her as a blanket.

I gently touched her shoulder, giving it a slight shake. "Ruby," I said to try and rouse her.

She murmured incoherently, then slowly opened her eyes, suddenly wincing at what I assume was a hangover too. "Eddie?" she said, still trying to focus.

"What're you doing here?" I asked. "Why didn't you knock on the door?"

"I was about to," she said, looking a little embarrassed in front of Daisy. "I tried a couple of times and then thought I'd just rest here, and bingo! Here we are!"

Then, as usual, there was a creak of a door from my neighbour as out came Miss Chambers.

"Well, what in the world is going on here?" she said. "The milkman delivers prostitutes now, does he?"

Ruby looked positively shocked, but I showed my palms in a keep-calm kind of way and shook my head.

"Good morning to you, Miss Chambers. Do you ever spend any time in your own house, or would you prefer to join our houses together?"

"Well, listen to Mr Smart-Mouth. Such a gentleman that he makes his fancy-woman sleep on his run-down porch!"

"It's rustic and well-loved."

"Well-loved by woodworm and mites! Ha ha!" I helped Ruby up, and we headed back into our house, leaving the old busy-body giggling to herself.

"D'you want a cup of tea?" I said as Ruby sat down on the sofa. She nodded as Daisy put the kettle on.

"I'm sorry, Ed. I'm not even sure why I'm here-" she started, but I waved this off.

"Don't be silly," I cut in. "We're friends. You're welcome to come here whenever you want. Maybe knock on the door next time though, yeah?" She nodded.

"Do you want sugar, Ruby?" Daisy called.

"One please, love," she replied, running her hand through her bright red hair. I was about to say something when my mobile went again.

"Hello," I said. Once again, I was met by static, but also some beeping of various tones. I'm pretty sure I made out someone cursing, but rather than in an offensive manner, it seemed borne out of frustration. "Hello? I can't hear you?" I said, but then I was met by a screech like you would get when a microphone and speaker object to being close to the other. Then it clicked off, and I was left looking confused at my phone.

"I had a call at the shop that was weird yesterday," Ruby said. "There was a sound like electrical interference on the other end. I could almost make out a voice, but it sounded a long, long way away."

I nodded. "Yeah, I got a call last night that was the same. I thought I heard my name, but I really can't be sure."

"So what happened to your hand and face? Did you get into a fight?"

"Something like that," I said as Daisy put Ruby's tea down on the wooden coffee table, before getting a couple of slices of toast and heading off to her room.

"I was jumped by a couple of blokes outside the back of the club."

"Why? Did they mug you, or, eh, what the hell, Ed?" She looked really confused but concerned.

"I've no idea. I didn't wait to find out. I defended myself the best I could, and they ran off."

Ruby shook her head in disbelief. Things like that didn't happen that often in Thornhill.

We both took a sip of our drinks before Ruby said, "Look, Ed. I was out to meet Tom last night-"

"Tom?" I said. I'm not sure whether or not I'd been told about Tom before or not.

"I met him online, and we decided to meet for a drink."

"And?" I pressed.

"And we had a drink. It was just like having a drink with my brother-"

"You don't have a brother."

"Nope, but if I did, I imagine that it would've felt like that." She flashed a smile.

"Was this guy tall and dark?"

"Yep, and handsome, but there you go. To be honest, he wasn't that interested in me either."

I smiled as I said, "I noticed. He looked like he was scouting the room when you were dancing."

She took a sip of her tea, and nodded. "But what about the other guy I saw buying you a drink?"

"Alfie?"

"I guess so. How many men bought you a drink last night?"

"Tom, Alfie, and some middle-aged guy near the end who thought he was going to get lucky!"

"Classy."

"Alfie is a guy I've known for years. We just talked for a while. I don't know, maybe I'm trying too hard to get someone. I want that fairytale romance, you know?"

"Ruby, life isn't about princesses, poetry, knights... and happy-ever-after endings. It's frustrating, but despite everything people say about being the holders of our own destiny, sometimes you have to just let things happen."

"I know," she said, putting down her tea. "And that's why I was here. Of all of the places I could've ended up, I end up on your front porch. I've been thinking, and-"

"Which one?" Daisy said, bursting in holding two tops. "Oh, sorry, you were talking."

Embarrassed, Ruby picked up her mug in both hands as I wondered what she was going to say.

"The dark long-sleeved one," I said. "If we're going to get the house sorted, then I don't want you getting cold. The wind whips off of the lake there."

"Dark one it is," she smiled.

"The house? You mean Caulfield Hall?" Ruby said.

"That's the one. I'm thinking of putting it on the market. I've held on to that money-pit for long enough."

"The cost of sentimentality."

"Exactly."

"It's a shame I have a couple of appointments today, else I would've tagged along," she softly said almost to her mug of tea.

"Maybe tomorrow?"

"Maybe."

"Oh, and, er," I looked at how the skin had started to go dark through the red swelling on the knuckle nearest my little finger. "Can you cancel my appointments for next week, or see if any of the guys can fit them in? This hand isn't going to be holding a machine for a few days."

"Of course. Have you got anything exciting coming up?"

"There's a guy coming in next weekend for a Japanese back-piece. I have it all sketched out, so it won't be too bad. I may be okay by then."

Ruby nodded. "That will be a long sitting though. D'you think he'll be okay?"

"Well, guess what?"

"He's not a blank, is he?" She grinned.

"Yep. His first tattoo, and he chooses a large back piece."

"I've got to be around for that one! I love to see a man faint."

"I think he'll be okay. I've explained how long it will take, and asked whether he would prefer it split into three sessions, but he didn't seem fazed by it."

"A coming of age."

"Yep, and you know what that means-"

She grinned cutting in with, "'When they get one, they get more done!'" It was something that was noticeable throughout all walks of life now. One tattoo really didn't mean anything anymore, and if it was small, then it no longer represented a hedonistic act, rather as acceptable a rite of passage as a drunken binge-drink session, or puffing on a thickly rolled cigarette containing any number of substances claiming to be 'good-shit,' which is itself an ironic oxymoron of proclamation. No longer a straight-forward sign of anarchy or individualism, the tattoo culture has now been embraced by all with a creative flair, from fashion and hairdressing, to artists and actors/actresses. The shock value is now left to tattoos sported on necks, knuckles, and faces, and once when punks and goths were feared for their looks, the new alternative scene is big business as an artistic expression of a person.

Ruby was a fine example of this alternative scene. With bright hair that matched her name and bright sleeves of tattoos, she had a nose ring and wore burgundy lipstick, although unusually, after a night on my front-porch, there was a slight smear to it, and her hair looked the way it might had it been nestled in a pillow the morning after the night before.

There was a definite emphasis on what was not being said as we made a little small talk before Ruby had to go. She wanted to grab a shower at home before going to work.

I had a full day ahead of clearing out of Caulfield Hall with the help of my glamorous assistant, Daisy.

It's an old cliché, but if I only knew then what I know now, then Daisy would not have been going with me. But this is Thornhill. It's not some movie that you roll your eyes at in disbelief; a snack of entertainment that we chew up and swallow without question.

Today was the day that I learnt a lot of things about myself and probably more than I ever needed to know about my family.

Chapter Eight

I had an enthusiastic drive to move forward and sort out the house. My granddad was fond of explaining this riddle by way of a sneering, "Sometimes you have to decide whether to shit or get off of the pot!" This was his take on ceasing any procrastinating desires and replacing with pragmatic common-sense, and I had been sitting there on that euphemistic pot for too long, with a quiver of my bowels being a twinge of nostalgia. The house, whilst beautiful in its elegance and unique by design, was also a money-pitted folly for someone with a lot more money than I.

I carried out some tools to the back of my 1968 VW Camper van (another money pit!), and was just returning to the house when I saw the familiar looking goon of Jez lost in his own world.

"Hey, Jez!" I shouted to snap him out of whatever reverie he was caught up in. I stole a quick smirk as he jumped out of his skin. It's these little things that keep me amused through life.

"Shit, man. I didn't see you there!" he said with an air of relief. I'm not sure what he was expecting. The war was over years ago, and as silly as he may be perceived, I'm sure he no longer believes in the bogeyman.

"Clearly. You sneaking around doing something you shouldn't?"

"That's how I live my life." He then proceeded to make some noises that I guess could be laughter, but sounds more like a seal with wind: "Arff! Arff!"

"You get back okay?" I ask, and with that, I have to concede that I do care on some level for his welfare. The very fact I was conducting this conversation was evidence enough.

"Sure did," he grinned, and things took an incredibly dark turn for the worse as a horrible glint sparked in his eyes. "When I got in, well-"

"Spare me the details!" I said with my hands raised in a defensive mode, and he was thrusting his hips forward like a jockey in the Grand National. Except there was no horse, and I was worried for the postman's sanity as he suddenly stopped dropping red rubber-bands for a second in horror and wondered whether or not to deliver to our houses ever again.

"It was like one of the first times again. She had this new underwear set and-"

"Seriously, I am happy for you, but I don't need to know the details-"

He suddenly fumbled with his phone. "Recorded it all!" I threw up both hands in a similar way that I would've had he threatened to throw dead kittens at me. "No thanks!" I waved off.

He shrugged and put the phone away. "Looks to me like you got lucky too!" He then added with an over-exaggerated wink. "I saw her leave about half an hour ago!"

"Oh, no. Nothing like that, she was on my front-porch-"

"What?!" He looked well and truly flummoxed by this. "Why didn't you let her in?"

"I didn't know she was there."

"I know bugger-all about how you work, mate," he said.

"That right."

"Anyway," he then said, "I've gotta get going."

"What are you up to?" I asked, though in reality I had little care especially if it had anything to do with his other-half and a replay of last night's red-hot wrestling.

"Haircut," he proclaimed proudly like this was something that was only undertaken by the rich and debonair.

"Really?" I said. "Your hair looks okay a little longer. Kind of surf-y."

He nodded and ran his hands through his hair. "Yeah, sod a haircut."

"Her indoors making you have it?" I said, throwing my head towards his humble abode.

He shrugged. "She said it needed a bit of tidying up."

"Uh-huh."

"But I think it's fine..." and with that he turned and loped back to his house, both of us knowing he'd be getting that haircut before the day was out.

I glanced at my watch, ready to get going in a way that can sometimes be seen as annoying by some. But I was on a schedule.

A familiar wrinkled face appeared in my rear-view mirror as I looked back from the house. I smiled as I mused to myself that my friendship with Father Dugan more often than not always seems to be the beginning of a joke: a vicar walked up to a camper-van...

"Where's that pretty girl of yours?" he asked, and I noticed a thick envelope in his hands.

"Still getting whatever essentials together that she feels she needs to clean out a house for a few hours. Females, huh?"

"Their beauty and their complex ways are what attracts us to them, and also why our love binds their every being."

"Pretty much, I guess," I added. "You're very poetic today."

He's used to ignoring my flippant comments. "Here," he said, thrusting forward the envelope in a way that seemed it might hold something dirty inside.

"What's this? Porn?" I smirked.

"Your father," he said flatly.

"I doubt it's my father." I took it, hiding my shock with a retort that was not in any way amusing. "How come you have this?"

"It's a long story."

"So why're you giving it to me now?"

He ran a hand through his beard, and with a sigh and an unenthusiastic whisper he said, "Amongst other things this is how to get into the study."

With a grin, I pulled out a large key. "Well, I was going to put this in the lock and turn it. Apparently, that is how these fancy mechanisms work nowadays in a fashion that is by no means ground-breaking or cutting edge...."

"My lad, that will not get you anywhere near the study. It's a false key bought at a car boot sale. It probably opens up Miss Chambers' garden shed. Your dad had a strange way about him, and one of these surrounds his mysterious study. I'm not sure much good came from inside that room, other than these fanciful ideas that he was some cross between Picasso and Thomas Edison-"

"Da Vinci? Wouldn't that be a better simile? A cross between Picasso and Thomas Edison would be Da Vinci, would it not?"

"An artist *and* has his father's smart mouth. Well, who would have thought it?"

I waved the key that was, or was not, what held me back from Miss Chambers' lawn-mower and hedge-trimmer, and conceded, "So this is basically useless?"

"For the purpose that you wish to use it for, yes."

"Hey!" Daisy squealed when she saw the vicar. Kids can be over-excitable. She threw her arms around him, and then chucked in her backpack full of God-knows-what in the van.

"How was *Twilight*?" I asked him.

"You liked it, didn't you?" Daisy jumped in.

"It was entertaining."

"Better than *Jaws*?" I pressed.

"Nothing is better than *Jaws*. Have fun, kids!" he said and walked off waving.

We set off to the sound of *Guns N' Roses* blasting from my stereo, but it wasn't long before

Daisy had intervened and changed the stereo to a band that, whilst still loud, were somewhat more melodic, adding a large dollop of pop to the rock.

"And who might this be?" I asked, prepared not to know who the band was.

"*Forever the Sickest Kids*," she replied, tapping her hands to the beat on her knees.

"They must've had patient parents,"

I didn't see the eye-roll, but it would've been there. "Not all bands' names should be taken so literally."

"What, you mean the *Pet Shop Boys* never actually worked in a pet shop?"

"Who?"

"'*West End Girls...*'" I sang in a deep monotone voice, adding the synthesiser too.

"Seriously, dad, other kids don't have to put up with this child-abuse."

It wasn't a long trip to Caulfield Hall, taking probably around 15 minutes, but in that time, I glanced more than half a dozen times at Daisy and felt a mixture of being proud and also how I had to be thankful for what I had. Yes, my romantic relationships had not fared so well through life, but I'd been the victim or indulger in acts of infidelity; things had just not worked out. I'd managed to raise a wonderful and sensible daughter, who was maturing better than I ever thought she would. Understandably, children can be deeply affected by parents' relationships breaking down, and whilst I know Daisy puts on a brave face, even joking about it to all who will listen, I know that she's upset by that whole escapade. This situation is an unfortunate one that plays out every day all over the world – a relationship ceases to be fruitful for both parties, and whilst both want it to work, the truth is they're not happy together anymore. People change for numerous reasons: perhaps they feel life is passing them by, and they want to grow; perhaps that romantic flame has gone out, and there is nothing that can reignite it again; maybe even some epiphany has occurred that opens the eyes of one or both of the parties. Whatever it is, these things can happen.

    Daisy was clearly still searching for her own identity. Today she had her hair pulled back into a pony-tail, but this was more out of practicality than of design. I could still see the red streak that she'd added a week ago, and whilst she favoured a more conservative dress-sense (albeit mixed with hippy undertones) of late, the fashion butterfly was starting to break free from its mundane chrysalis. Thicker eyeliner had appeared, and the additional hint of lipstick was now apparent.

Chapter Nine

The winding country road took us west a mile to the edge of Thornhill and around White Horse Lake. Caulfield Hall sat domineeringly on its own. There was some distance around the lake until the next few houses that spanned the two-mile diameter. From our house, the lake was a brisk fifteen-minute walk. When you got there and looked out across the large lake, you could just make out the boathouse, and then further up the grand building of the house that was known as Caulfield Hall.

We turned into the drive of Caulfield Hall, which started off as tarmac and slowly turned into pot-hole filled gravel.

The house with its Neo-Gothic architecture appeared to sneer and reach out menacingly at me, and like my childhood, I was unsure whether there was any warmth behind it. It was designed over a hundred and fifty years ago by James Thomson, who designed many houses throughout Wiltshire, and also with the help of John Nash, with whom he designed building developments in London's Notting Hill too. This was, for the most part, a folly, and slightly more abstract and creative than James Thomson's normal Tudor influence. Somewhere inside the false-grandeur was a family home, but this was distorted by the pointed and slightly ecclesiastical windows and by a large spiral tower. The house is large, although perhaps considered on the slightly smaller side for a country house, that could cater servants and hold fancy social events. Although, that is exactly what it did. Stories from my youth hinted at this albeit on a smaller scale. Behind it, hidden away, was the aforementioned boathouse and a sprawling thirteen-acres of land.

"It's like a house from a horror movie," Daisy said wide-eyed. "It's been a while since I've been here."

"Yeah, not since you were a small child. We came over a fair few times, but since your granddad went missing, we've only been here a couple of times." I had no reason to come back here. There was nothing here for me, so I felt no need to unleash it upon my own child. I'm not sure what I was trying to protect her from, and considering what was going to happen, this was certainly a slice of irony that was not lost on me when I later looked back at this.

As we stopped, Daisy got out and ran to the door. I was grabbing for the front door key when Daisy shouted, "It's open."

As I walked up to it, I could see this was not out of someone's forgetfulness, but judging by the crude gouges in the wood frame, it had been forced open. Instantly, I scolded myself for not making the house more secure, what with it being so isolated out here, but I also knew deep down, there was a part of me that hoped my dad would return. So why should I mess with his house?

It's easy to wonder why I did not venture here more often, but really, what was the point? There was no one here to visit, other than the ghosts from my past. This was not a place of fond memories, and I held dear to the thought that at some point, my father would return with that determined look in his eye, nod at me with acknowledgement, and then lock himself away in the study, forgetting all who lived outside of those walls.

"Stay behind me," I said to Daisy, wondering whether I should actually make her stay in the van. I couldn't help but think that I felt better with her here with me and not outside on her own.

The first room on the right was a sitting room, and at first glance, it looked undisturbed. Whenever I see burglarised rooms on the television, they are a complete mess of drawers thrown out, books strewn everywhere, and cushions slashed. You could argue that due to the location, there wasn't the urgency to gust through like a whirlwind, but then I also wondered whether they were actually looking for something in particular. But what would that be? Or more specifically, where would they be looking for it?

The study.

The room that I knew the least about. The room that my father loved the most. The room Father Harry Dugan had said was not straightforward in opening.

Out of the door we walked. Daisy was almost pushing past me to see what was going on. There was an air of excitement coming from her. I guess the naivety of youth was prominent, and in time, this would most likely be swallowed by the experience of life and replaced by cynicism.

Down the hall we pressed on, bypassing the kitchen where I could see the wooden panels of the outside of the study wall were scratched and discoloured. This was not the patina of age, but evidence that someone had tried to gain entry. I pushed the door and turned the handle, but the door remained locked.

The lid to a Pandora's Box of emotions was suddenly open. This house had ceased to be my home in many years, so I did not have that longing of a safe haven attached to it. I was also void of the abundance of happy memories that others later pang for, but the importance of the house to my family did tug on some emotion that was possibly a sadness by proxy. Then there was the smell that– had this scene been recreated in a cartoon– would have had wiggly stench lines floating vertically to the ceiling. I recognised that smell from the club– or the club toilets to be more exact.

Urine.

Disappointment had led them to commit one of life's most basic acts– a bully's parting gift.

"What were they after?" Daisy asked, trailing a finger along one of the many chips of wood. "How come they couldn't get in?"

I pointed out the answer by pulling away a bit more of the wood, exposing a metal membrane. "My dad built steel walls from the inside," I explained. "But I think this was out of some sort of paranoia."

"What is in there then?"

"Look, Daze. My dad was quite eccentric. It would surprise me if there is nothing there but a desk, some old paintings, and a whole pile of junk. He most likely started some rumour about something he found or bought that supposedly is worth a lot of money-"

Daisy wasn't buying this, but again, this was more than likely due to her want to believe that her granddad was some sort of hero. She was still of an age that believes in buried treasure, adventure, and excitement without risk and danger.

"What if there is something there?"

"Look, he was a man that either spent a lot of time trying to find something out of nothing, or he was trying to be someone important."

"Yes, but-"

"But nothing. He never lived up to his dreams. It's a sad fact, and that is what eventually made him disappear− again another ruse to be part of something fantastical. Part of his own riddle." And wondered whether that had been passed on to me. Life was nothing like I'd anticipated it to be. I guess I lacked the desire for the dramatic, instead deciding on whisky shots and depressive contemplation to fill my evenings.

"You've got the key to this room though, haven't you?" she said, and there was that magic in her eyes again− the sort that wanted to believe in fairy tales, true love, and happy-ever-afters.

"Supposedly, but let's see the rest of the house first."

We went up the big staircase first, our footsteps echoing around.

Daisy pushed past me, wanting to be engulfed fully in the history and the excitement and adventure of exploration; again, the risk of rot and decay far from her mind. "Be careful!" I called.

"Jesus. This place is the bomb!"

"It's what?" I replied. It's funny how you never thought just how old you would feel in your mid-thirties until you have children, and they are absorbing the new trends and language of the young. And whilst you may try to keep up with it, you will invariably fall flat on your face and just look old.

Daisy ran ahead, still with the large grin on her face.

I was drinking up the sights that were so thick with nostalgia that it was almost like walking through a stream. Each step it got deeper.

I stopped to look at a picture of my father and mother. It was outside by the lake, taken on a sunny day, which in memory was a little short of perfect, but in reality, may only have been that way for this exact snapshot. My father is looking out towards the lake with a far-off gaze and a look of wonder that suggests his mind is anywhere but there.

His own private Shangri-La.

My mother has a smile that is small and looks like it might be the tail end of a grin that she has managed to control. Experience tells me it's probably a resigned look of amusement at how she should feel, rather than what she does.

My granddad took the photograph on a warm July day. I watched them from the tower where I'd been told to stay. I wanted to join them, and for years later when I looked at that photograph, I pretended to be just out of shot chasing a ball and giggling gaily.

Life is certainly, and for the most part, what you make of it. However, you can also be dictated and coerced into living a life you think is grand and normal until you find out that you are different. So a lot of my memories are filled with some kind of love, but there are always niggling repressed emotions too, like neglect, shame, loneliness, and control that makes me feel slightly scarred.

I found my little girl in a room that was sort of a play room for me. She was sat cross-legged, looking through old LP's that I'd neglected to take with me when I'd left. I thought straight away that after the break-in, I should really collect these items and take them back to my house.

"You've got some of these on CD now, haven't you?" she said matter-of-factly, holding up an early *Alice Cooper* LP. She'd been trying to convert me into downloading music for a while now.

"You bet. That's a classic, by the way," I nodded to the 1973 '*Million Dollar Babies*' LP that was the rare version that included the 'Alice' dollar bill.

Daisy smiled as she flipped it over to read the song titles, and I looked at the other LP's fanned out. *The Stones, Aerosmith, Bob Dylan, The*

Ramones, Patti Smith, then a couple that I had yet to purchase again on CD like *Quiet Riot, Suicidal Tendencies, Johnny Crash, Springsteen.* These were the soundtrack to my youth– the outlet for my frustrations – and ironically, also the fuel to them too. The American youth seemed far more exciting and exhilarating than the lonely grey and rain-filled reality that I lived in.

I smiled to myself as I looked over to the full-length mirror that stood innocently on the wall adjacent to the window. As I looked in, a scared boy looked back. I smiled, recognising the boy as myself all of those years ago as he faded away to be replaced by a man beginning to look rough around the edges.

"Hey, Daisy. Go over to that mirror there."

She rolled her eyes and dutifully did as she was told.

"On the top left corner, you will find a small button. Press it and pull." As she did this, the mirror opened up towards her, showing a doorway to a cupboard that had a ladder leading straight up and small walkway barely wide enough for a person going off in both directions.

"Welcome to the first of many secret passages in this house."

"Oh, man, this place is freaking cool!"

"Freaking, eh?"

"I know you don't like me swearing."

"You're freakin' right, I don't."

Holding on to the ladder, she asked, "So where does this go?"

"My old bedroom. Let's take the stairs though. I don't know how strong that old ladder is anymore."

We closed the mirror back up and took a left out of the door, the opposite direction from which I had come to find Daisy.

Whilst the air was musty from the dust and atmosphere that longed to be filtered through the lungs of humans, there was still that underlying familiarity in the house's own unique perfume of polishing wax and natural deterioration of books and fabrics. The bleaching sun rays cutting through the rooms doing their worst. I walked to the door of the staircase, hardly seeing anything as my mind flashed through a compendium of memories in a painful sentimentality that almost drained me.

Although it had been many years since I'd last climbed these unvarnished stairs, I still knew which step would creak and which one had the slight raise in the head of a loose nail. Opening the door was like stepping back into the past, and I even had to glance back at Daisy to make sure I hadn't just woken up from a deep sleep or another episode of regaining consciousness.

In the corner was my Swindon Town scarf from the few times I'd been to see them play football years ago. There were posters of bands that have since split up and rock stars who had died, or slipped out of the limelight. There was an old Gibson Les Paul copy guitar, with well-worn chipped blue paint left on the floor discarded for years. A bookcase packed with Richard Laymon,

Jack Ketchum, Shaun Hutson, Christopher Fowler, and Ed Gorman books, and a pin board that held many sketches that would be the first signs of my interest in art.

There were two large dormer windows which flooded the room with light. However, it didn't take too long before you realised that this room was in the attic, and whilst it seemed big, it wasn't anywhere near the size of what an attic would be had you looked from the outside. Again the answer to this was behind the side wall, where when a button near the floor was pressed, would then slide open, revealing another large room fitted out with a chair and a large square television. Although there were two more dormer windows, the room was always darker due to the large trees that huddled over this part of the house.

"This place is truly amazing," Daisy said as I revealed the room to her. I could easily forgive her for this as I have always loved to explore places like this. How could she know exactly what this place meant to me and the pain I felt? Even knowing there was no longer any danger, I still felt cold chills dancing up and down my spine.

"Well," I said, pointing to the far corner. "I suspect you'll appreciate what is behind the door over there." And she trotted off, bouncing from one foot to the other as she went, each step echoing around awaking any lost souls that had been trapped here over the years.

I thought of Jack for the first time in many years.

Jack was a boy who had hidden up here in 1924. He'd been playing hide and seek crouching in the opposite corner to the door, when he thought that he was about to be found and made the tragic decision to step out of the window onto the roof. He fell not long after and died instantly from a head injury.

I used to talk to Jack, and sometimes he'd talk back. Of course, this may have been my overactive imagination or the fever that had befriended me more than once.

"Wow, a spiral staircase," she grinned before heading up. This was the tower.

I loved the tower, as this was mine, for whatever that was worth, of course. In contrast to the playroom that was large and dark, this was small and surrounded by glass. It was my favourite place to read books or simply to daydream. When I look back, I admit that a lot of my time was spent daydreaming.

Daisy was quiet with awe for almost ten minutes as she looked out at everything there was to be seen from the vast view which looked out over the back of the house at the large lake and where the small boathouse was. It is two stories tall, with the top floor being my mother's retreat whilst my father did God-Knows-What in the dungeon of this house.

"The view is amazing! It sure beats what I see from my bedroom." To that I could only smile. She'd never understand. And definitely never needed to know.

I thought about one particular night that I was watching fireworks going off dancing with my own silhouettes off of the walls as I wondered what it would be like to be with all of the people below laughing, grinning and 'ooooing' and 'ahhhing.' On the inside looking out, but feeling like I was on the outside looking in.

"Okay, let's go. I need a coffee," I said, walking back towards the stairs.

Daisy looked slightly worried, suddenly understanding my discomfort. "Where does the ladder come out?"

"In that other room. There is a trapdoor in the corner." I tried a smile that came out a little lopsided. "I've one more thing to show you."

As we got to the bottom of the other stairs, I told Daisy to go into the landing, shut the door, and wait for ten seconds before opening the door again, whilst I stayed on the staircase.

Behind a picture of a smiling cartoon cat was a red plastic button that I pushed with the same excitement at showing someone as I had on many occasions as a boy.

After the ten seconds, she opened the door. However, I wasn't there, and nor was the staircase. Instead, there was shelving that looked like you had opened up an airing cupboard.

From behind it all, I heard was a timid, "Da-ad?" I cranked the lever that raised up the shelving to see my daughter in a mix of surprise, wonderment, and a little worry.

"What do you think?" But the answers were written on her face like an over-excited brainstorm.

"I think I could play in this house for hours, Dad!"

"You have to remember that you come from a long line of eccentric and paranoid ancestors."

Chapter Ten

"Can I look outside?" Daisy asked, and I nodded, opening up the envelope that Father Dugan had given me.

"Don't go in the boathouse though. I don't know what condition it is in, okay?"

"Yep!" And she was gone.

I looked at the stack of pages in my hands and then had a quick flick through. My father was a very detailed and meticulous man. He would've spent a long time writing down these details through the pages and pages of text, and I can hear his deep sigh at the very thought of me scanning the paragraphs to get to the bits that I need.

It looked like there was a key, but I had to find it in some elaborate treasure hunt. Each clue appeared to have a short riddle, and was also accompanied by a longer paragraph of detail attached to the text that was either irrelevant, or perhaps extra clues should I fail to decipher the riddle.

A minute or so later, though, I had to smile, whilst at first glance it was easy to dismiss this as a pointless game, and another example of my father's eccentricities; when you looked closer it was actually quite clever. The riddle read like a poem, but the text was a little more like a diary entry, so actually, like all things associated with my father, the obvious was a complete red herring. I was sure the riddle meant nothing, but the clue was in the text, and the text was a vague recollection of a time that only I would know. So what at first seems like a security risk in the wrong hands, was in fact a map that only I can read.

Genius.

There was a slight niggling feeling that I had that asked a question as to why Harry had this envelope and its contents. Why was he only giving it to me now? There would have been no way that I would ever have been able to open the door without these clues.

I looked at the first clue:

"Walk up the hallway to that between floors, on number 12 another clue will be yours!'

And then underneath, the following passage:

"I will not forget that look upon your face when you were about nine. For three days, you had had a strong fever, and your strength was almost seen dripping out of your body like someone had turned on a valve. I gave you this, and whilst your mouth only twitched, your eyes beamed happiness, and I have rarely felt that satisfaction from you before. It was always in your eyes; later on I would see many things in those eyes, emotions that I would pretend not to notice, and whilst your mouth was a fine actor in remaining non-committal for the most part, it was always your eyes that told me the truth. Windows to the soul, they say – barometer of truth, I prefer."

I walked up to the grand staircase and counted each step. At step thirteen I bent down and pulled back the carpet. A folded piece of paper was there. I hadn't expected it. But as I opened it out, I smiled at the short line: *Fool, your search ends here.*

I knew this was not the staircase that was talked about. It was, of course, the secret staircase up to my room that I had shown Daisy earlier. There weren't thirteen steps; there were only ten, but halfway up on a shelf was a Ford Mustang car with the number thirteen on the door and bonnet. I was sure that I would find the clue here.

And of course, 45 seconds later, I did just that. I unfolded it and looked at the riddle and paragraph.

This carried on for another couple of clues, and to be honest I was beginning to get a little bored. There was a slight fun aspect to this riddle-hunt, but I had a lot of work to do, and my hands were still aching from the fight the night before.

I was on my hands and knees in the lounge. Daisy was now around the front sweeping up. I pushed at one of the floorboards in the corner as instructed and was about pull it up when I heard the voices.

If the next few minutes of my life were to be on an old VHS video tape, then it would've been well worn, like the copy of *The Goonies* that I had recorded, and that had been played and rewound so many times that the picture quality had deteriorated long before I bought it again on DVD.

I can see the dust still dancing in the sunlight.

The musty smell lingers with the memory, and my stomach sinks.

The sound of my daughter's voice dries my throat and wets my eyes.

How can this happen to me? I've done nothing wrong to deserve this. I've spent my life fighting against the odds to live a semblance of normality. I made decisions to help Daisy rather than myself, and yet –

And yet I am the one left here, unable to fathom quite what has happened.

I'm never one to point the finger of blame, but I cannot help it. Just when I thought that my father might end up bringing something to the family, all that he brings is pure destruction. Maybe it's my good-natured manner, but I'm sure that he didn't mean to leave me in this cesspool of complete shit, but that is the cold, hard fact.

As my memory replays the events it will see the van, the men, my scared daughter, and the bright white light that stops me even being able to take in one last look at her before she is taken.

Thanks, Dad. Thanks a bloody lot.

I hope that you are happy with making me feel the worse pain that I've ever experienced in my life.

Chapter Eleven

Present day

I've never particularly wanted to be in the Forces. No real reason, it just never appealed to me. Aside from not having family in the Forces, you may think that I would've been a good candidate for that vocation.

A troubled childhood that lacked direction, trained as a fighter, but without a sense of belonging, but this was the closest thing I've ever felt to being actually under attack.

The 'flash bang' grenade (or a stun grenade) is a military non-lethal weapon, and whilst it doesn't do any long term damage, it is usually used to confuse and stun a person with temporary blindness, deafness, and balance – often when used as part of an attack, the 'stunned' are then left as sitting ducks to be finished off by actual lethal weapons.

In this case, the lethal weapon was kidnap, and that hurt more than any bullet ever could.

At first, I tried to get up, but my balance was all over the place. It was like being drunk– it took great effort to get my body to react to what my brain was trying to tell it. Slowly, my vision cleared in what I can only describe as being like woken up from a deep sleep to a bright lamp shone directly into your eyes. Rapidly, I blinked, half to slowly get used to the sudden light, and half to add a little more moisture to my eyeballs. I imagine my pupils are so wide now that my eyes must look like some drugged-out raver.

The dust had settled on the floor...but my baby was gone.

The sudden sense of loss was overwhelming.

Through all of her years, there were things that I'd kept her away from, or slowly spoon fed her so as she would be streetwise without being suddenly exposed to the horrors of life. I'd worried myself to sleep over situations that she may get herself into when I'm not around her, and yet here I was, no more than twenty feet away when I allowed someone to take her.

If this had happened to someone else then I would be full of sympathetic advice: You cannot have known that this would happen, and you cannot legislate for something that is incredibly unusual, and of course, this is not your fault.

But this was me, and I could see nowhere else to throw the guilt but at myself. I felt defeated, but more than that, I felt totally inadequate as a father. And worse still, I was totally inadequate as a man and a human being.

My pragmatic nature was eradicated as I felt myself drowning in self-pity. I tried to snap myself out of it, but my options seemed to be lacking. What should I do?

Adrenaline was pumping through my veins, but I had no outlet for it. My mind was still cloudy, and I was slightly worried that my hearing would never return.

In my head, I screamed. Later on, when my throat remained burning sore, I knew I'd actually screamed out loud.

But as I looked to where the van had been, I saw something in the gravel. A small, black mobile phone.

I walked to it, and with my t-shirt, I picked it up.

Hope – That is what I felt. This hadn't been dropped; they had seemed too slick and professional. This had been left for me. There would be no fingerprints on it, but I wanted to make sure I didn't taint it any further.

And of course, if it did ring, I wouldn't be able to hear it.

Talk about buggered.

I needed someone else here. I pretended that it was to help me answer the phone, but deep down, I knew I needed someone to talk to. I'd had dealt with things on my own for too long. This was too much for me to handle. I knew that mentally I was suddenly fragile.

Very slowly, my hearing returned, but with a slight ringing at first.

I took out my own mobile and kicked the now empty small canister that had deemed useless in staving off the attack. I hardly made good contact and it skidded to a halt a few feet away.

I badly wanted to call Father Dugan, but in spite of our joking about in regards to him being hip, he also kept his phone on silent, and could not be relied upon for a quick response. Jason would be my next port of call, but he was out of town today meeting a new supplier, and whilst I could rely on a quick response, he is about three hours away. Jez would answer, but would be giddy with excitement with the situation, and lacking so much in regards to tact and understanding that there is a good and very genuine chance that I might murder him in a sudden fit of rage.

For a second, I thought of Jean. The bottom fell out of my stomach again. I'd protected Daisy from Jean for years, sure that she would be better off with me, and Jean to her credit, admitted that I was more of a parent that she would ever be. For all of her bad decisions and wild ways, the two of us were completely convinced that living with me, Daisy would be better off. And now I feel that I've let Daisy and Jean down.

That was an almost paralysing feeling.

I had to get home to somewhere familiar.

Away from this place that seemed to hold tight some family curse, that was not within reality. It was slowly forming a synopsis of a new *Stephen King* tale.

I put away my phone.

Part of me knew I was leaving the front door unlocked and open, but it was not the conscious part. I stumbled to the camper-van, knowing that I shouldn't drive, but I just wanted to get away from here.

I looked again at the phone that I'd found and saw that there was a text message. I pressed the button to read it and the words flashed up:

DON'T SPEAK TO THE POLICE, OR YOU WILL NEVER SEE HER AGAIN. WE WILL KNOW. WAIT FOR INSTRUCTIONS.

I read and re-read the text about ten times. It was certainly to the point. There was a suggestion that I would see Daisy again. At least, that's what my optimistic side told me, by way of being told that I wouldn't see her again if I didn't comply. And then I was filled with dread that actually the important word that was missing was – ALIVE.

This time, I didn't think as I pulled my mobile out and scrolled down the names until I came to Ruby's: *Please meet me at my house ASAP,* I typed and started up the van.

Off I went, numb with an overload of emotions on the longest drive back home that I'd had in years.

Chapter Twelve

I pulled up outside of my house still completely numb to my core.

The rest of the world moved around me unaware of the horror I'd experienced. I was struggling to function. I recognised the onset of shock. It was only now I understood when I'd caught my girlfriend naked with another man, the awful feeling was nothing compared to what I felt now. Back then, I felt lonely, but I had Daisy to hold tightly. I had gently kissed her soft infant skin and longed to protect her from this feeling. And now that she was lost, I felt truly alone. It is not often I indulged in self-pity, but now I wallowed and was almost engulfed in it.

I didn't want to go into my house alone. I knew everywhere I looked I was reminded of Daisy.

And reminded of how I'd failed.

I sat gazing out of the windscreen, hoping that neither Miss Chambers or Jez would come out. I don't want you to get the wrong impression of me, but I may well have been liable to have punched either of them when they both opened their mouths. Of course, I'm sure I would never had – Jez would start crying, and Miss Chambers would probably laugh at me and hit me back. Neither one was a good scenario.

And then I spotted the magpie.

For the past few years, the same magpie has habitually flown around my street like a cross between a stalker and a guardian angel. He has decided that my rubbish bag alone is filled with all the dietary requirements needed for an eighteen-inch bird. In return, I get the occasional and slightly annoying vocal 'thank you' of the bird's crow-like squawk. I have no idea how old said bird is, but I do know that they can live between twenty-five and thirty years, so I don't see my rubbish bags being left in peace anytime soon.

I call him Sorrow, and after feasting on my leftovers, I'd like to imagine that he thinks of me as Joy.

One for sorrow, just like the rhyme. I searched, but he'd not brought a friend.

Typical.

In my rear-view mirror, the familiar sight of a new-shaped white VW Beetle pulled up behind me. I got out to meet Ruby.

"I-it's bad," I stammered as she walked to me, not trusting myself to speak much more than this.

"What's happened?" I could make out her lips saying. My eyes jumped around, and I saw flashes of her black clothing, bright pink lipstick, and dyed red-hair.

"Someone has taken Daisy," I said, hearing the quiver in my voice.

"What do you mean, taken? Like, kidnapped?" One of her hands now comforted her face as she said it, her silver rings and bright bangles contrasting against slightly pale skin as she looked in shock.

Forgetting to not worry about prints, I showed her the message on the mobile.

"Shit," she said as I fell into her arms. For a while, we stood there clutching tightly, and on any other occasion, this may well have been a moment.

I pulled away, and we stumbled in to the house.

I collapsed into the sofa, and Ruby sat on the edge, clearly unsure what to say.

After a little while of silence, I mumbled out a few words, "It's something to do with my father," I said. "They were asking about him. Something in the study."

"I take it you have no idea what it is they're after?" Ruby said.

I shook my head. "My father spent a long time there working on something. To be honest, we never really thought it was anything of importance. He was-" I paused trying to arrange the words in my mind, "-disconnected with us. I assumed it was some sort of escape. He worked feverishly in there, sometimes days at a time, barely stopping to eat. I thought that he was in some sort of psychological breakdown. Perhaps he thought he was searching for some ground-breaking cure, or inventing something beyond the rest of our comprehension." I was sure that I was babbling, but I also realised that I needed to say these things out loud. It never seemed appropriate to speak to Daisy so deeply, and I've had a number of trust issues with adults. Finding your girlfriend naked with another man will do that.

Ruby nodded encouragingly as I ran my hands through my short hair. "He was so guarded with what he was doing that we gave up asking. He made out he was just painting, and we allowed him to carry on with the guise. But the paintings were becoming less frequent, and when they did make it out of the study, they seemed rushed and not of the same quality of his original pieces.

"My mother showed obvious signs of frustration, and having once supported him, became suddenly disenchanted. I think I always knew he wasn't painting. You don't spend that much time doing something with such focus and dedication, to then produce something of sub-standard quality. If only he had told me."

Looking at the phone in my hand, Ruby then added carefully, "We should look in the study."

I nodded. Why had I not thought to go straight there? The answer could well be staring us in the face once we got inside.

"Text them," she said simply. Ruby was a sweet lady, but there was a strong backbone under the Rockabilly-chick style that she favoured. Her tattoos also showed the same contrast: a cupcake on her wrist and a skull and poison bottle above. The stars and pin-up girl on her bicep and a smoking pistol below. A dragon on her shoulder looked over a cartoon swallow, and so on. Sugar and spice. Good and evil. Beauty and the beast.

"But they said to wait."

"Time is everything though, right?" And I could hear the words from a thousand movies, and read the lines in a thousand books about the importance of the first 48hrs.

With shaking fingers and a heavy heart that pumped solidly in my chest, I pressed the reply button: *How can I get my daughter back? What do you want?*

Then, as if this small black object held some incredible power, we were again lost in silence, only speculating in our minds how this might play out. The phone suddenly became very heavy.

And then it vibrated with a response.

And at the same time, someone banged the front door.

Chapter Thirteen

1986

It was lunchtime on a Saturday, and it had been raining ever since I got up this morning. My mother was busy preparing for another party tonight, and once again, she was mad at my father. He was lost in his own world, deep in the silence of the study painting. His paintings are really good, and I bet one day he'll sell one for thousands of pounds. He does spend a long time in the study, but I heard that you have to dedicate a long time to something in order to be really good at it. Roy Castle always says that on *Record Breakers*, and he knows loads of people that are great at things. It's all about practise!

I've been drawing pictures myself, but I'm not that good at drawing from my mind. I can copy things pretty good. My friend, Peter says I should get Dad to show me how to paint, as he reckons I'd be able to copy expensive paintings and make a bomb!

Yesterday was a strange day at school (stranger than normal!), and I'm not sure what Monday will bring. Derek Wallace had an accident, and by an accident, I mean that he shit his pants! Ha ha!

Derek Wallace is a big fat bully. He likes to treat everyone like crap just because he's about seven-feet tall, and fat. He thinks he's special just 'cause his dad's in the RAF. So what? To me, he's over-grown, over-fed, and his dad pisses about with planes. Big f-ing deal.

Anyway, Derek has decided that he's not happy with filling his fat face with his own crisps, chips, burgers, and pies, but he's also entitled to everyone else's, and has spent the last week going around those that are either smaller (so that's like everyone!) or keep to themselves, helping himself to their lunch. I knew at some point his fat arse would want to take my lunch too.

"What you got for me today, Ed-ward?" he sneered, looking around at his peers and enjoying their laughs. He always over pronounces my name like it's a big old joke.

I hate bullies, and I'm not a huge fan of confrontation, especially with big-boned Neanderthals looking to swipe my lunch. "Look, just leave me alone," I started. "You can have a couple of chips, but stay away from my lemonade, as that's the only drink I've got."

"Chips, huh? I've had some chips, Eddie-bear!" Again he glanced around for approval. "What I really need is your drink, I'm afraid!" He laughed as he snatched it up.

"I wouldn't," I said in a low, defeated voice.

He stopped for a second with the plastic bottle against his lips, growled, "Really!" and guzzled the whole lot down.

The great thing about a high-strength liquid laxative is its speed to work when ingested at three times the recommended amount. In this case, I used magnesium citrate (in liquid form), specifically because it tastes of lemonade and is fast working. Just as Derek's grin was about to drop, and using an element of surprise, I punched him as hard as I could in the stomach. The scene was completed with the bully falling off balance through surprise onto his chubby backside, and then followed by a God-awful guttural sound as his intestines bubbled like a water-cooler, and his bowels gave way, and in front of his peers, and the whole of the canteen, Derek Wallace shit himself. Not once or twice, but all the way to the toilets. The odd discoloured drops marking the way like rancid liquefied breadcrumbs were all that was left. And of course, my great big cheesy grin as I shouted, "You had better run away, wimp!"

I've always hated people that think that they can bully their way through life. My granddad has been teaching me boxing at his friend Harry Dugan's gym. They think that I am pretty good, but I've no intention of fighting at school. So I am not worried if Fatty Wallace wants to try and get me back. Harry taught me a couple of moves that involved slipping under any swinging punch and landing a good solid punch just under the rib-cage. If well executed, they could well either end the fight there and then or allow you to pick whatever punch you wanted. The David and Goliath concept is heavily flawed, as some of the larger guys down the gym are more cumbersome, with less balance, but can pack a punch. Small and quick can out manoeuvre the bigger guy, especially if they are not as well-schooled as I am at boxing.

For five years, I have been coming down here to the gym with my granddad, and apart from the times that I'm ill, I'm hanging out here listening to the rock music playing on a stereo as the deep rhythmic thud of fists on heavy bags pound out, metal clangs of weights, whirling skipping ropes, and machine-gun rapid fire hits of the speed-bag become the sound of my youth.

Last week, I remember being put through a hard session with Harry on the pads. It was hard because Harry was speeding up the position of the pads so I nearly missed them, and more than a couple of times when he swung for me to duck under, he caught me on the side of the head. There was no apology. "Focus," was all that he would reply, to which I remained silent, save for my quick breaths. I sometimes think I'm like that Daniel kid in *The Karate Kid*, and Harry is an English version of Mr. Miyagi, although there is no way I would be painting his fence or waxing his car. I'd tell him to get stuffed if he ever mentioned it!

When it was finally over, I sat back with a glass of water, panting and sweating buckets, listening to *AC/DC* play *Back In Black*. When it was over, I felt totally revived. That's why there's very little pop music played here, I reckon. *Whitney Houston* and *Madonna* may well be scoring hits in the music charts, but there is no place for them here. We have things like *Iron Maiden* with *Somewhere In Time*, *Motorhead*'s *Orgasmatron*, and *Metallica* thrashing out *Master Of Puppets* to keep us focused.

So I already know that I'm to stay upstairs tonight. Mother doesn't like me coming down when she has guests, as everyone fusses over me, especially when they've been drinking. My dad may or may not make an appearance. He's spent almost three days solid in the study, and I'm not even sure that he comes out to sleep. I wonder whether he's ill. Not like the flu, but in his head. Nobody talks to me about his obsession with the study, but it doesn't seem normal. I sometimes wonder whether he can go off to another world there like they did in the *Narnia* books that I read a few years ago. Lately, this wonder has become real. Why would you spend so long in there? I sometimes joke to myself that I should stand at the study door and shout, "Father, come home to us!"

I like to look out of my window as the guests arrive. They're all smiles and giggles. Sometimes I play hide & seek with Jack or we just talk. I told him about my secret. Jack won't tell anyone....

Chapter Fourteen

Daisy

Everything happened so quickly. It was like, one minute I was talking to this strange bloke, and the next thing, I'm being bundled into the back of a van!

I'm babbling here and sorta getting ahead of myself, 'cause at some point there was a flash of light and a bang, and I was convinced that it was a bomb and I was dead. Horrible.

That would be typical, especially when I'm wearing my stupid old clothes. I'm not sure what I'd like to be wearing, should I know I'm about to – you know - die, but ideally not something from *Primark*, even if it is a favourite of mine. I'm not snobby, but given a choice, it might be something a little more, er, hard wearing.

The movement of the van, but the lack of sight or sound had made me wonder whether I was really off to Heaven. Unlikely, right? For a second, I smiled at how my father was wrong in his assumption of no afterlife, but this is soon replaced by a fearful sinking feeling in my stomach. Who knows, really?

It's not long before my sight returns, and my journey to Heaven appears to be in a rather beaten up van. I mean, I'm not sure how I expect to make the transition from living to the afterlife, but I'd like to think I'd at least be worthy of a horse and carriage or even some space-age pod full of comfort and harp-playing. Even *Cliff Richard* would be better than nothing. Well, sort of.

There's this big guy sat next to me on some bench seat, he has a smell that suggests bulk. It's hard to describe, but it's a manly sweat made up of greasy chips, onions, and beer, I think, although of course I've no reason for this. I can see that he knows that I am staring at him, but he doesn't even try and make me feel at ease. I want to shout, but my lack of hearing stops me. I want to take my small fists and bang on his head until, like in a cartoon, it explodes. I don't, of course. I am not one of those stupid girls.

I quickly try to get to the back door, but as I start to move, I feel a large vice-like grip on my arm and turn to see him mouth, "Stupid bitch" and smile a toothless grin. Actually, he has teeth, but there is one missing, and so I want to describe him as toothless, so he sounds as horrible as I think of him to be:

This large, over-grown, toothless man with huge pointy ears and green scaly-skin, sat like some giant slug next to me, ready to eat me up in one great big bite before letting out an incredibly loud belch that will reverberate around the van so loudly that the slimy little man in the front may very well crash into a tree.

However, he is just a slightly larger man than my dad with a shaved head and some ear plug thingies hanging from normal looking ears. I guess you would say he was 'thick-set,' which is a good way of saying chunky, when you don't know whether they are packed with muscle or packed with pies!

I should also point out that I am trying to make light of this situation, as I am scared shitless. I know dad wouldn't like me to say that, but I also know that he would forgive me in this unfortunate situation. I mean WTF??? I've been kidnapped. For real. It's like #callthepolice!

I feel a tear escape from my left eye, but I turn away to the tinted window quickly so the horrible men can't see. I'll not give them that satisfaction.

They would most likely love to see me show this girlie weakness. I still want to smash his ogre-like face in. I want to see my dad again.

This is the worst feeling that I have ever had. Period.

Come and find me, Dad, please.

And soon.

Chapter Fifteen

I snatched up the phone desperately, almost dropping it with haste and sloppiness. Ruby got up to answer the door, although this hardly registered with me. I needed to know what the text said. My stomach was in knots. I was about as low as I had ever been.

The text message replied: We r not fucking around. Either u bring it to us, or yr daughter is gone forever. u have 24hrs from now.

So what the Hell was I supposed to do? I had no idea what they were looking for. They were the only people that knew what was hidden – apart from my dad.

Harry. Just what did he know? He knew to finally give me the details to get into the study. So what else was he hiding from me?

I thought that all of the surprises of my life had occurred, until I looked up to see Miss Chambers striding in and Ruby behind looking slack-jawed.

"You've turned her into the maid now, I see," she said. "I guess that's a promotion in your book."

At that moment, I wanted to get up and punch Miss Chambers square in the face. I know this would be a totally irrational act, but the emotional cocktail that had been fed to me had almost taken me outside of my body. My laid back sensibilities had been shocked into an uncharacteristic reaction. One punch would lay the old snoop out on her back for ten minutes. *Lead us not unto temptation*, I thought quickly. Then by way of an automatic response, I found myself weighing up which cushion would be best to smother her with.

"Look-" I started sharply, before Ruby cut me off.

"Ma'am, something awful has happened." It was visible to see that Miss Chambers was about to come out with another smart retort, but Ruby rebuffed this with reality, "Daisy has been kidnapped."

"What!?" Miss Chambers seemed visibly shaken, and this was a sobering sight. "Have you two been sniffing something?" This iron-lady, so normally impenetrable, almost aged in front of my eyes and showed that she was mortal after all, albeit trying hard to mask with a quip.

"It's true," I said, and had to take a deep breath so as not to show just how close I was to completely shutting down emotionally.

Ruby, to her credit, stepped in. "It was from Caulfield Hall. Two men in a van came looking for something and, without warning, took Daisy."

I looked up and quietly said, "They've just sent me a text to say I have 24hrs to give them what they want, or I will never see Dai-" I coughed back the tears and felt the warm embrace from Ruby.

"Two men," Miss Chambers said. "The ones from yesterday, they came to see me a few hours ago. That's what I came to speak to you about."

I had completely forgotten about the men that Miss Chambers had mentioned before. Sometimes the woman just winds me up without uttering a word, and therefore whilst she is trying to engage in idle chatter (by which I mean her putting me down in some way), I am imagining large objects falling on her head.

I half smiled at how Miss Chambers could still keep up our banter.

"What did they want?" I asked mechanically, looking up, but seeing nothing that was in the room. All I could picture was the men that I'd seen moments before they ripped my heart out.

"They wanted you. They seemed quite adamant and forceful about that. I told them that as far as I knew, I was not your mother, so I had no idea where you were."

"What were they driving? Did you see it?" I asked.

With one fluid move, Miss Chambers brandished something from her house-coat. "Better than that. I took a Polaroid!" she beamed, showing us a set of good strong teeth.

And as I looked at the photograph of the familiar white van, the memories came flooding back. I had to swallow again and grasp as much composure as possible.

My heart fluttered slightly with hope as I saw the number plate. It wasn't conclusive, but we could find out who this vehicle was registered to, and from there, possibly find our way to these two shits. But 24 hours was a short period of time.

In my book, these two individuals were dead men walking. I was trying out the tough-talk in my mind, but honestly, to have my daughter back, I would buy them lunch and clean their van. I'm not *The Krays*, and despite the tattooed exterior, I'm just a family man who loves his daughter more than life itself.

There are very few things that will guarantee to turn a man from a normal, law-abiding citizen, to crazy Neanderthal man, but anything to do with a man's daughter is a punishable offence.

"They were awfully rude about my music," Miss Chambers continued, like this might be on par with your offspring's kidnapping. Normally, I would've chipped in with something like, "At least they understood music then!" But I couldn't bat the ball back on this one. Somewhere, the ball fell to the floor and rolled to a stop.

"Oh, dear," Ruby said, slightly forced.

"I'm not looking to be patronised, young lady," Miss Chambers said, and then suddenly with a shake of a hand and a click of her fingers, she appeared to have an epiphany. "Look, I don't know exactly what it is these ghastly men could be after, but I've got something that your dad gave me a while back. Some prototype thing, although it looked like a fancy walkie-talkie if you asked me." Whilst I stood there unable to put together a proper sentence, she turned and was out the door with a, "I'll look for it and pop back around later!"

"Why would she have that?" Ruby asked. "Is that what they want?"

"It's beyond me as to why that woman seems to be imprinted into my life more each day. I can't see them doing this for a prototype, although it depends on whether or not the thing works." I picked up my own mobile and sent a text message to Jez. He may be able to run the plates (as they say in the movies). I was still a little wary of bringing his immaturity into my life and this situation, but sometimes you have to put up with these little things. I certainly had no problem with punching him full in the face if he dared to joke.

Ruby then excused herself to use the bathroom, and I was left with my thoughts— my sad and lonely thoughts.

I went to a photo album on my bookshelf and pulled out a picture of Daisy. It's a few years old, and in it, we had been on a holiday in Coombe Martin in Devon. Daisy is looking out over the swimming pool, with the sea in the background. Her young innocence is so apparent that a new lump appears in my throat. Two separate tears escape from both eyes, one slightly after the other.

To think that yesterday I got drunk and then carried on drinking until I passed out looking at pictures of my ex-girlfriend like it was some fairytale that went wrong— some unwanted longing that only the inebriated mind can conjure up, and all whilst my beautiful daughter slept above, and also whilst Ruby was asleep outside on the porch. I was certainly what the phrase 'blind drunk' was coined for, unable to see exactly what I had until it was gone— something I think *Joni Mitchell* once sang about, although she was talking about nature being turned into parking lots, but the idea was still the same.

My dissatisfaction with normality kept me focused and striving for better, but refused to allow me to appreciate what I had. I mean, even my relationship with Daisy's mother wasn't that bad; it was sort of on the level as with an annoying little sister. I still loved her, but just not in that romantic way anymore. I was still prone to bouts of being in love with the idea of being together, but these were (as aforementioned) fuelled by alcohol or by waves of loneliness. I missed what I'd lost and not what I had to hold. You also can't help but concede that as your daughter's mother, maybe you could overlook her funny ways, her want for attention, whether it be at home or elsewhere.

And then it hit me. I was the apple looking up at the tree that I'd not fallen too far from, not knowing whom I should feel sorry for the most. Self-pity can be a slippery spiral that is incredibly hard to slow down and get off from. It's easier to point your finger at anyone but yourself, and sometimes the ability to lie to yourself is so easy that you never change, always believing it's not your fault.

And sometimes you need a horrific wake up call.

LOST CONNECTIONS

Chapter Sixteen

Daisy

I don't know where I am, obviously, but I can tell I'm out in the countryside. I was blindfolded with some musty-old rag as we turned up a country lane, and I'm gonna take this as a positive sign. The only thing is, though, I can't think of too many times when people have been taken hostage and then let go. Or rather, the chances of getting away with kidnapping nowadays are pretty damn slim. So this doesn't bode well. I get that. I'm usually quite a positive person, rarely used to speaking in bad language, but if I am completely honest, I don't see much of a happy ending to this story. I see ugly headlines in the papers and an extended episode of *Crimewatch*, but for me: I'm fucked. Seriously, like, how could this end well?

So anyway, having been pulled out of the van and walked a while, I can hear the echo of our footsteps, which tell me that we've gone inside somewhere (I could tell the change in light).

They like to shove me a lot. It doesn't hurt much, but catches me off balance.

The floor is hard, and we've just slowly gone down some stairs. I am guessing we've gone into some sort of basement, but this may be my mind assuming that as we have gone downstairs, we are in a house and not some other sort of structure built for kidnapping and murdering in. I don't suppose the décor will be all that.

I hope there's not blood splattered all over the walls.

I'm not so good at guessing the distance that we travelled, but it's not long before we stop. There's a horrible moment when I think they're going to do something to me, as I can feel large rough hands all over my body, but they don't linger or squeeze me, and soon my blindfold is taken off.

I'm not sure what I expected.

Well, that's not strictly true. What I expected was a stone cell with no window and a large steel door, perhaps a chain in the corner and a bowl for food. A classic dungeon feel. Or something out of a *SAW* movie (I've seen clips on YouTube). But this was not a crime novel about serial killers with loose-cannon cops, or alcoholic detectives; this was some failed theft that had a kidnap twist. They needed me to be okay. At least that's what I hoped.

There was a bed and a bookcase with a handful of paperbacks, a couple of small dirty windows too tiny to climb through, and a single doll abandoned by an unknown. The walls were covered in an old floral design wallpaper that reminded me of cheap B&B's we'd stayed the weekend in years before, or the rooms of strange old aunts that we would put our coats down in, the thick smell of potpourri bothering our nostrils with its floral fragrance. This could be Miss Chambers' house, I thought, trying to keep my spirits up.

"Stay here," they said to me, although really I had no choice. Then the door closed. There was a fumble of a key in the lock, and they were gone.

I walked to the door and was about to try the handle, just in case it was some strange psychological experiment to see whether the captured would ever try to escape, or whether the fear of what was behind the door would be enough to keep them away from even trying the door, like an electric wire fence to a cow. However, I could hear talking, and as I strained to hear, a few words could be made out.

"...They said that they would be at Caulfield Hall..."

Another voice replies, "But can they be trusted?"

"Of course.........is with him now, and he is beside himself with ...."

I wasn't too sure what I'd heard, as they must've been turning away from me when speaking, so I was missing key words. But it sounded like someone that my dad knows and trusts was in on this. That really sucks. And now I want to just kill someone! Dad doesn't deserve this.

As the voices get further away, I reached into my bra and retrieved my mobile phone. Those blokes are idiots. If you kidnap a teenage girl, then for God sake search her. We will always have a mobile phone. Our dads buy them for us because they never want us to be stranded, and always want us to be at the end of the phone should they ever need to call. How many times do we use it for that purpose? Once or twice a month? The rest of the time I am texting my friends about boys, homework, and music.

I look at the screen, and the first thing I do is make sure that it's on silent. It is. If it wasn't, then my dad would go all detective on me every time it beeped a message or rang.

Then I checked the battery. It still had a pretty good charge. But then I notice the signal, and I'm not surprised to find that there is just the one bar.

Quickly, I tap out a text to my dad:

Dad am ok. Am in a room somewhere. Dont tell ne1 about this. Heard them talking and saying that sum1 u know is in on this. B careful. I'll b ok. D XX

I stare at the phone, and my heart sinks at the message that comes back: ***Text Failed***

I move as close to the window as I can, hold the phone right up to the glass, and press Resend.

My heart beats fast, and relief then washes over me as I see the words ***Sent*** flash back at me. I quickly try to go on the internet by pressing the *Google Map App*, that way I could tell where I was and then get some help. However, my hopes are dashed as I get the ***No Internet Connection*** message back.

I slip the phone back into my bra, sit down on the bed, and begin to look around the room.

It doesn't look like a cell. And whilst there's a lock on the door, the fact that there are a number of items here giving an air of comfort suggests this could've been a bedroom designed for relaxation. My mind works overtime looking around the corners of the room, the door, the window, because comfort means structural weakness somewhere along the line– a glimmer of hope that I may be able to get out of here.

The door is not solid, but it doesn't look like I'm able to pull it open. The lock is bolted from the other side, and whilst I may well be able to remove the handle, the door would still remain locked, and therefore, my efforts would be useless.

The windows are both just too small for me to get through, although it would be a matter of inches.

I open the other door that I assume to be a closet, and there in front of me is a wardrobe with a handful of clothes on hangers. But as I look at the clothes, a chilling thought stops and manifests into my brain.

These clothes seem dated from current fashions. So what happened to the owner of the clothes?

I'm suddenly wondering whether or not these men are professionals. I then wonder not only whether I will see my father again, but whether I will ever step outside of this room again. Amateurs are notoriously bad planners and prone to rash decisions leading to panic – I've seen enough Netflix documentaries to tell me as much. In this case, if they feel some heat, then my goose is cooked.

I stumble back to the bed, drop down on the mattress, and silently sob. I'm not normally a person to feel sorry for myself, but shit, I'm definitely going to do that now.

I don't know what to do anymore.

I close my eyes and feel the comfort of my dad's arms around me. The scratchy stubble as he kisses my cheek, then a fatherly warning about something, whilst still trusting me fully. I would love to think that between the two of us, we'll find our way back together again, but this was a situation that may take even more than love to conquer.

Dad, please find me.

Chapter Seventeen

I sat down on the sofa looking around the room at all of the people that were now here, and do you know what I thought? This was like somebody's wake after their funeral. I'm here feeling all sorry for myself – and I make no apologies over that – and here were all of these people around me. It brought a lump to my throat to think that these people cared enough to want to help. They were certainly a band of motley-looking folk. Not many of them would you sit down and design from scratch into perfection of a friend, neighbour, or family member, but this was reality. This wasn't a Hollywood remake. Here were people with wobbly bits, crooked noses, limps, lumps, and bad habits – each idiosyncrasy shaped that person, forming the familiar memories of them, as well a handful of bad ones – but that is life.

It wasn't long, though, before the feelings changed inside me. I know I should be grateful that all of these people were here to show me support, but frustration overwhelmed my want to say "thanks," and instead I resented that this may bring some excitement to a couple of their boring lives. Yes, immediately I feel guilty for thinking this, *but why shouldn't I?* I don't want to express such dramatics from me, but without Daisy, I really have nothing to live for. Losing a child is probably one of the worst things that could happen to someone. And all these do-gooders will then have the unfortunate 'awkward' moments with me until I can pull myself together again. Even Jean may well shrug it off like it was happening to someone else. That's probably not fair, but that's just how I was feeling.

Jean was now sitting opposite me, unable to look at me for more than a few seconds. She said that she didn't blame me for what has happened, but her eyes tell me something different. They're bloodshot and red from crying, and her hands are visibly shaking, but she tries to pull the sleeves of her GAP hoodie down over them so as not to be noticed. And all I can think of is that it makes a pleasant change for her not to be trying to show the world her breasts in a low-cut vest or dress.

Her new boyfriend, Bob, is pacing around the room looking at all of my personal effects, slightly embarrassed with the situation and totally at a loss as to what he can offer. In another situation, I might even feel sorry for the poor bugger. Him there with hair that has been highlighted, and a gold ring in one earlobe, looking like someone that may've been cool with the same style in the eighties, but now resembles a loss of identity and a refusal to move on. Maybe I'm just being deliberately harsh. There's a small part of me that remains jealous of each of Jean's boyfriends; *how messed up is that?*

Jez is sitting at the dining room table like a kid at Christmas playing with a new toy. He's finding out the registration details of the van with his laptop and a couple of small boxed IT attachments, unable to believe his luck as to the adventure he's found himself thrust into. He's smiling and practising his lines of a hero. He longs to be the guy in the movie sitting in the back of the surveillance van tapping away at the keys, with no use for a mouse or having to put in a password that he recently changed and cannot remember. I wish that just once in one of those movies, they'd get an error message that they'd have to ring through to their IT Support to help with, only to be told that they had to try 'turning the PC off and then back on again.' Or clearing their cache and cookies.

Ruby is in the kitchen sorting out refreshments, and Father Dugan and Miss Chambers are looking at some sort of telephone handset that was around when Bob first got highlights. This was what my father had left with her. The thing looked old and antiquated. It was a complete dud and certainly not what was required. You'd have more chance of making a call with one of my beaten-up trainers than you would that thing. We'd busted it open, but like Jez's skull, it was an anti-climax revealing nothing much inside.

For a second, I wondered whether or not I could pass it of as the real thing, but for all that I know, the real thing may well be something completely different.

If this is it, then what the Hell is so special? You can get cheap phones at any of the shops in your high street that is not a betting shop, pound shop, or charity shop. These guys also appear to not be against mugging, should they desperately want one, not to mention the fact they left one with me.

Did my father have an antique one? And honestly, I'm making a huge assumption that it has anything remotely to do with telecommunications at all. It could be a picture, a DVD, a treasure map. It could be just about anything, and I have nothing to go on at all.

I'm at a total loss.

I glance over at Bob, who keeps checking his phone, but there is something I'm not quite sure about him. It's not that he's got a strong Northern accent, or that he resembles a *Viz* character that never quite made it to the comic. There's just something. He suddenly looks at me and looks extremely guilty. He wipes his nose with the back of his hand, then swiftly makes an exit. Jean doesn't seem to notice, but I make sure he doesn't have any of my CD's in his hand.

"She was the best thing that ever happened to us," Jean said, looking into her hands. "We made that sweet girl. You and me."

I swallowed. "Yes. Life can be full of regrets if you let it be, but I don't regret having her with you, Jean."

"We could've had something good, eh?" she thought out loud with a hint of regret. Without thinking, I place my hand on hers. "We're better for her, as we are, don't you think?"

A beat passed, whereby she seemed to think deeply about this, and then she sighed, "It just seems like we missed an opportunity. We had it all, and we messed it up."

I'm never one to deliberately go for an argument or one to rock a boat, but inside my head, I wondered about what she was saying. Our equality of guilt shared over the slippery hands of our relationship, but in truth, I was working many hours and coming home to look after Daisy, and Jean went out and ended up in another man's bed. As easy as it can be to try and make up a justification of needing space and time away from looking after a child, with neglect from a hard-working man, the reality is that a jury would not see this situation fit for philandering. This was no cause to be driven into the arms of another man, and of course, if the result had only been into his arms then perhaps forgiveness could have been gained, and wounds could have healed.

Looking around the room again, it was a shame that my best friend, Jason wasn't here.

I tried to think of what business he was on. Normally, I know— that's what business partners do. But then every once in a while, Jason will keep something from me, and the problem is, it usually blows up into a big storm of shit. He doesn't mean it to, he just gets a hunch and follows it rather than speak to me about it.

Like the cheap alcohol he got hold of that was a 'real bargain' and almost got us shut down. For the most part Jason has a wonderful head for business, but sometimes the 'networking' turns him into someone that seeks out high-risk for the sole purpose of looking cool.

Another time, there was a guy that he followed to the other side of the country and almost beat him black and blue. Something to do with a bar-tab.

But the major fuck up of our lives was the night all those many years ago when I caught him having sex in the office. I'm not sure who looked more surprised: him or Jean. I'd ushered a very young Daisy back out, not wanting her to see what I had witnessed.

I couldn't help it, there was a part of me that blamed Jason for our relationship breakdown, even though my rational side knows that had it not been Jason, then it would've been someone else. And of course, from there, many came and went. I suspect that Jason didn't leave it there with the one liaison, but we've never talked directly about it. We skirt around the subject when talking about relationships, and it is always the elephant in the room with us. Jason will, in fact, go out of his way never to talk about Jean or mention her name. In front of me, she doesn't exist.

Jean has always been attractive, and in some ways, that's been her problem. She craves the attention. But of late, she's showing signs that her best days are behind her, and dare I say, you only have to look at her current beau to know that her tastes now verge on the slightly desperate.

There are the signs of wrinkles beginning to appear as crow's feet next to her eyes and mouth. Under her hoodie is a shirt that is a size too small and so cannot be done up over breasts that were once firm, but now sag slightly, almost forcing her to wear a low-cut vest to prove that a fine cleavage is there for the taking.

She notices me looking at her this way, and a small smile plays on her lips, and to her credit, it's not in seduction, but more in a resignation that whilst an attraction will always be there, only a foolish man will settle on what is not right for him.

Contemplation is a time waster and a thought-provoker, but at that point, the most prominent thought I had was that I wanted my little girl back. All of these people were nothing more than a mere distraction for me. Was anyone here able to get Daisy back? This was hardly an extended version of The A-Team.

Only one person here could do that. And that was me.

I got up, placed my hand on Jean's shoulder, and smiled. I didn't always have to say things to her.

I turned and saw Ruby staring at me, wondering just what the hell I was doing. Sometimes, though, the bond that a child brings is just that little bit too strong.

"I'm just getting some air," I mumbled to Father Dugan as I walked passed and as I turned back, he replied, "Be careful, lad."

Thankfully, no one had blocked me in. I got in my van and sped off to the place I probably never should've left.

Caulfield Hall.

I had to open that damned study, and I had to find what it was that they were looking for.

I started the engine and began to turn around the van. As I glanced back out to my house, I saw Ruby step out. Her face showed a touch of concern, but most of all, it showed disappointment. We were like waves and shoreline, getting closer and closer, but then retreating just as quickly.

My daughter was not going to get back to me whilst I sat wallowing in pity; I had to go and find out what it is that would drive someone to commit such a desperate act as kidnapping. I just couldn't believe that my old fool of a father would have anything of importance there.

It turns out that it couldn't have been further away from the truth.

Chapter Eighteen

The roads couldn't have been more winding, nor the trees and hedgerows so absorbing to my ability to concentrate. Various shades of green flashed past me along with the odd broken colour of wild flowers, but it was the sound of the crunching gravel that had me speed up as I got closer to the old house.

I had no memory of stopping the car, and I was living in a constant auto-pilot. I desperately wanted my daughter back. I was scared that I would never see her alive again.

I was scared of going back to my house alone.

I was also scared that I would slowly go crazy until I found out who was to blame.

I flew open the door and actually jogged into the house, stopping only momentarily to look at both phones.

One message from Ruby:

Let me know if you need company. XX

It was a nice short sweet text, but I knew this was down to me.

And of course, since you asked, there was also the way I felt— or the confusion in my feelings more to the point. This current situation only added to that confusion, having me long for normality, and that of course, was not venturing into a new relationship. I like Ruby. I've liked

Ruby as a bit more than a friend for a while, but life is never that easy.

This isn't some throwaway romance of two hearts coming together ready to explode into passion, connecting on both an intellectual and physical level perfectly— a tale of soul-mates finding each other, and meandering walks off into the sunset of happy-ever-afters.

Reality bites. I've not paid too much attention to this before, but this describes us equivocally as a slice of our current situation, but mainly that when you add all of the emotional baggage, I'm cynical at the longevity of any deeper relationship.

I've already burdened you with my feelings towards Jean, and with Ruby there's a similar sense of positives and negatives. We're great friends, but she has this longing for a relationship that burns slowly with desperation. Being at the end of a long line of one-night-stands does not make me feel wanted. She also has this wild side that, admittedly, could stem from the desire to be wanted herself, but also raises question marks for someone who has a daughter...

...My lost daughter. And so it is her that I focus all of my attention to, not some teenage feelings. My hopes of living out a John Hughes-style romance got waylaid in the 90's and never returned to me.

I'm back staring at the door that could unlock my world.

I tried the door handle again, forgetting the thing has not been opened in years, no matter who had tried to break in.

I walked down the hallway and back into the room where I'd been when I had heard voices. The memories nearly brought me to my knees— memory bullets spraying over me like a Japanese assault rifle funnelling them all to my heart.

I pried open the floorboard and looked inside to where a ring with one large and one small key sat. It was almost strange to think I'd left earlier with the front door wide open and the hints book sat on the floor next to the screwdriver and the floorboard. I'd only stopped short of leaving the study door wide open with a neon sign inviting guests to peruse at their own risk.

I snatched up the keys and hurriedly walked to the study door.

One of my first smiles twitched on my lips as I got to the door. Having read on further in the hints book, I followed exactly what it said. I pulled gently on each of the hinges and watched as they came away. The door handle was a dummy, and its use was purely to help slide the door from right to left, and not to push in as anyone else would've expected.

When slid back as far as the handle would allow, a metal door now appeared with a small keyhole just to the right of eye level. I placed the small key in the hole and turned.

A clank sound could be heard, and another larger keyhole appeared, and the inside of the hole seemed to implode. I took out the small key, placed the larger one in the hole, and turned.

I could well be mistaken, but there was the sound of a seal being broken as I opened the door to my father's study.

For the most part, it was a mess. Not dirty, or full of rubbish, but a picture of organised chaos and regretful neglect. It was a large room, and the size was on par with the dining room that my mother spent all of the neglected evenings entertaining guests in.

Paintings donned the walls in a haphazard state, and a couple of easels attempted to feign 'in-the-middle-of-a-masterpiece' set up. This was a mock-up of what a painter's studio might look like, and then I spotted three things.

The first was a pack of paints that I'd saved up my money for to buy my dad for his birthday. I'd found out what ones he used and had bought them in the little gift box, and here they were, unused and unopened.

The second thing was my boxing trophy that sat proudly next to his chair. I had won it in an under 12's amateur boxing tournament, and had raced home to show it off to my parents.

"Congratulations," Mum had said sarcastically. "Deliberately giving yourself brain-damage. Don't think I'm looking after you when you can't feed yourself or wipe your own backside." Hurt, I'd grunted and knocked on the door of the study.

"Wow! Look at that!" Dad had said. "Your granddad is teaching you well, huh?"

I had nodded. "And Harry!"

"Of course, the great Harry Dugan." And he had glanced up at the picture on the wall, and of course that had done two things: stopped the conversation flat and turned my proud, happy moment into a sudden deep melancholy.

The picture seemed so innocent. The smiling face bordered on cheeky, and whilst I looked a lot like my mum, this face was the spitting image of my father.

This was my brother, Ben.

The true apple of my father's eye.

Chapter Nineteen

October 1985

"How was school, Ed?" my dad asked as I walked in, having endured another school bus journey home. I shrugged, but smiled. It had been alright when all was said and done. I was in the top group in Maths, but felt like I only just qualified, which meant I had to work hard to keep up with the others, and I often wondered whether I'd feel better being top of the group below rather than near the bottom of the group above. Somehow, though, this seemed like taking the easy option, and I had never done that, so I was not going to start now.

"That good, huh?" he said, but it was often this way. He and my brother were in the middle of something, and it seemed like politeness, or something bordering on duty that would make them engage with me. There were things I wanted to say, questions I wanted to ask, but to do this would take up too much of their time. When I'd ever attempted such a thing, there was almost a silent sigh before either would reply to me. Any response was done with the attempt to move the subject back to what they were doing. The two-member club that I could never join.

"It gets better, kid!" Ben laughed, but I wasn't sure whether or not it was just a throwaway comment or not. I was too young for him to take much interest in, and it was a similar scenario as with my Maths conundrum. He could live an easy life teaching me and playing with me, but then it would not be a challenge. Therefore, he followed my dad around trying to play at being my dad's best friend rather than his son.

I don't know the 'ins and outs' of my being here on this earth, but I find it hard to believe that either of my parents had planned to have me.

"So they say," I mumbled, walking to my room, though of course I'd never heard this. It was just a non-committal reply.

There were times it seemed like I was an only child, but with two dads and a mum. Ben was ten years older than me, and he and dad had this bond that I could not come between, nor recreate. There were also times it felt like I was dead and observing life of a perfect family. I was, however, the annoying distraction to the harmonic tune of their life— a burden or curse bestowed upon them.

Ben seemed to be the perfect child, getting great exam results, the captain of a number of his school and college sports teams, and having women keel over at the very thought that he had looked their way. In fact, the only slightly odd thing about him was on the many occasions that he would be talking to himself in his bedroom. I assumed that my dad had run an extension cable up from the telephone downstairs, but when I looked, there was nothing there. I would hear him laughing away in there. It was the first time that I thought perhaps my brother did drugs, or that he was slightly mentally unstable.

I sat and drew pictures of far off lands, or started on another of my comic books about *'Ricky's Grand Adventures!'* a character that I had created, completely moulding on myself. There is something great about writing yourself into a world with complete control. Ricky had a friend called Seth and a string of girlfriends. Adventure was always just around the corner! Ricky was popular, because Ricky was great.

I wanted to see my friend, Dave, but his family moved north a month ago, and so all we had was a couple of scribbled letters back and forth, as we went from best friends to pen friends.

I spent a lot of time on my own, and sometimes my imagination ran wild. I remember one time when our telephone rang, and I casually picked it up.

I'd had a good day writing another story about Ricky fighting for justice, and later that day, granddad was going to take me to get a video of my choice (well, one that he allowed me to have!), so I was full of good cheer as I picked up the telephone receiver and said, "Good afternoon. Welcome to the circus. I am the ringmaster!"

For a second, I thought that there was a problem with the phone-line, as it crackled and there was a pause before I heard, "Hello? Who is this?" This was followed by a loud clang that sounded like the person on the other end of the phone had dropped their receiver, the idiot! I almost giggled, but then managed to compose myself to reply.

"Edward," I said. "Who are you?" Again, there was a pause before a response.

"A friend," they said, then, "Is Ben there?" That explains it, I thought, all of Ben's friends were idiots.

"Nope. He's off with some girl. He should be back either later, *or tomorrow-*"

"*If he got lucky,*" he said at exactly the same time as me.

"Jinx!" we both said simultaneously, and then neither of us said a word.

Just as I was about to speak again, the phone went dead -as they say – I heard the dial tone was the real sound that I heard.

It was strange, so I went upstairs, and I laid back onto my bed and put on some music. *Alice Cooper* was telling me about his nightmares, and I had a strange fascination with the non-mainstream lyrical content and how it conjured up stories and scenes that the likes of *Wham!* and *Shakin' Stevens* were unable to produce, although I was also known to drift off to sleep listening to the Rock-Opera of *Meat Loaf* on many an occasion, quite unapologetically.

I think it was through the guitar solo in the necrophilia song, '*Cold Ethel*' that I heard raised voices. I pulled off my large headphones and heard a door slam, I looked out of my window to see Ben jump into his *White Ford Capri*, the engine growl, and the wheels spun a shower of gravel before twin red lights sped off into the night.

I casually wandered down the stairs to where my parents were in the kitchen.

"What was that all about?" I asked.

"Girl-trouble," my dad winked, and could easily have added 'the sly old dog' to the end. My mum was drying up the plates from dinner and shaking her head. "He's too good for her!"

The girl in question was called Sally. I'd only met her a couple of times, and despite the fact that she felt the need to pat me on the head like I was the family pet, she seemed okay. She was pretty, but not TV gorgeous. She had big red hair that had a kink in it, and she wore sweaters that were a little too tight. Not that I was complaining – but then, I'm only the pet.

Apparently, Sally had been seen at the cinema with a guy called Tony, and they'd been locked together with the mouths for the majority of the film. One of Ben's friends had seen this, and had gone straight to the phone-box to ring our house and divulge this heinous act.

An hour later and the phone would ring again, but this time it would be with the news that my brother was dead....

His car had collided with another car a few miles away on a tight bend.

This would prove to be the catalyst for the self-destruction of the family. My dad lost more than a son that day, and the wonderful paintings that he produced suddenly turned into dark images, before seemingly to dry up altogether.

Painting and socialising were no longer his hobby anymore. At first, he was withdrawn and then a recluse to his beloved study. If I hadn't known better, I may have even thought that he had my brother's body in there and was trying to recreate some Frankenstein re-animation of life.

My mum, on the contrary, almost revelled in her new position of forever entertaining, throwing dinner parties and luncheons at the drop of a hat, soaking up the sympathy in some twisted way. When people began to stop feeling sorry for her, I mysteriously came down with a sickness off and on for a few weeks, where I would be violently sick, with sharp stabbing pains in my abdomen. At this point, my grandfather took me to live with him for a spell. Within 24 hours, I was fully recovered.

Whilst I was back living at home within 6 months, things were never quite the same. In the same way that we recognise 'BC' as Before Christ, there was definitely a change in our family dynamics before and after Ben's death, aside from the obvious. I soon became more of my granddad's son than my own father's. I spent every other weekend around his house and much of the holidays. My parents got on with their lives, albeit separately from each other. My mum would still throw large parties that would either end up with her drunk and crying in the arms of friends in dire need of sympathy, or else she would disappear out to the boathouse with someone, usually male, but not exclusively until the morning.

My granddad and Harry took care of me, they'd already introduce me to boxing as a way of distilling some discipline into me, along with focus and routine. As a result of my brother's passing, I kept to myself at school, but boxing gave me the confidence to know that I could succeed through hard work, and also meant that I would not go looking for trouble, but if it were to find me, then I would be able to finish it. I'm not boasting; it was just the way that things panned out.

It's strange that for a time, I felt a longing to go back to the time when I was just being ignored by my family, because little did I know that the neglect I felt then seemed so warm and comforting compared to the way they treated me later. We all know without a shadow of a doubt that my family (aside from my granddad) would've swapped me for Ben in a heartbeat that fateful night.

Chapter Twenty

In the same way a person would react when their team scored a goal, or perhaps got a call to say they'd got the job they'd always wanted, Jez leapt up ready to high-five someone.

"Who is the fucking daddy!" he shouted, to which Miss Chambers, who'd made the mistake of sitting next to him with a cup of tea replied, "Well, if you carry on with that foul-language then it won't be you, my lad! I'll give you a swift kick in the old dangly-bits!"

"Sorry, ma'am," he said, clearly scolded, but then remembered what his outburst had been about. However, Miss Chambers was not finished. "You are a very strange person. Has anyone ever told you that?"

"Um-"

"Aside from that, a bit of tact wouldn't go amiss, would it? Remember why we're all here?"

"Sorry, ma'am," he mumbled again. "It's just that I've got the details. You know, who the van is registered to."

Harry and Ruby wandered over, and Jean looked up from her untouched mug of coffee.

"Well?" Harry pressed. For someone quick to try and pat themselves on the back, this guy was certainly milking the suspense and enjoying the centre stage.

"It says here ITC Solutions. Now, I've done a quick check, and they are a consultancy company in Swindon."

"So why would-" Harry started, but Jez had not quite finished.

"Now, that company rang a bell with me, and a quick look on the old Facebook told me something very interesting." He paused, pleased that his audience was captivated.

"Jez, just tell us, will you?" Ruby said. "If we had wanted a Columbo impression, then we would've called him."

"Ed's mate, Billy, has his job description as a Financial Analyst at none other than...drumroll!"

"I'm assuming ITC Solutions," Ruby finished.

"#Spoiler alert!" Jez said with a big grin, almost jumping up and down on the spot.

"Hash-what?" Miss Chambers firmly said.

"Tag," Ruby said. "A *Twitter*-thing."

Miss Chambers frowned and then looked accusingly back at Jez. "Have you got learning difficulties?" She waved her arm in frustration. "Daisy is missing and you are enjoying this a little too much. I assume that your wife was part of an arranged marriage? I cannot imagine that she would choose to be with you!" Ruby giggled at that, and whilst Harry did all that he could to stop any sort of smile, his eyes were laughing.

"Well, I found it," was all that he could think of to reply, almost by way of an apology. "Our love is one that is deep."

"Well, before we start some sort of witch hunt, this doesn't necessarily mean that Billy had anything to do with this. Yes, he knows Ed, but I assume that a Financial Analyst would not usually be driving or have access to the company van, right? Jez, any idea on the size of this company?"

Jez looked at his screen, toggled to another webpage then looked up with a big beam, "It says here around 50 members of staff."

"Okay, so anyone of those could have access. Also, we have to think that just because it is registered to ITC Solutions, it doesn't mean that it is still their vehicle. We have the vehicle registration, so why don't we ring them and find out whether this vehicle is still part of their fleet?"

It was at that point that Jean got up, and slowly as she walked forward said, "Should we not contact the police? I know what they said, but this is all too much. The police are professionals."

"Let's give it a bit longer, huh?" Harry added. "Let's just see how this pans out and if Ed comes up with something. If we messed up and anything happened to her...well."

"Ed..." she says as if remembering the name of a forgotten person. "What is going on here? He says that he is popping out for air, but that is clearly not the case. You and her..." She points accusingly to Ruby. "...know what he's up to, and-" She stops at the table, looking to steady herself, clumsily pulls out a chair, and plops down onto it. Running her hand through her dark-blonde hair, she continues, "Look, I've not been the best mother in the world, you know?" She looks around at the faces that are all unsure how to reply to this. Miss Chambers looks like she may be the first to speak, but Jean carries on. "I just want her back. My baby girl. I just want my baby girl back."

Harry waited a beat before saying, "Ed is a clever guy. He'll do all he can without putting her at risk."

"Harry, what is he doing?"

"I suspect that he's out at Caulfield Hall. All the nightmares in his life always lead him back there. If you blindfolded him and threw him out in the middle-of-nowhere, he would always find his way back there."

"That was the first place he went to when we split up," Jean mused to herself. "I never understood with all of the things that happened, why he went back there so easily."

"Solace," Harry replied. "The things that have given him much pain have tended to be people. Caulfield Hall was, and still is, his sanctuary, a place he understands and that he believes also understands him. He loves and hates it in equal measures."

Jez looked up from his screen. "Like a church?"

"Exactly like a church. Ed has no place for religion in his life, which is fine; it is not for everyone. But Caulfield Hall, whilst paved with what we perceive as bad memories, in some way offers comfort to him. It's a family home built by his ancestors, known by all around. I suspect also that he knows a lot of people were jealous of him living there, and in some way, he feels more privileged than the stories that we know of his upbringing truthfully were."

"I don't get it," Jez said, looking somewhat perplexed at the way the conversation had gone. Things were certainly moving away from his Sherlock-like discovery. Always the bloody way with him.

"A place he has overcome his demons," Ruby offered quietly, still remembering Jean's comment and the fact that this woman refused to look at her.

Harry and Miss Chambers both nodded. "Correct," Harry agreed. "His bedroom and the attic are places that he's very fond of."

"But not the boathouse," Jean added, looking up at Harry.

"No. He refuses to go anywhere near the boathouse."

"Terrible business," Miss Chambers commented, and Ruby and Jez glanced at each other, unsure exactly what that was all about, feeling completely out of the loop, but unable to ask what it was that had now produced even more gloom into the room.

Chapter Twenty-One

Daisy

I've been looking out of the window, or at least trying to look out of the window. It's smudged with that green-mossy stuff you see on old outbuildings. I rubbed one of the panes, but whilst a dark smear appeared on my hand, the window seemed to have the majority of dirt on the outside.

From what I can make out, the view looks like trees, but there is a slight clearing. I cannot hear a road or any other sounds, except for something that sounded like a creature outside. The sun appears to be high, offering me hope. I don't know why. It's just some female intuition, I guess.

There's a deep damp smell that tells me that this place doesn't have heating. Not good news if I'm still here tonight, but damp and old can also show structural weakness. Bonus! But it also shows me that the air is not entirely clean, and I hate to think of the tiny particles of mould spores floating around. We learnt about this at school. At best, it can make it hard to breathe, bringing on asthma or other respiratory issues or allergic reactions, and then there's the possibility of poisoning by mycotoxins (leading to neurological issues and/or death). None of these things fill me with joy. I stretch my sleeve up over my hand and try breathing through it like it is some magical air sieve.

There's no way I'm going to just sit here and wait to find out my fate. My dad didn't raise me like that. *Think outside of the box*, I can hear him saying. I look at everything around me like I'm *Jonathan Creek*. I'm not going to lie to you, my teachers love me when I think of things that no one else does. *"Trust Daisy!"* some say, whilst I also hear kids mutter, *"Crazy Daisy!"* though this is from girls with empty heads and stuffed bras, unable to think past their next fumble in order to be popular with the older boys. Bitches.

I had already tried the door, and as usual, the obvious was a no go. The door was locked, not only at the handle, but judging by the movement when I pushed it, by a lock at the top, which I assume is a bolt or a padlock. I don't remember hearing either, so it might even be some sort of bar. I'm getting side-tracked here. If this weren't so life and death, I might actually enjoy it.

I walked to the closet to check that out. I'm already thinking about hiding and jumping out on them. The back and side walls are wooden, so I put my ear up against them and gently tap all around to see if they are solid and strong.

The back wall has a slightly different sound, and for a second my heart jumps, but the wood still remains strong. It could be that there is a passageway or possibly a toilet behind here. The thought of the latter only makes me need to pee suddenly.

I move my hands gently to the corners and edges to try and find nails, screws, or some sort of join, but there is nothing. I sit down on the floor, hug my legs, and feel the tears again escape.

For the first time in many years, I pray. I feel a little like a novice, unsure of what I am doing, and also, I cannot help but feel like a hypocrite. I love Harry to bits, but his talk of God, redemption, embracing one's faith, etcetera, it has washed over me for years with little or no effect. I now feel almost too far gone for any of it to matter or take effect. I don't have faith; I have a strong level of desperation. I see the world as a scientist would. I don't pin my hopes on miracles. I look around at the tools that I have, the environment, and I try to make them work for me. But when I feel that all avenues have been exhausted, then I resort to despair and desperation. I've tried nearly everything that I can think of, and now in the eleventh hour, my last resort is God. But of course, the true answer to my conundrum is that I know my limits, and I know that my dad will be doing all that he can to find me. However, it's not God that I am calling on. I am actually sending out a message to Harry to ask him to intervene and show me that if there is a God which he himself serves, then please help my family to reunite.

I pull out my phone to look at a couple of pictures to give me hope and most of all, comfort. The picture of my dad pulling a silly face almost makes me sob, and I put my head back against the wooden panel and look up to stop the tears.

The light from my phone shines to the ceiling where a dark patch is. The ceiling looks to be boards overlapping, rather than a proper ceiling. I stand up and reach as high as I can, but I am still a foot or so away. I grab a dress to remove from the hanger, but in doing so, see the name '*Alice*', and this again fills me with wonder as to what may have happened to Alice.

I tap the wooden coat-hanger against the ceiling and am able to move the board by pushing up and sliding. The gap is not large, but is bigger than any of the windows. I need to be able to look up there. I think about trying to fashion something out of coat hangers and my phone on camcorder, but I have no way of securing it, and let's face it, I need to see whether or not I can get up there if it is a possible escape route.

I go back into the room and look around. The bed will not fit into the closet, and I momentarily think about trying to climb up by using my legs and my back to push myself like I've seen in movies, but when I try, I get nowhere; in addition, I now have a bruised back and burning leg muscles. *Great going, Crazy Daisy!*

My next idea is the books. If I can balance the half a dozen hardbacks on top of each other, then I should be able to reach the gap by just over a finger's length.

It's not the most stable of towers, but as I take my first tentative step up, it holds my weight. Then with my other foot up, I tip-toe and feel around inside, trying not to think about things that might live in dark, damp places.

I suddenly wobble as I touch something cold and hard, but realise that it is a bar, possibly a pipe, although it feels thicker than the normal pipes you see going into and out of a radiator. I can slip my hands either side of it, so I prepare to try and pull myself up. I have always had good upper body strength, but still, I've not done anything remotely similar to this since I tried climbing a tree around Rachel's house a few years back. That ended with a branch breaking and a mild concussion.

I take a deep breath, think of my dad, and pull with all of my strength. I manage to get my elbows up to a ridge with the help of my legs on top of the clothes rail, and then pull my legs up.

I open up my phone and prepare to see what else is up here.

I scan around and then almost jump out of my skin as I see a person with their back to me. I'm paralysed with shock more than fear.

There is a slow movement as I turn the phone, and it is then that I realise that this is not the person, but an illusion caused by the shadows. The person is not a person, but a retail dummy. A glance around shows boxes and old-fashioned trunks thick with dust, and I then realise that there is a thick blanket on the wall which I see is giving off the only light, so must cover a window.

So what is my next move? Surely as soon as they realise I've left the room below, they'll know that I'm up here? But wait, I'm sure that I can bluff them and escape another way....

Sometimes in life you never know whether the choices that you make are going to be the best. Will they get you to that desired destination? Will you really get to your hopes and dreams? My mind is rambling now; I know this is my body's reaction to the day and my current unfortunate situation.

I gently lower myself down, having seen the obvious sign below of books-used-as-a-stool. One look at these and they will look up, and I will be rumbled. Even if I kick the pile over, I would think an enquiring mind would wonder why someone would take a pile of books into the closet. Not to read, that's for sure, what with the lack of light and all. Therefore, I have to re-create the success of the books, and find a way of getting rid of them too. A conundrum for you, Mr. Creek...

First things first, though. I need to create the diversion. This will involve smashing one of the windows in order to create the illusion that I have used this means of escape. I need to scan the room again. Ideally, I could do with some tape, but unfortunately, there is a lack of a stationery cupboard here packed with what I need! I could then crack and break the glass with hardly any sound.

The good news is that the room is partly underground, which means that the drop from the window to the floor is a matter of a couple of feet. If I'm really lucky then there will only be grass underneath.

I walk to the door and listen carefully to see whether I can hear voices. Nothing.

I grab the blanket and eiderdown from the bed, and one of the coat hangers and move towards the window. I look out carefully, and whilst I know I can still only see dirty smudges, I look for movement or bright colours that may suggest someone around.

When I'm as happy as I can be, I get a wad of the blanket and eiderdown and press against the window pane. Then gently, with the coat hanger I begin to tap, adding more and more pressure each time. I stop after 3 taps to listen for any noises, but when I hear nothing, I carry on. With one more hard blow, there is a sudden release, and my hands, along with the blanket, go through the window. The sound is not loud, but the fear of being heard makes it louder. I feel my anxiety shoot through my shoulders and my neck like something physical has touched it.

I feel the scrap of glass on my skin under the blanket, and whilst it draws blood, it is only a scratch. Again, I listen out, but there is nothing.

I proceed to push out as much of the glass as possible, and then I use one of the few pieces to cut some of my t-shirt. I place this on the last shard of glass so it looks like it was snagged there as I squeezed through.

I pulled back the blanket and eiderdown and place them quickly back onto the bed. I then grab the bottom pillow, open it up and take out the pillow so as I am left with the case. I really cannot be sure whether this will work, but the clock is ticking now as the broken window can be seen from the outside.

I saw a driveway, but more importantly I saw a lake. There is only one lake around here that is that size:

White Horse Lake.

And somewhere on the other side of that lake is Caulfield Hall.

Anyway, distractions aside, I go into the closet and place the books inside the pillowcase. I grab two coat hangers. I then realise that the hardbacks will be too heavy, so I remove these and go back and get some paperbacks instead. I'm thinking on my feet here, and again, make another tweak, which is to go and get the second pillowcase. I put this over the first one and pierce a hole through for the hook of the coat hanger to go through. The plan is that I will bend the hook around so it will not come out. The hole is below the seam, so hopefully this will reinforce it, and I will then put legs through the triangles of the coat hangers, in an attempt to pull them up through the hole too. I'm hoping that the books won't be too heavy, and if they are, then I'll just go back to the original plan and hope that when I am discovered missing, they think that I've escaped by the open window and not check out the closet.

My heart is suddenly beating faster, like I've self-induced an adrenaline rush around my veins. I go into the closet, put my legs into the coat hangers, and then pull the closet door closed.

Damn! It is now almost too dark to see. Only the thin strips of light seep under the door, and momentarily, it feels somewhat symbolic that I am turning my back on what I know in order to take a risk at what I don't.

This is the point in the movie where we go, "What the Hell are you doing?" But until you are in this situation, you cannot possibly make the decisions. It is all about getting out alive with zero risk, and sometimes that means turning your back on the obvious.

I pull out my mobile and slide a finger across the screen to light it up. I look up at the hole, then glance at the bar and the wall. *Here we go.*

I step carefully and am cautious that too much weight will cause the books to slide and then topple. It is definitely harder with the books around my ankles. I roll my eyes to myself, *Little Miss Obvious*, I think!

I have a strong grip, but I'm not sure whether or not I can still swing my legs up. Before, I could get momentum by swinging my legs wildly, and quite un-lady-like, I might add. However, now, with the restriction of the heavy pillow cases, it is proving to be something worse than doing PE at school.

I have just got one leg up when I hear something.

It's the door to the room below.

As quickly as possible I pull up my leg, but I can feel that the angle is tipping the pillowcase, and there is movement from the books.

If one of them falls now, then as my dad says, *"Your goose will be cooked, young lady!"*

This is like one of those skill games manufactured and sold at Christmas by MB Games. *A game of skill and agility for all of the family!*

Someone makes an unpleasant sound deep from within, and I am guessing that they have realised that I am not there.

Finally, I reach and pull the pillowcase up carefully and slowly slide the wood over the hole.

And as I do I hear the closet door swing open...

A deep voice says, "Shit!" and I hear him walk out. I then realise that I'm holding my breath. A lungful of oxygen rushes in with relief, and I allow a smile to linger a while, whilst I congratulate myself on a well-organised plan.

My congratulations are short-lived.

"Hello, my pretty," came a voice from behind me. "You didn't find the camera then?"

"Shit!" I say, feeling the blood drain from my face.

Chapter Twenty-Two

October 1985 - Harry

I never really thought that life would be like this. Back when I was young, working hard through Grammar School, I had these big, wild, and some might say, fanciful ideas. And now what do I have to show for them? Okay, maybe nothing as an answer is a little defeatist, but I have not amounted to the man that my potential suggested. I also realise that this is an answer more common than is ever admitted between adults. The truth of the matter is that life is built on the foundations of hope and dreams, and as you grow, your hopes and dreams evolve, and with the scale of evolution, the hopes and dreams peak and then slowly diminish to wants and needs surrounding health and longevity. My personal hopes and dreams came from a dose of over self-confidence built on easy goals achieved and listening to those around me telling me the things I wanted to hear— pandering to an overly inflated ego.

I wasted my life chasing a girl called Mary O'Donnel. She was a Catholic girl that acted anything but. My blinkered infatuation is almost a cause for embarrassment, and Alfie told me as much, the old bugger.

But then he would, wouldn't he? He went right ahead and married her. Broke my bloody heart.

I've mulled over the riddle for so long that I cannot believe the outcome never changes. The one woman that I want is somehow repelled by my charms. At first, her gentle put downs to my advances seemed like a non-contact joust– a battle of wits both entertaining and endearing. However, as my enthusiasm peaked, hers began to wane, and her defences remained strong. I was humbled into a revelation that perhaps this time, I would not catch this beautiful fish, this graceful creature with an inability to be tamed by my heart. The frustration that I felt bordered on consuming, and for a while, my thoughts turned dark.

Alfie talked for long periods to me, listening, and finally brought me back into the realms of reality and helped me see the error to my ways and regain the charm and confidence that I was about to throw away on some solo path of destruction.

And I know that Alfie only had my best interests at heart, and sometimes – not very often – I allow myself to indulge in a few minutes of envious hate to my best friend, before embracing once again the friendship of a caring and kind man.

The caring and kind man that seemingly, and unashamedly swooped in and swept Miss Mary O'Donnel off of her feet, with his quiet and thoughtful ways.

However, here I am off to try and woo a woman who, again, has tried to fend off my advances. I cannot bear to be second best again. I also get the psychology behind it: the increased desire of the chase– the classic male concept of pursuit and conquer– the Biblical forbidden fruit, the quick-wit and on-my-toes waltz that I am led – shooting hormones around my body like a ball-bearing around a human pinball machine. Now, there is an epitaph waiting to be written – *Shot often, scored big, but lost his balls...*

There's something competitive about this with Alfie and me, and I will probably be the first to admit that since Alfie's beloved wife, Mary, died a few years back, his sparkle died with it. The only time that I see a fleeting glimpse of that sparkle is when his grandson, Edward is around.

Little Edward takes after his granddad more than his dad, although all three have a quiet way about them. Thinkers, surveying the situation and analysing the details. The difference between them is that Alfie and Edward are selfless, almost lacking of backbone to a point, but stubborn in their morals. Gordon, however, is single-minded, and as much as he loves his sons, he would swap them for success in a heartbeat. And he's a very good artist, but he would see no problem in making a deal with the devil if the opportunity arose.

However, my strength (along with my dashing personality), is that I know when to go and get it. I don't get bogged down with the details, wondering what they are thinking, contemplating a future and what it may bring – no, I'll shake the tree and see what falls out. So whilst Alfie is still thinking about this friendship, the possibilities of the slow magnetic pull towards a relationship with her, I am going to bite the lead pellet and express my love. Perhaps this time, I will finally get the girl, and Alfie will be left wondering in the wings.

Feisty Alice will be mine!

Distracted, I jumped into my car, a large Rover so wide, it was almost square in shape, and reversed out of my drive at speed. Little did I know this enthusiasm would be so catastrophic, as I would pump hard on my brakes, before putting the car into first gear, and this act would squeeze out the last of the brake fluid in the pipes next to my back wheels that had been severed by a human hand....

Traffic was light, so I'd hardly had to stop. So for the most part, the simple act of taking my foot off of the accelerator was enough to reduce the speed of my car, apart from when I was heading towards log lane, a shortcut on the outskirts of the town.

Replaying over in my mind is the scene that I will never forget.

I headed up towards the junction, ready to turn right, and I pumped the brake, but to no avail. I saw the headlights of the other vehicle, and as the horror of what was going to happen became apparent, I tried first to put the car in a lower gear, and then with desperation, grabbed the handbrake.

Everything seemed to slow down, then my senses exploded with a bright light, and a loud bang deafened me as the windscreen shattered, cutting my face as I was thrust towards a thousand razor-sharp shards washing over me with menace and unstoppable force.

Then there was darkness and the burnt smell of oil and metal.

I spent two days in hospital, and I never got to declare my love for Alice Chambers.

But things were worse than that. The driver of the other car – a Ford Capri - had died instantly.

The driver was Alfie's grandson, Ben.

Everything that I knew and held dear to my heart changed that night. The fact that the police found evidence that my brakes had been cut, and that Ben was driving erratically, and at speed, could never be seen as comfort. I didn't want people telling me that I wasn't to blame. How could I not be? Yes, someone had tampered with my car, but it was my animal lust– the want and need of pure pumping red blood– that made up my mind to get in my car and take that fateful journey. I had to be held accountable. I had to give up more than just guilt.

My story is a little different from others. When they say they found God, it is as if by chance some small act enlightened them, filled them with wonder, and an unbelievable warmth of love. I actually searched for God, almost pleaded with him to help me to help others.

I would later become a vicar, which caused much stirring within the community, and whilst one boy died because of me, my life's worth was to then look out for his younger brother, Edward, no matter what.

The very act of being a vicar brought forth so much responsibility that the motivation to do the right thing was almost overwhelming. Each day when I put on the dog-collar, it is as much to remind me of the journey that I've made, as much as it is for the love of God. Please do not misunderstand my intentions. This is not some elaborate confession presiding as a life-long martyr act. I truly believe in God and a higher being, and strive to promote a Christian lifestyle wherever possible. Edward and I share the same need to convert the misconceptions of others: I, to prove that a vicar is to once again be seen and a trustworthy member of the community, and Edward, to prove that whilst the world is still naturally prejudiced, his tattooed-skin and my dog-collar represent who we are, but that we both share Christian values of looking after each other and loving thy neighbour. Even when she plays country & western music louder than a rebellious teenager!

Alfie lost a grandson that night, but I gained an unspoken bond with Edward. Later, when Alfie passed on, there was almost an unspoken regard of grandfather to grandson between us, and this would grow to almost a father and son relationship in a somewhat unconventional way, but a way that worked for us.

Chapter Twenty-Three

Jez

Jez was buzzing. It was like a movie, and he was more than just an extra. He was sat in front of his laptop updating his Vlog:

"Don't get me wrong, I'm really sorry at what has happened to old Eddie, truly I am, but bugger me this is a rush. This is like being in some CSI-like programme searching the evidence, and they're all looking towards yours-truly to find the answers! Un-bloody-believable!

"I have slipped back to my own pad next door with my laptop, under the premise that I'm going to make a few phone calls and what-not, but I couldn't carry on without updating you guys, my loyal followers," Jez winked into the web-cam, picturing all of his 'fans' wondering just what was going on. He liked to think that there were hundreds of folk from many different countries, endeared by his wit and charm, and equally as cross and frustrated that they lived nowhere near him. *This guy is so cool, he is frozen!* they would tell their friends and work colleagues. That was his own line, and he was proud of it. The cost of getting this printed onto a t-shirt was reasonable, and any day now when he finally went viral, he would get these printed up and sell them. He wasn't sure how many views it took to go viral, but he was sure he wasn't far off. He hit one hundred last week. Only eighty of them by him.

The truth of the matter was he had in the region of 12 followers, of which most were non-descript names like Toothfairy91, Riotgrl5, Satansandwich, and Sk8Goth whom had started to following him, but had declined to comment or try to make contact. Schoolkids or Paedo's most likely, he concluded, not quite understanding the implication of this. However, a few had left comments, and he had struck up an online friendship with three: Sexygrl90 - a model-looking female from Bournemouth, Doc85 – a middle-aged guy doing research for a book, and Pinkchic – a secretive woman from Norwich who kept asking him for nude pictures, but so far, he'd declined.

"So I've traced the registration number," he was telling the webcam again, although he was picturing Sexygrl90, fluttering her eyelids, and waiting for him to stop talking in order to reply, *"My hero!"* She would be wondering ways that they could meet up, and she could ravish him in a way that a woman had never done before. "I found out that the vehicle was registered to ITC Solutions!" he paused, wondering whether he should be revealing this now. "And it just so happens that we-I, er, Eddie knows someone who works there..." He let that thought hang there, again convinced that all 12 followers were watching the details of this unfold before their very eyes, unable to draw themselves away to their own lives, that obviously by comparison, would be mundane and paint-drying-ly boring. No, they were listening to every detail, like this was an audio recording of a *Simon Kernick* novel. They wanted to be part of it, even if they were just the select audience, chosen to be part of it. They were experiencing the highs and lows with no ability to help out. This was the experience of the future. This was better than a movie or a videogame.

With a loud beep, a message came through:

Sexygrl90: Hey! What's going on? Is this actually happening?

Bigman84: Sure is. I have to stay focused though.

Jez was of course Bigman84, originally he was called Biguy69 (instead of Big Guy), but Eddie pointed out that it could be read Bi Guy, and along with the childish number, may give the wrong impression. Jez's response was Bigman84. The 84 was a hope that people thought he was only 30 and not his actual age of 44. It was on the same basis that he assumed that Sexygrl90 was 25 years old. Whilst Jez is married, the word 'happily' is not only silent, but conspicuous in its absence. This is something of a fantasy that Jez is living. Slowly he moulds Sexygrl90 into his ideal woman, knowing on some level that they will never meet. And if they did...well, he'd cross that structure when he came to it (winking emoji!).

Sexygrl90: What are you going to do?

Bigman84: I've got some ideas. I might be a while. Things could get dangerous!

Sexygrl90: LOL! X

Jez never knew how to end, and if he was honest, he was a little disappointed with the 'LOL,' which he found both immature, and given the current situation that he found himself in, highly inappropriate.

The kiss though, well, he held that dear to his heart – a sure sign that she was flirting, and therefore wanted to have sex with him. Even a blind man could see this.

He logged out of the website and brought up the telephone number to ITC Solutions.

On the fourth ring, which Jez found extremely unprofessional, a distracted girl answered, and he remembered then that it was Saturday, so by all accounts, this was not the peak time for this job, and she was probably in the middle of texting her friends, painting her nails, or exploding sweets on *Candy Crush*. A million things you could do rather than sit waiting for the phone to ring.

"ITC Solutions. How can I help?" she said with as much enthusiasm as her paygrade would allow. She was probably doing well on the current level and frustrated that he'd stopped her in mid flow.

"Hi. Yes, I would like to enquire about the whereabouts of one of your vans, please?" Jez said.

"Vans?" she replied as if he'd actually enquired about one of her cucumbers.

"Yep, big things. No backseats, generally white, used for shifting things."

"O-kay," she said, splitting the word into two drawn-out syllables, sounding like she was really confused, and he was the simpleton. "We don't sell vans, sir; we sell solutions to commercial business."

"But as a business, you own some vans that you carry around the commercial business solutions in?"

"Um – I'm not sure you've come through to the right number. Maybe you should ring back on Monday."

"No can doody, lady. I'm talking about the vans that your handymen and staff drive."

"What, facilities?"

"The very same."

"Okay, so what did you want to know again?" She sounded slightly less like she was about to self-harm or put the phone down now.

"The whereabouts of one of these vans. Can I give you a reg?"

"Sure," she said, and so he did.

"Bassett Garage," she said triumphantly. "Been there all week. Pete took it there."

"Pete?"

"Yes, Pete Grimes."

"Okay, thank you very much. That is all that I require at this point in time." He hung up before she could reply. So the van was at the garage.

Within a minute, the phone to Bassett Garage was ringing. It was picked up on the second ring, which was a lot more business-like.

"'Llo, Bassett Garage, Tristan speakin'"

"Tristan, hi, it's Pete calling from ITC Solutions, how are you?"

"Very good, thanks," he said, stalling for time, clearly racking his brains as to who Pete from ITC Solutions was. Then the penny dropped. "Ah, yes, the Transit? Should be out by Monday."

"Can I pop down and see it now?"

He was met by silence. Then in a smaller voice he heard, "Why would you want to do that?"

"Oh, I just left something in the glove box that I was after, that's all," Jez silently thrust his fist in the air with his ability to think on his feet.

"Well, if you let me know what it is that you're after, then I could see whether it is there and save you a trip, yeah?" His voice ended an octave higher than he started, halfway between pleading and whining.

"Tristan, mate, it is of a personal matter that I care not to divulge. I'm sure that you understand – *yeah*?"

"See, thing is, Paul-"

"Pete."

"Uh, Pete, sorry. Thing is, it needed a part and had to go over to another garage."

"Ah ha," Jez agreed.

"They're closed at the moment – some family issue."

Jez was actually beginning to enjoy himself. Too many times, it was him that was caught up in a lie, stammering out responses and unbelievable webs of half-truths, and to his credit Tristan seemed to have a real aptitude for it. He should work in sales. Or Parliament.

"You should work in sales, Tristan," he said.

"Excuse me?" Tristan answered.

"Sales. A vocation whereby it is advantageous to bend the rules, stretch the truth, and spin a yarn so long my granny would be happy as pie."

"I'm not sure that I get you?"

"Tristan, mate. My van is not there, and nor is it at another garage, is it? Let's stop pissing about."

"Yes, it is, it's at another-"

"Garage," Jez mimicked. "I know what you said. But I also know that it is a lie. Look, the fact of the matter is that I don't care about your involvement. I only want to know the details of its whereabouts."

"Okay. Okay," he said in defeat.

Chapter Twenty-Four

Ruby

I have found myself caught up in some situations before, but this is truly strange. I'm not even sure what I'm doing here. I'm so confused that I want to either go to a bar and drink myself sober or lock myself away in a dark room somewhere – hiding until the world is right again.

Eddie and I are caught up in that strange relationship dance. We circle each other, waiting for the other to make the first move. We pretend that we're 'just good friends,' and technically, we are just that, but we're also something deeper. We have a magnetic pull that keeps us close together, but sometimes I wonder whether it is pulling us together, or like when you turn the magnets over, an invisible force is keeping us apart.

Last night, I went out to do what I always do– that stupid childish thing of trying to make Eddie jealous. The irony is that I do this to try and make him want me, but I'm beginning to think this act could well be the thing that's keeping us apart. What a mess. I know this, and yet next time, you can bet a bottle of vodka I'll do the same damn thing again. The stupidity cycle is what my mother would call it.

I kept throwing glances over to him, but he gently glides through life, sometimes bumping into things, and sometimes with an air of elegance. Even with his mate, he seems at arm's length, but then he caught his mate shagging his ex, so I guess underneath that laidback persona is a sensitive guy who doesn't want to get hurt again.

It has all built up, and I need to tell him how I feel, which of course is the reason why I walked in those death heels all the way to his house before sleeping outside on his porch and putting up with the comments from the Wicked Witch next door.

But even then− even after doing all that− something held me back, and this morning I was sat looking at the real elephant in the room.

Jean.

From my awkward position across the room busying myself with cups of tea that for the most part was ignored; I could see there was almost a moment. The two grieving parents together grasping at snapshots of happier times together, their invisible rose-tinted glasses there for all to see...

I hate this. Eddie has had his daughter kidnapped, and I'm here snivelling away through utter unadulterated envy. I just can't help the way I'm feeling.

One minute, the two of them were a second away from an embrace, and the next Eddie was off − without so much as a word to me. I know I'm being selfish, but it hurts.

Then that human muppet, Jez springs to life on his laptop, probably realising that he can do more than play games against 12-year-old boys from America on it, and suddenly thinks that he's *Peter Falk* as *Columbo*. With a finger in the air and a giant grin, he's gone. We all just look at each other, similarly thinking the same thing– that whatever he's up to, it's probably best done away from us.

Old Mopey Jean's boyfriend disappeared long before Eddie's Lord Lucan act. So then Miss Chambers decides to go home, probably to take some pills, have a nap, or make voodoo dolls, and I'm left with Harry and Mopey.

This is about as comfortable as a cactus in my bra. Harry is good at this though– most likely the vicar in him– and delves into his vast vault of stories....

Chapter Twenty-Five

Harry

Things have got completely out of hand. Just when I think everything is moving gently on an even keel, someone comes along and shakes the snow globe of life, showering me in a blizzard of confusion.

I've always been there for Eddie, slowly guiding him forward with vague gestures and subtleties, and we bicker like a father and son, but of course, it is all within jest.

My own son grew up away from me. His mother was someone who in my younger years, I chased, caught, and then grew bored of very quickly. My shame runs deep now, but after losing to Alfie with Mary, I became disillusioned with ever finding 'The One.' I was convinced that Mary was 'The One,' and so now I filled my time with a string of women that I didn't need to worry about in terms of depth, feelings, and a whole-hearted relationship. Kenny was the bi-product of one of these liaisons, and whilst we still talk on occasion, this has become out of duty, and not because of want or need. We both never fit into the idealist vision of a father or son, so with mutual disappointment, both kept our distance. Eddie was, and still is, by no means perfect, but just the simple way that he respects me is enough, and as he is related to my best mate, he certainly feels like family.

Eddie always had something that little bit special about him, and I couldn't help but feel his dad was the biggest fool for letting this special person grow up around him and be ignored the way that he was. It used to break my heart to watch how that family interacted.

Eddie was an independent child, but there was also a need that he kept hidden of wanting love and acceptance. Alfie gave him this and more, but at home, things were always a bit odd. By all accounts, Eddie was an accidental pregnancy, and if I was to be a little bit mean, then one wonders whether the hushed whispers of rumour as to the identity of the father were unsubstantiated or not.

Eddie's father and mother got together young, and before you roll your eyes at that, I'm thinking the same thing: that cannot be the reason their love went cold. No, the main reason for this was that Gordon was easily distracted by life, and Collette was easily distracted by other men. But the thing is, there was a time when these two were caught up in the usual rush and flourish of love and lust.

Gordon lived in Caulfield Hall with Alfie and Mary, but Alfie was never fully comfortable there. He was a quiet man, humbled into still working as a teacher at the local school, even though he didn't need to work. His wealth through inheritance embarrassed him, and it was almost a relief when Gordon started dating the very elegant Collette LeStange, a daughter of a French artist. She was tall and athletic, with long, lithe legs and a mouth that was on the verge of twitching with a smile. Who could blame him for being taken in by her charms? And he was not beaten with the ugly stick either, and being known as a hard worker, and coming from an upper-class background, the two of them in a town like Thornhill were bound to be drawn to each other eventually. I'm not talking about fate, chance, or even serendipity− just two strong-minded individuals pushing aside the advances of others until they met. And when they did, they looked like they belonged together, holidaying all around the world from Kenya to Copenhagen, lunch in Paris and a weekend in Barcelona. Wealth feeds whims with little thought or wisdom.

A large wedding followed, and these two socialites were almost local celebrities, but the hysteria of it all built up until it could go no further.

Then the pregnancy of Ben occurred, and things changed. Firstly, Collette became obsessed with taking it easy whilst carrying her baby. The weekends away stopped, and a maid came in to help clean and cook. Alfie mentioned that the 'Lord and Lady of The Manor' had even talked about a butler, but that was pushed to the side. The laughed-off blame falling heavily to the door of wine and sherry indulgence.

Gordon was drawn into his painting, but he felt the pressure of marrying the daughter of a French painter, and grew frustrated with his own work. It was good, but he allowed himself to not express, expand, and explore his own artistic vision, but be influenced and intimidated, and was intransigent by wanting to be better than someone else's. The hardest thing in life is to try and be better than a woman's father. Every man knows this.

When Ben came along, the beautiful family lived and loved together. They soon began to travel with Baby Ben in tow or staying with Alfie and Mary.

Then Lady Luck grew annoyed with the family, and Mary was taken ill with cancer. Within four months, she had lost three stone in weight, and behind her eyes, she had left the world as her body fought on for another few weeks, a sad empty vessel parading as nothing more than a worn-out deflated beauty. It was heart wrenching for those with vivid memories of a vibrant and joyful past.

This was enough for Alfie, who moved into the house that Eddie and Daisy live in now. But something had changed in that place. Ben was doted on by both parents, but to an almost competitive gain for affection. Ben grew confused and ultimately angry, but would always insist he loved both parents equally.

The maid was a sturdy built girl chosen by Collette to be her opposite, with the assumption that men coming to parties and visits would only spare thoughts of pity towards her, whereas any flirtatious advances would be directed her way. However, it wasn't long before she understood that men cannot be coerced easily, as the fact of the matter is that their choices can derive from many strange criteria or be a simple toss-of-a-coin irreverence. Of course, there were plenty of sweet comments and more than a few borderline innuendos, but facts are facts, and when men have been drinking they are more likely to look for the more nubile single female than the married mother. It's a simple calculation of statistical likelihood at mate-finding, completely irrelevant of whether or not they themselves are married.

It was easy to see the looks passing among some of the men as the quiet buxom brunette smiled shyly whilst serving drinks, and Collette dismissed their winks again with pity. However, she was not so lucky after the New Year's party, having only just fallen pregnant with Eddie. She had uncharacteristically gone out to the garden to get some air, and taken as she was with the moonlight gleaming off of the lake, she was drawn down towards it. Feeling a sudden chill, she headed into the boathouse to get a blanket. And that is when she got more than a glimpse of her naked maid serving two of her male guests in a way that she had not been taught. How dare she take advantage of her guests? She stormed off without interrupting anything. She was going to bring the episode up the next day, but instead decided that it could be used as an advantage.

And so began Collette's calculated hatred towards the maid. The sullen look never too far away, and whilst she was never a captive, at times that is exactly what she seemed to be.

Never one to fully understand a situation, Gordon, of course, took pity on her, but as far as I know, other than some kind words, the odd bonus and gift once in a while, that was where it ended. However, now with another small child and an older child too, Collette was able to conjure up all kinds of carnal images that she assumed was happening between her maid and her husband.

Eddie was six years old when he heard noises coming from the boathouse, and upon looking through the window, was shocked to see a man doing something to his mother. She was gasping and clawing at him, and in confusion, he ran in and disturbed the pair. "Get off of her!" he screamed through tears.

"Get lost!" the man had said with a large swoosh of his arm as if trying to fend off a cat. His mum, understanding the full implications of this, spoke calmly to her son, "Eddie, this man is sorry for hurting me, aren't you?"

Looking up to Heaven, he replied, "Yes."

"Now run back up to the house and get yourself a biscuit, okay?"

Eddie had nodded and made off to the house. He didn't see his mother for another hour.

This wasn't the worst thing that happened in the boathouse though. That would happen when Eddie was eight. He had been playing by the side of the lake when he heard a bang− not the bang of a gun or something bursting, but of something hard falling over. It was late in the afternoon; the day was losing light, and the night was drawing in. As he turned to walk back up to the house, he saw a flashing light coming from the boathouse. As he got closer, he realised that it wasn't a flashing light but something swinging back and forth in front of the light.

Through the very same window that he caught a glimpse of his mother in a compromised position, he was shocked further by what was in front of him now.

Swinging like a human metronome was the maid.

We later found out that her name was Sally Dennison. Though confirmed as a suicide, many folks had theories that could well be the work of over-active imaginations or perhaps half-truths liberally sprinkled with rumour.

Chapter Twenty-Six

I'm not sure how long I've been in here now. This study is a mixture of familiar and new. There are items that, when I see or touch them, they spark off memories. I'm elated with nostalgia at one point, and filled with sadness and close to tears at others. I often wonder as to the healthy properties of nostalgia− the way our memories surface in an anaesthetic clarity, shielding us from any true pain from the whole historic episode, leaving us with a longing to return to that time. It raises false feelings of satisfaction and elation that were more than likely never present in real-time, but our minds conduct this perfection built with feelings that we think we felt, rather than a facsimile of those original emotions. Yes, I'm over thinking this, but that's what I do.

My sole purpose is to search and find something that someone is after, but it's like walking through a thick sea of memories. Ghosts all around seem to paw at me, making the air thick and the oxygen levels low. I'm suddenly tired and lethargic.

There are canvasses strewn around the room, and not many are carefully stacked or hung. I can only assume the ones that are must be my father's favourites. I quickly look at a pile. The first is of Caulfield Hall, with the lake in the background.

The many glints on the water smile up at the sun in the sky. But just to the side is the boathouse, and this has a real eerie look to it. The windows have some sort of menace about them, and I am transported back to those times of tragedy as a child. For years, I thought that my mother had been attacked. When I was old enough to hear about and learn what rape was all about, I was convinced that this was what had happened to her. She was the victim, and I wept many times for her. But years went by, and suddenly I was exposed to the notion that sex and violence are not always the poles-apart acts we've come to believe. So whilst that was a riddle that was never truly understood, then the night that Sally committed suicide was even worse.

It wasn't the way that she was swinging by her neck, like there was still a hope that life remained within her. Or the fetid smell whereby on her deathbed her bowels had released its contents. Or her grey face, with a loping thick tongue and an expected mournful look that I hope never to see again in the whole of my life. It was all just a great big shame.

There are a lot of things from my past that I don't know. I had so many questions. There were things that were either secretively hidden from me by my parents, or shielded from me as an act of protection by my granddad or Harry.

As I look at the painting below, I once again have questions. There without the grey face, but in all of her naked glory is Sally, a playful smile that looks like it was captured just before she laughed.

Her full figure, whilst sturdy, is shaped beautifully. Never has a woman with a few extra pounds looked so good. There didn't seem to be much flab on her— just ripeness from breasts to buttocks.

But what was she doing posing naked for my father? I wonder if I will have answers to these questions.

I wonder whether I will ever see my father again.

I wonder whether I will ever see Daisy again.

I look at my phone, but there is no answer from Daisy. I'm glad that she contacted me, but that seemed so long ago.

I glance around again. What is hidden here that they could be after? It has got to be of great value, but really everything is of standard junk-slash-artist-studio-slash-study. The desk and chair, whilst old, are mass-produced, as is the bookcase and other furniture.

I walk over to the bookcase in the corner and scan along some of the titles. There are reference books to art and artists. There are a handful of local history. Then there are books on symbols and symbolism, cults and secret societies.

My mind is now spinning with wonder. Was my father caught up with some secret society? There were a lot of things that could feed this theory. The large house and the wealth and status. The many parties thrown for people I didn't know. But there was something that derailed this train of thought. My father was not interested in the social gatherings, so either my mother was the one that, by choice, recruited, entertained, or headed up the society, or my father was an unknown leader, so important that he need not make an appearance, but would make decisions in a cloud of suspicion. I didn't buy it. Now Harry, I certainly could see being involved in something like that, but he'd found his own cult in religion. Although Miss Chambers certainly had a Thatcher-esque feel to her, she was only ever an occasional guest. She didn't mix well with others, with her tendency to buck heads with most.

Then I noticed the books on Benjamin Franklin, Leonardo Da Vinci, Thomas Edison, Albert Einstein, George Westinghouse, Nikola Tesla. There were also copies of *'A Briefer History Of Time'* & *'The Theory Of Everything'* by Professor Stephen Hawking. I also remembered a weekend that my father had enjoyed with a guy by the name of James Dyson, and how as Mr. Dyson's brand grew, my father dropped his name into conversation time and time again.

I picked up one of the books on inventions called 'Spy,' but as I pulled it, I firstly noticed that it felt somewhat solid, and then I realised that it didn't come out, but tilted back to me. As I did this, I heard a little click, so faint that it could easily have been missed. As nothing happened, I rolled my eyes, knowing that this would open something, but one point of release would be open to an accidental finding, whereas two pulled together would be perfect. I glanced over all of the book spines trying to read them as quickly as possible when to my left, I spotted it. In fact, you could say that I spied it. It also proclaimed to be about inventions, albeit not with the other books (suspicious!), but was entitled 'Eye.' So with my left hand on 'Eye,' and my right hand on 'Spy,' I pulled and pushed first left, and when nothing happened, I pushed right.

The bookcase swivelled slightly, producing a gap about two feet wide. I could see nothing beyond. However, a couple of steps in there must've been a sensor, as first there was a couple of flashes, and then some light appeared.

The only thing that I could see was a staircase leading down to a basement that I never knew was here.

Almost twenty years I'd spent in this house, and I'd never known there was anything below. I was a mixture of excitement and disappointment.

I put my hand on the rail and began my descent down the spiral staircase to God-knows-what!

Chapter Twenty-Seven

Daisy

"Who are you?" I said, which is a pretty silly thing to say, of course. I was in a room, having climbed up from some stinky cellar, and here is a guy hiding in the dark calling me, *"My pretty."* Talk about frying-pan and fire! This wasn't the best scenario in the world, if you asked me, but suddenly, he was holding up his hands. So by the very fact that he was doing this and not trying to grope me– or slit my throat from ear to ear– I considered it a moderately good sign.

"Look, I'm just trying to get out of here. I came to pick up the van." He fumbled in his pocket, and I was holding the book bag tightly, prepared to swing it at him at any moment (whilst knowing I probably didn't have the strength to do any real damage). He pulled out some keys that could well belong to a van – although they could just as easily belong to a car, a motorbike, or a ride-on-mower for all of the good my automotive-key knowledge was.

"You came to pick up a van, but ended up whispering in a store-room of some old building?" I pressed.

"Look, I work at the garage that this van should be at, but I lent it to someone, but actually the van wasn't mine to lend, and now I have to get it back."

"So you were given the van to mend, but you decided you were in the van hire business, but you are about to get rumbled, so you are coming to pick the van up and finish on a race-against-time type of scenario?"

"Yeah, that's about the size of it," he nodded, and she could make out that he wasn't one of the men from earlier. He smiled, but it wasn't totally natural. Either he was lying or a little embarrassed.

"How come you have the van keys? Don't tell me they were left behind the sun-visor, or perhaps under the wheel arch."

"Spare key."

"So when you get the van back, how are you going to explain that the main key is missing?"

"They look alike. This afternoon I'll go to my mate at a Main Dealer, and within a day or so, he'll have me a replacement. Job done."

"So-" I started, but abruptly stopped when we heard shouting from below. It seems like I'm officially missing now for the second time today, and judging by the unchristian language, they're none-too pleased either.

I looked up at the man, but he put his fingers to his lips. I'm not sure what sort of idiot he takes me for, but having just spent the last hour hatching a plan and then squeezing up through a hole in the ceiling in order to escape, why the heck would I deliberately make a noise so as to let them know where I am.

I couldn't help it; I pulled a face at him which silently said, "Duurr!"

My heart was beating again with adrenaline, but it was also nice to be with someone else, even if I was far from trusting him. He didn't seem all that surprised to see a very attractive (why not?) girl appear through the floor hatch, and had made no attempt to ask me my name or who I was. It smelt less fishy at the local fishmongers, but what choice did I have?

After a few minutes, he slowly got up and carefully picked his way over some piles of stuff covered in blankets and placed his ear up against the door.

He then walked over to one of the covered windows and peaked behind. This let a strong beam of light cut across the room. He put his thumb up to me, which I took to be a sign of triumph, rather than a confirmation of friendship.

"They're both running around out there like a pair of bumpkins!" He grinned and headed back over to the door. "Come on."

I tentatively went with him, but it seemed too good to be true that he'd stumbled upon me. I just couldn't get my head around it.

I covered my eyes as we went out into a hallway that was bright with sunlight from an open door. I glanced back and saw a staircase going up and a door underneath. I wondered whether it went downstairs to where I'd been held.

"Quick, straight to the van," he said, and I then had a feeling there was something familiar about him. But more than that was the black eye and a definite bruise on his cheek.

"You walk into a wall or something?" I found myself saying, then cursed myself for saying it out loud. He grunted, and his left hand unconsciously almost made it to his face before he realised what he was doing.

The back of the van was to us as we jogged up.

"You go to the passenger side, and I'll let you in from the inside." I nodded, but as soon as he disappeared behind the van, I legged it.

I ran as fast as my legs would carry me. I'd got probably 30 metres away before I heard him yell, and that was the moment I knew I'd done the right thing. If you're sneaking away, then there's no way you'd let anyone know that you were there.

I was running towards the lake without a plan other than not being caught and not falling over. I hate it when the poor female is running away in a book or movie, and she trips over something and falls down. It just doesn't seem right. I also don't mess around looking behind me, as this very act will slow me down and make me lose concentration – not to mention balance.

"Hey!" another voice shouts, but he's further off. I don't even look to see who it is. This is my chance. This is what a lot of people in my position want and hope and pray for. This simple gift may even take me to see one of Uncle Harry's sermon-things if I make it out of this.

The house has been left behind me now, and I'm following a path along the side of the lake. My running is a lot stronger than my swimming, so I am gambling that this might be the best option. I can see a building up ahead, and there is a jetty, but I'm still running hard and thinking on my feet. Fight or flight, I think they call this. Well, mister, I am a bird all of the way. My dad would fight. He has a great determination, and his reflexes are almost superhuman. Uncle Harry said that my dad could've become a professional boxer. He looks at some of the Super-Middle weights and tells me, "In his day, your dad could've given these boys a run for their money!" It seems funny now to think about this as I am running for my life. Or even that I notice the natural beauty of the wild flowers that line the bank so randomly at this time.

I'm pretty sure this is the other side of White Horse Lake, but this isn't the side that I've been to very often. I spring over a gate that has a padlock on like it's nothing.

"I've got a gun!" shouts a voice from behind, but I'm not going to stop unless I get shot. This is England and the countryside. A gun is as rare as a rainless summer. Unless it was a shotgun used for game, and this would slow you down – although I'm a large ambling clay-pigeon – but I quickly dismissed this thought. It sounded like a desperate shout, rather than a threat.

And then I see the boat.

It's not very big and has oars, and it does have a motor in the back.

I glance behind, something I didn't want to do, and see that the two men are almost together. But they're still half a football field away from me, and there was no shotgun. A handgun will not shoot accurately that far, this I am sure of. CSI has taught me many things – possibly inaccurately – but they have taught me nevertheless.

I quickly untie the rope and jump into the boat.

I know nothing about motors, so trying to start this could be the same as me signing my own death warrant, so I grit my teeth, with my lungs burning and prepare to row. Thankfully, I had done this a few times with my dad and with Uncle Harry, and I knew that it wasn't the speed, but the long hard pull on the oars and finding that rhythm that would then keep me away from the men. I only had to row faster than they could swim, and I was hopeful of that.

My first couple of attempts sent me off course slightly, as I took some strokes to get my two arms working together. I could now see them getting to the beginning of the jetty near the bank, as I was about 15 feet out. For a second, I thought that the fitter of the two was going to run and dive into the lake and chase me, but they slowed as they got to the end. Thankfully, they didn't have a gun.

But as they turned and looked back at the building, I could see that there was a speed boat.

But surely they couldn't get that started, could they?

They ran off in its direction, and I paddled my arms like I have never done before.

Chapter Twenty-Eight

Miss Alice Chambers

I sometimes wonder about people of today's society. Of mankind as a whole, if I may be so bold and convey some of my feelings. Of course, there are still some gentlemen in this world and plenty of folk that appreciate all that has been given to them by their forefathers. There have been a whole host of uncles, grandparents, and great-grandparents that all gave their lives for this wonderful nation, but what have we got to show for it, I ask? We have a youth culture that glorifies the horrors that we endured in wars by fantasising it as a glorious way to live. They bring it to their own backyards, like they are proudly showing off this imported lifestyle that they have cheaply stolen from a disadvantaged country. Refugees left homeless and living in a Hell unknown to most, risk life and limb to travel and what are they met with, open arms of compassion? Certainly not. Only snivelling hoodlums trying to emulate the very thing they're trying to escape from. I mean, goodness gracious alive, the lack of mental capacity and common sense would have slain war heroes the land over turning over in their graves.

We're not producing soldiers; we're producing inmates. And what for?

Young lads are still dying, protecting innocent people in foreign lands, and here we are killing each other over land that is owned by the council, not ourselves, and then ultimately it doesn't matter who owns what, as people live out their years in a cell provided by the government and paid for by us, the tax payers.

I don't apologise for my feelings in the same way the youth don't apologise for their actions. I was brought up in a world where we were all on the same side and fighting for the same thing; somewhere along the line these things got forgotten and the lines blurred. Now we're surrounded by selfish leeches trying to get as much as they can from the government and with the audacity to complain at the Prime Minister's decisions, but not even bothering to understand politics, nor move their lazy posteriors to vote.

I grew up in a basement of a house that I was sent to as a refugee in the war. My father died for his country, and to a certain extent, so did my mother – she was put to work in a workhouse and had an industrial accident. I was sent out of London and into the countryside, working for my keep. Pay no attention to any misconception that you have over these details. I'm not trying to wet-your-eyes or pick-pocket your sympathies. No, this is a simple background to my life and quite possibly the key to my personality. I'm a strong and independent woman. I was not born this way; or if I was, then this only reinforced these characteristics. I worked hard for little return, and again I say this not as a sob story but as fact. I'm by no means alone in this. I wasn't having to hide out whilst Nazi's stampeded through the house killing whoever did not conform to their idealistic super-nation, and therefore, I had it better than most.

In my late teens, I found my way over to Caulfield Hall on large celebration dinners and dances, and I was rather taken with the place, allowing teenage fantasies to fill my spare time. These romantic notions, of course, never blossomed into real life. There were many roads of opportunity that presented themselves to me, and often I've wondered just where these would've taken me had I dared to follow them instead.

Eddie is a lad that will always remain in my heart, as his daughter does. There is something so very gentle about the way he baits me. He is amused at our relationship, but I know that I keep him on his toes, and I think that we both enjoy the unpredictability of it all. I have very few pleasures or hobbies that keep me sharp, and that is why we jab at each other the way we do. Gerald, though, is something completely different. He is some sort of man-child loping around. It is a fine thing that he is so good on those computers, as he would be just as happy claiming benefits, whilst playing on whatever games console is currently considered the best. I'm at a loss with the infatuation of these— grown men playing childish games, a complete reversal of what I grew up with, whereby most of the boys never returned from playing the adult game with guns....

Gordon should never have been a father to Eddie. Many people say that officially, he never was, but that is a debate for another time. At least they both have Harry. Good old dependable Harry.

It may surprise you, but I was married once to a rather dashing man, if you understand what this description to be. Theodore was tall and debonair, strong in his principles and of course a brave man, although ultimately a stupid man. I, of course, do not mean the last bit, but it is a comment that slips from my tongue rather easily, as his decision to go to war was one that cost him his life. I resent him for that wrong choice and the hole in my life that has never been filled since. I will not entertain you with the precious and personal details of our courtship, and ours was probably not a tale that has been retold by others through sentimental reminiscing, but let us say that he had the ability to take a strong independent woman and make her follow him rather embarrassingly, like a deluded virgin maiden.

In later years, there could well have been opportunities for me to enter into some sort of courtship with another man, but this has never been an avenue that I'd wished to explore. Half of me never required that sort of commitment or companionship, but the other half that did failed to make it back to the shores from the bloody war all of those years ago. I may admit to a form of friendship with Harry, but we flitter about with a relationship that neither one of us understands and certainly not that we pursue to a deeper level. Who would've thought that I could ever find anything remotely attractive about a vicar? Well, I'll be damned. He may try and be all Rock Hudson, but there is an insecure man under that ecclesiastical attire, and well, who wouldn't enjoy the thrill of hooking a man like that, especially a woman of my age and vintage.

However, this is an extremely unfortunate turn of events and another prime example of how the world has gone to ruin. I mean jeepers-creepers, if you want something in this world, you bloody well get off of your backside and go and get it. You don't go and kidnap someone. This isn't the Victorian era. I have been racking my old brains over that thing that Gordon gave me, but I cannot be sure that it is anything to do with what those unscrupulous individuals are after, and anyway, what gives them the right to threaten and commit such a cowardly act as to take a defenceless, innocent girl, without giving her dad the chance to hand them what they want? I know Eddie, and for all of his fight, he would give up his life for the safety of his child. And that is the problem. I do not think they have properly thought this through, and if this is indeed the case then they may well panic and do something extremely bad with a half-cocked plan.

And who has Eddie got in his corner? A wrinkly old vicar, a dithering old woman, an idiotic side-show of a neighbour, a stupid ex-girlfriend, and a slutty-love-interest. Well, someone was surely scraping the barrel for this cast of misfits.

Chapter Twenty-Nine

Jean

Sometimes you sit and review your life, wondering just what you were thinking. How your priorities were never as they should've been. I know this. I don't need people telling me, and I don't need the looks that I receive.

They have all been nice enough, but behind each empty 'I'm sorry,' I can't help but wonder whether there is a finger of judgment pointing my way.

I wanted more from life than to be weighed down with a husband and child. I know how that must sound, but that is the truth. Eddie is a good man, and I would be lying if I didn't admit to wanting to get back together with him. But in all honesty, I know it wouldn't work. I love him for an evening or a weekend, but not for a lifetime.

I miss Daisy, but I enjoy her more seeing her once in a while, rather than her living with me. I know that must sound strange coming from a mother, but I don't see myself as a mother. I want to be free and single, but be able to fall back into the groove with Eddie once in a while. But he's not like that. He's traditional, and it's all or nothing for him. I also know that finding me with his best mate really hurt him. Yeah, I know, *like, obvious*, right? But I don't see anything wrong with wanting to have sex with different men. I don't want to be an old woman, or even a middle-aged woman, so why can't I just be young and free to do whatever I want? I smile a bit at that. In those last few lines, I've managed to say stuff that has been in a number of popular songs over the years, and that tells me that I'm not the only one to feel this way. I mean, fuck it, who wants to stay at home and clean and shit? Not me, that's for sure. I want to be taken out and bought fancy clothes, and then have some man slowly take off those fancy clothes with that excitement in his eyes and bulge in his pants! But I also feel a little empty.

I've seen the way that Ruby looks at him, with her tattoos and her '*alternative*' look. But I also know that she has a wild side, and I'm not sure that Eddie will go for her long term. They do sort of look like they might be a match, but I dunno. I think I'm better looking than her, even if I have puffy eyes. My stomach is flatter, for one thing, and although I cannot be sure, my breasts are bigger.

I should probably worry about Bob and where he has disappeared off to, but Bob is Bob. He takes me out to posh restaurants and shows me off to his golfing buddies, unaware that when I go out in the week it is to have sex with other men. He has no idea how to interact with people, so being around the friends and family of my ex-boyfriend is likened to a person with arachnophobia surrounded by tarantulas. He's more than likely either at the pub or the bookies. Northern Bob with his funny accent and old ways, but completely out of his comfort zone when he gets south of Birmingham.

"You holding up okay, Jean?" Harry asked. I know that he's a man of God, but he has never judged me. Eddie used to tell me stories of the things that Harry got up to before he found God, but he has always been Father Harry Dugan to me.

I shrugged, "I suppose."

He walked over, still holding the walkie-talkie looking thing. "What the Hell is this?" he smiled, looking at the strange ugly object.

"Gordon told me about it once. It was his big thing," I sighed, thinking back to one of the many chats that we'd had. Gordon wasn't as bad as everyone made out, but then I guess we were similar. He loved Eddie, but he was focused on his work. That is why his relationship with Eddie was better when Eddie went and lived with his granddad.

"Well, his big thing had already been invented. It's called a walkie-talkie! And now there are smaller versions with a lot larger coverage called mobile phones!"

"This was different," I said, looking up at him.

"How so?"

"He told me that you could talk to the dead." Harry looked at me like I was on drugs.

But imagine if you really could?

Chapter Thirty

I'd only gone down two steps when I heard my mobile ring. With one hand, I grabbed it out of my pocket, whilst I jumped back up and into the study, just in case I lost signal going down into the bowels of unknown.

There was no name and no number, just a bunch of symbols that I've never seen on a phone in my life. My mobile is not exactly cutting edge, unless of course the year was 2005.

"Hello?" I said, and really it could be any number of people about to give me great or terrible news.

"Eddie?" a faint voice asked. "Eddie, is that you?" Then there was static again.

"Yes," I said.

"It's me," an excited familiar voice replied. "Your dad!"

I wasn't sure how to take the news. I mean, I had wondered whether he was still alive, and certainly, the two men this morning had hinted that they thought he was definitely still with us.

"D-dad?" was all that I could muster.

Then there was a buzz and an ear-piercing sound, which made me pull away from the phone abruptly. When I could hear that it had stopped, I tentatively put it back again.

"You're breaking up. What was that?"

"I said, let them have them if-" but a whizzing sound drowned out what he was saying.

"Dad, I can't hear you anymore. They have Daisy. They want something from you. What is it, and where can I find it?" I reeled off the questions as quickly as possible.

"Find the cellar...I-Spy books... Go behind the clock. It's all there. Everything tha-" with a crackle and a bang, he was gone. I looked at the phone, but it looked dead. Somehow the battery had gone flat in minutes.

I pushed the button again to turn on the phone, but it was not having it. I remembered back to all of the phone calls that I'd received over the past couple of days. It must've been my dad trying to contact me. But why was he trying to reach me so bad? And how come he seemed to know that he had something that someone wanted? There were so many times I felt disconnected with my father, that actually this was almost the perfect description of our relationship. For the most part, he was dead to me, with a slight wonder that he may turn up at some stage, with that crooked grin that he had that said, "Here I am. I bet you weren't expecting me!" And I would gloss over those slight feelings of neglect from my childhood, and that's exactly what it was. I've made excuses for him to nearly everyone that I've spoken to about my childhood, but deep down when I'm on my own with a bout of melancholy, then the word 'neglect' doesn't seem too strong a description.

I'm not being overly dramatic; I know that there are children that you'd really consider having being neglected– ones who aren't fed for days or who are left on their own whilst their parents are drunk, high, or in another county or country. Ones who didn't survive or the ones who did, but were physically and/or mentally scarred. I'm not in either of these categories, but I still cried myself to sleep some nights. I grew up wondering why my parents didn't love me. I asked friends whether I could stay with them, and when I finally started to live with my granddad, I begged him not to make me go back home. I shouldn't have felt like that. So I make no apologies for using the word 'neglect,' because I was hurt inside over how I was raised. I fell into a relationship with Jean because she seemed to care about me. We got pregnant, and that didn't seem to be such a big thing, because I knew that I would be the best dad in the world. But then Jean decided to start sleeping with other people, and I had horrible flashes that she was my mother, and so was I no better than my father? My family and I had seriously lost connections.

I put my phone on my father's desk and was drawn to the pile of paperwork. Perhaps this might give me an idea as to his whereabouts.

There were a couple of invoices for electrical and telecommunications companies for the purchase of components and an interesting letter from a company called 'Cutting Edge Technologies,' expressing their interest in seeing the prototype in action. It was dated two weeks before my father disappeared....

Then I noticed a couple more invoices, except I recognised the letterhead, as I had helped design it. *'Capers'* it said. But when I looked closely, they weren't invoices, but credit notes. They amounted to a little under twenty thousand pounds. I cannot understand why we would've been giving back my father this money....

And then the penny dropped.

Jason had given my father the money, putting it through the books for the purposes of some tax fiddle. So had we as owners/shareholders of *Capers*, been financing my father's little project all along?

This so say unknown project? Surely then, Jason must know more about it to warrant paying out this money. And if this was the money that was paid out seven years ago, then how much has been paid out since? I thought that *Capers* was doing well, but the profit margin always seemed to be quite small. I put it down to the economic climate, so whilst we were filling out the place, the supplier charges were increasing at a higher percentage.

So does Jason know where my father is?

And is it a coincidence that Jason had gone out of town on business the very weekend that my daughter got kidnapped? Who goes out on business on a Saturday?

Jason screwed me over once before – well, technically, he screwed my girlfriend – so what's to say that he won't do that again?

This just gets worse and worse....

Chapter Thirty-One

Jez sat outside the Garage, looking at how closed the place seemed. This was interesting. This is where he was told the van was, and it was neither in the car park, and judging by the gap in the door and the large window, it did not seem to be inside either.

He pulled out his phone and was about to ring, when he decided that he might as well update his followers on what was going on.

"Interesting developments," he started, like he was a lead investigator on the crime of the century. "I have arrived at the aforementioned garage, but alas, the said van is nowhere to be seen. It looks like I may've come to a dead end...for now!" He signed off, and was about to leave when he heard a telephone ring from inside. There was a large bell that was attached so the mechanics could hear it ring too.

Jez walked over to the door of the office, just as he heard the answerphone click in, and thankfully like most things around here in this tin-pot garage, it was old and therefore of the variety that play the message out loud.

Jez missed the beginning, but managed to tune in to the rest. "-escaped. Tell Jason that some weird guy is looking for the van, and I get the feeling he knows what is going on. If you don't ring me in an hour, then I am going to the club. I should be able to catch Jason there."

This was all getting a bit strange. Jason was Eddie's best friend, but seemed to know about the van. So if he knew about the van, then he must know about the two meatheads, and there is then a very good likelihood that he knows about the kidnapping too.

But what the hell was the motive behind all of this? It can't be a ransom, as Eddie doesn't have that much disposable cash. Maybe they thought that he would sell Caulfield Hall, but then you would be talking at least six weeks, and more like thirteen to sixteen weeks before there was any money – and that would be if it was snapped up quickly.

Jez had a feeling it may have something to do with Eddie's dad and his disappearance. Hell, maybe his dad kidnapped Daisy? What about that for a kick in the nuts?

Jez went back to his car and got in. He looked through his CD's and put on some *Coldplay*. He pulled out of the garage and was indicating to go right, when he saw the Range Rover Evoke pass him with the registration number of J4SON. Quickly, he turned left instead and followed. *What are the chances of that?* he wondered, although someone was clearly expecting him around the area, hence the phone call.

Maybe the mouse would lead the cat....

Tailing someone wasn't as easy as it appeared to be in the movies. You can't get too close, but you can't be seen to be just lagging back. The trick is to look and act normal – these are two things that Jez has struggled with throughout the whole of his adult life.

They were heading out of town, this was clear, and at one point he lost sight of the Range Rover altogether and panicked. He couldn't help it; he still had this feeling inside that this was going to make him a hero.

Thankfully, he saw the vehicle turn left just as he was thinking that maybe that guy Adam Driver from the new Star Wars movie might play him, when this was turned into a movie. Eddie remarked that they were similar looking – well, in truth Eddie had said, "You two could be brothers, except you are the older and slightly more redneck looking, with a dash of Marilyn Manson thrown in!" But that was good enough.

It looked like they were following the road around White Horse Lake, and the Range Rover pulled into a drive that went down to Tulip House. If Jez wasn't mistaken, this was the house that Miss Chambers grew up in, although Eddie said that he shouldn't spread it around, on account of some horror that went on there in her childhood. Jez had long decided that this was probably the reason she was close to the devil now. But it didn't stop him throwing dog poo over her fence a few years back! He still smiled at that one every time it popped back into his head. A move so good that there really should be an area on your CV for such antics.

Jez stopped the car, knowing that there was no way that he could just drive down there. I mean, what would he say? Jason knows him – not well – but still knows him nevertheless. It would all seem fishy. And Jez suddenly had visions of himself on the edge of a jetty with his arms and legs tied together and some mafia-type bloke with a thick New Jersey accent mumbling, "No loose ends," before shooting him in the stomach. He would fall, and everything would be in slow motion. The splash and initial freezing cold water. His useless struggle with the ropes, unable to loosen them as the water around him turns crimson and his lungs burned to hell.

They say that drowning is one of the worst ways to die. Well, that's what Jez had read once in a crime novel. So he was going to play it safe. He pulled into an open gateway and drove slowly into the field, making sure that the ground was hard enough for him to not get stuck. His car was by no means hidden; the solid red paint hindered any chance he had of it merging into the background, but it couldn't be seen from the road, so that was the main idea.

He was fully aware that every breath and with each footstep, there was a noise that he was sure could be heard for miles. Nevertheless, he walked along the hedgerow alongside where the drive went in some bumbling fashion that may well have seemed comical to the wildlife. Then through the trees, he saw the house. It was a fair-sized house, certainly not as big as Caulfield Hall; although in truth, Jez had only seen it once in the flesh, and that was a few years ago.

Tulip House would be considered a large family house if it were situated in the town. It was quite picturesque in its surroundings, and whilst it seemed a little run-down and unloved now, it sat with the land in a wonderfully complimentary fashion. The whole view would be lost if either were to disappear. So whereas Caulfield Hall was grand, standing proud with its large architectural chest puffed out, demanding, "Look at me!" and the lake behind resigned in the knowledge that it was an also-ran in the race for attention, Tulip House stood arm-in-arm with the lake, and they both smiled, "Look at us!" before giggling gaily. But both buildings had their dark pasts. Jez had even heard the lake spoken of as White Curse Lake instead of White Horse, as the local taletellers told of the hearsay of abuse to Miss Chambers as a girl and also to that of Eddie a few years later in Caulfield Hall, which also had the story of adultery and suicide. Then just around the corner, was the remains of White Horse House, which caught fire in the 1930's and remains a shell. It is now a sometime party place for teens in the summer, who tell the tales of Eddie's great granddad Truman, who had a feud with Old Man Abe of White Horse House. The two would go at it over fishing trips in the lake, both accusing the other of some wrong-doing, until one night White Horse House went up in flames, killing Old Man Abe, his wife, and their two children. Fingers were pointed, but nobody was ever charged. However, there was a story – or possibly you could call it a legend – that told of Truman's youngest son Jack, drowning in White Horse Lake. At the time, it was put down to Accident By Misadventure, but there are some who say that Old Man Abe was seen rowing away from where Jack's body was later seen, and this filled in the gaps of motive in the eyes of those looking for one when it came to the house fire a month or two later.

Jez saw Jason come running out of the house and start shouting something loudly. Jason didn't look very happy at all.

Jez momentarily wanted to update his blog and let his viewers know exactly what was happening, but he also wanted to get closer to the house. He felt the obligation to his fans, but he knew that they would want the full story more.

He couldn't actually believe he was thinking this, but what if Daisy was in that house? What if Jason had been tipped off this and was running in to rescue her? Or what if he'd kidnapped her? He didn't mean actually take her, as Eddie had seen the two blokes that did that, but what if he was masterminding it?

He was suddenly unsure of what he should do. He suddenly saw his film character role changing, and he was incredibly worried that he would now play the part of a victim, rather than the hero role that he'd envisaged. Of course, sometimes there is a fine line between the two, with only fate sandwiched there rolling the dice to determine which they would be.

Would it not be a better thing to ring Eddie? Or tell him at least?

He pulled out his phone and pressed a couple of buttons that would then start Eddie's mobile ringing, but when it clicked to answerphone, Jez gave up, cancelled the call, and quickly sent a brief text instead:

Jason is sumhow connected to the van. Have followed him to Tulip House. Sumthin is happening here. J

He always signed off with 'J.' The text didn't like the word 'Jez,' like it was some completely foreign word or something. Bloody annoying really, but perhaps when he became famous, Apple, Samsung, Huawei, and the such-like will programme his name automatically to be recognised.

With that done, he made his move. It was slightly foolhardy, but he ran up to the house and through the door. He'd never been much of a runner, and his running style often brought comments from others that he looked like he had special needs, or that he was in the throes of a heart-attack. It was unkind, but an accurate description.

It was pitch black, or it seemed to be, having come in from outside. He walked forward, and just as his eyes adjusted to the light, a deep accented voice to the side of him said, "An' who du voock are you?" Jez involuntarily let out a loud squeal in fear. Maybe he wouldn't be the hero after all....

LOST CONNECTIONS

Chapter Thirty-Two

Daisy

My arms were beginning to ache. The lactic acid was building up in my biceps and triceps from pulling back the oars – not to mention my chest and shoulders! I can see why there are rowing machines in gyms (not that I ever frequent them) as this gives you one hell of a workout, tipping and pushing, dropping and pulling. My legs were shaking as I dug my heels into the bottom of the boat, clenching my butt-muscles as hard as I could. When you watch it in the Olympics or the Annual Oxford & Cambridge Boat Race, the boat glides effortlessly over the top of the water like it's a large water-ski, filled with people moving back and forth without much of a care in the world. Well, bollocks to that thought from now on!

I was in the middle of the lake. Maybe I should've headed off to the side, so as to make an escape on foot, but then they could get to me just as quick. The plan was to row right over to Caulfield Hall. It was incredibly ambitious, not to mention lightly stupid. This quick flash of inspiration lacked perspective in both actual and virtual vision. Water has a horrible way of tricking the mind into misinterpreting range. Even though

I'd been out here before, there is a major difference between being in a motorised boat and rowing on your own. We can all recall times when we have had to walk a journey that previously was done by car, miscalculating the distance by a long way. Well, the prosecution rests, your Honour. It is official: Daisy is a stupid cow!

But whilst part of me is dismissive, the defence comes to the stand full of hope and belief: If I could make it to the other side, then I had a chance. The size of the house, the corridors and hidden rooms would be enough to hide me. I was adamant, and I'm sure I've never used that word before so there you go! That must be a sign.

I just had to get there.

And then in the distance, I saw and heard something start up.

The speedboat. There was no way that I was going to be able to out-row the speedboat. I was slowing down, and the truth was, I wasn't even sure that I was moving anymore.

The motor was my only hope, other than jumping into the lake trying to swim as fast as I ever had.

I pulled in the oars and looked at the motor. I knew that it was a pull-start motor, but that was about where my mechanical knowledge ended. I looked closely, pushed a button that seemed right, and pulled the rip-cord. This was pretty similar to my dad's large lawnmower motor. I'm no petrol-head, but I'm guessing the principle is the same. There was a sound, but it was more like an old man with a chesty cough than a young, fit motor. I tugged again with more of a snap movement. This time, there was a more enthusiastic stutter of the engine as it almost said, 'Nearly!" I tried again, but this was a poor effort, and I felt my grip slip right at the point when I needed that snap. I took a deep breath. This time picturing my dad again, I pulled the cord as hard and fast as I could, letting out almost a guttural growl as I did so. The motor started up fine. I lowered it into the water, and off I went. Girl Power!

The speedboat was bouncing along, still building up speed. I looked over at Caulfield Hall and saw it getting nearer and nearer.

Another glance over my shoulder told me that the speedboat was gaining, bullying its way across the lake like a predator homing in on its prey.

This was going to be so close.

As a movie scene, the audience would be captivated, willing the young heroine to make it unscathed to safety. Surely, the pointless killing of the heroine would ruin the storyline, right? Or would this be some melancholy ending, deliberately dodging the safe Hollywood ending to puncture hearts with a painful scene before the credits rolled, the audience left with an uncomfortable and unnerving ending? Quietly exiting the theatres, unable to speak to one another, stunned into silence. The final scene burnt into their minds as they made their way home. Still there as they closed their eyes, and they were left feeling like they had lost a family member. *But, if only...*they start, with an inability to finish the sentence, and unsure on how they would function the very next day....

As the jetty came within twenty feet, I stood up. I didn't even think about whether what I was going to do was sensible or not.

I refused to look behind me anymore.

I jumped over the side, and with a splash, the water came up to my middle. I fought hard as the water got shallower. I could hear the speedboat getting closer and nonsensical shouting just over it.

Then I was onto dry land, and I felt suddenly unshackled. Completely liberated, I ran as fast as I could, tired limbs pumping with a never-ending supply of adrenaline.

I ran as fast as a person was able to, having not eaten since breakfast and having been in a stressful environment for most of the day. Whilst Caulfield Hall was not a home to me, there was something about it being part of my family that reached out and gave me energy.

I ran past the boathouse, as it was too close, and for some reason, Dad had been reluctant for me to venture near it. I knew if I got to the front of the house, it would be open, and I could hide.

But the front seemed so far away.

I looked ahead and saw someone waving at me.

It was a small boy, smartly dressed in a black blazer, grey shorts, and black cap. He motioned for me to come to him behind a hedge on the front of the house. It was a good 200 metres away. How I wished I had kept in shape again.

He disappeared behind the hedge, which had bright pink roses welcoming me, and I momentarily glanced over my shoulder to see that the two men were running after me. I had about twenty metres on them, and with a bit of luck, that might be enough.

As I made it to the other side of the hedge, I saw a door open and the boy's arm beckoning me inside. I certainly needed no invitation and skidded down the last bit into the darkness. I turned and pulled the door shut.

Relief washed over me as I saw a bolt, and quickly I slid it across and locked the bad men out. I could hardly breathe, and my hair stuck to my forehead with sweat that I had not had since some army-type PE lesson a few months back. I could only imagine what a state I looked. I scrunched up my nose as I noticed the wet rings around my armpits. *How unladylike*, I thought.

In less than five seconds, banging on the door told me that my followers had made it just too late. I was just about to shout out something stupid, almost goading, or even a clever one-liner like you might get from an 80's action movie, but nothing but relief came to mind, and I was far from safe, I reminded myself.

I smiled and turned around to a long empty corridor.

The boy had disappeared.

Chapter Thirty-Three

Bob

Shit, what the fuck? I'm looking inta the mirror long and hard, wondering just what sort o'Muppet I am. I never signed up to be part of some bloody Jerry Springer meets Jeremy Kyle family thing. It were almost like some Big Brother reality-crap. Don't get ma wrong, I love thee, Jean. She's a nice lass, but shit, there have been, and there will be tuther Jeans.

I'm there in that house standing out like some prize cock, whilst everyone else is moping around. What am I meant to do there? Heck, Jean is looking all dreamy-eyed at her ex, and the thing is, if he were to take her by the arm, up them stairs and throw her onta bed, she wouldn't be able ta get 'er knickers off quick enough. It feckin' winds me up.

I'm not Eddie. I'm not mister Fancy-Drawings-On-Peoples-Arms. Old Captain Father Of The Year. Shitting Billy-Big-Balls-Do-Nowt-Wrong.

Fuck this. I don't need this.

I pull a load of ma clothes out and stuff 'em in ta large holdall from under tha bed. I ignore the love-letters, cards, an' keepsakes hidden next to it from King Dick. Even the shoebox of Polaroids that she has o' naked men that I had the misfortune of kicking t'over once. I've never seen that many men's cocks inma entire life, and I hope ta God I never do again. Why tha fuck would ya keep that shit? She is a fuckin' wild one – the were time when thee liked that 'bout'er, but even I wants a bit more than sex.

I don't have much else if I'm truthful.

I grab ma phone. Flick though the names o'people I've not spoken ta in while. Stop and hover a little bit before pressing ta number. Shit, why not? Grab thee bull by thee cock, or whatever thee say is.

On the second ring, the familiar sweet voice answers, "Hi, Bob? Is that you?"

I smile. Her voice gives the impression of an innocent 18-year-old and whatever else your dirty mind cares to conjure up when hearing that high-pitched girlie voice.

"It is indeed, darling," I reply, all Mr. Smooth. Of course, she is exactly what is meant by that phrase that some blokes yatter: '*Sounds nice on the phone? Then add four stone.*' Cally is a solidly-built woman in her twen'ies, half ma age, but twice ma stamina, if ye get ma meaning. She'll help me ta get over this episode, that lass'll. I can then scope out a woman to take thee and p'raps be me wife.

"You going to come see me?" she asks.

"You betcha, chick. Ya free now?"

She giggles. "I've never been free. But for you, I always make an exception!"

"That ya do, Cally-baby. That ya do. I'll see ye in ten."

I put the phone in ma pocket and look one last time at the picture of us stuck to the fridge. Happier times. I'd always known since tha day we got tagether that someone had turned over tha egg-timer on t'our relationship. I got a lot out o' it – I chuckled at a couple of the photos that I still had on my phone. But today was inevitable.

It wasn't just her doe-eyed over her ex today. Or all of them other oddballs sat around drinking shitty tea. Or her daughter getting herself taken by some blokes that have probably murdered her by now.

No, I think the real issue here was coming in from work this morning and finding Jean in a not too pleasant position with Eddie's best mate Jason.

That's how fucked up this whole thing is.

Apparently, it's not the first time either.

I slam the door. Chuck the keys over into next door's garden and wheel spin my BMW the fuck outta there.

Cally may not be as much of a looker as our-Jean, but fuck-me-sideways, she knows how to treat a man....

Fuck it, I'm gonna head back up north. They're just a bunch of soft-fuckin'-imbreds down 'ere.

Chapter Thirty-Four

Harry

Ruby looks up at me, and I can tell that there is a question brewing behind her eyes. I wonder again how Eddie is so blind as to not see her beauty, and, indeed, the way she looks at him. He's a clever lad at reading people, but with Ruby, the guy is as thick as pig shit– please excuse my language. Sure, Jean was his first deep love, but that was always a fiery encounter. The passion was full-on, with the whole relationship being completely bipolar. As far as I could see, they were either shouting at each other through arguments or ripping each other's clothes off for carnal acts of satisfaction. There was never a middle ground – until Daisy came along.

Eddie was never someone I would've put money on as being caught up in that sort of relationship, and I can tell you, I had placed many a bet in my life. I'd won big, but lost bigger. It never quite made it to a full addiction, but I'd that destination locked into my personal Sat-Nav, and my ETA was imminent. Thankfully, God came calling, and my addictive personality was wholly (pardon the pun) taken up with religion.

Jean, for the most part, was a nice woman. She had that way about her that made you think she was really listening to you, and as you got to know the real her, you found out that she was, indeed, listening to you, but generally so as she could work out the benefits of engaging further. And of course, there was always that underlining sadness about her— the girl that was given away at birth by a mother shamed into becoming a maid.

Jean Palmer should actually have been called Jean Dennison after her unmarried mother, Sally, but her mum was the 'swinger' in the boathouse that traumatised Eddie and was dead before Jean was four. I know for a fact that Eddie knew exactly who she was, because I was the one that told him. I thought it would make a good reason for them to remain apart and not get involved, but somehow, this plan failed, and there was some underlined guilt that Eddie felt, which only seemed to build some bond between them, whilst also adding this fire to their relationship. In hindsight, I probably wouldn't have told him, but we all know how that song plays out.

But whatever I say, however I portray this doomed relationship, they did bring Daisy into the world, and that is something they both deserve to feel proud over.

"What's that thing that you and Miss Chambers were looking over?" Ruby asked. I was slightly taken back, not just because of the question, but because of how my thoughts had gone in full circle. In Ruby, there was an opposite of Jean, a woman that looked wilder than she probably was.

A woman that wanted to be seen as daring and care-free, whilst underneath, she was a sweet girl who just wanted a little romance.

"Beats me," I said. "Gordon once said it was a form of communication. And Jean there tells me it's something to do with speaking to the dead."

Ruby laughed. "I'm sorry," she apologised. "I'm not sure about any of this ghost-talking malarkey. I can just about buy into this energy-memory stuff to a point, but the dead speaking on a telephone? It sounds like the beginning of a joke."

Even I had to chuckle at that. "You know, I'm there with you. But Gordon was really serious when he lent them to us. I think he truly believed that he was onto something."

"It wouldn't be the first time..." Ruby started, but then when nothing else followed, I encouraged her with a, "Go on."

"People believe a lot of things, but it doesn't mean they're right. Nor does it mean they're wrong."

I nodded. This was, indeed, correct.

"Harry, you believe in God. Many people don't."

"Like you?" This slipped out before I could bring it back in.

"This is not about me, Harry," she said neutrally.

I held up a hand in peace. "I apologise. I shouldn't have said that."

"It doesn't matter. The point is, Gordon wanted to believe his telephone worked, but maybe he was picking up voices via a frequency, like on a walkie-talkie."

"Could be," I agreed.

Jean had been left on the sofa, and I thought that with the emotional struggle of it all she had fallen asleep. That was until she spoke. "What if he had actually done it? Somehow had put together some means of communication between the living and the dead? That would be huge." Her eyes remained closed throughout the conversation.

"Worth a lot of money," Ruby added.

"Worth kidnapping a child for," I said. Jean's eyes snapped open. Then I felt both sets of eyes looking at me.

"That's it, Harry!" Ruby said. "I know it's all rumour and theory, but what else could someone be after?"

She was right. To me, kidnapping somebody was the action of either someone powerful or someone desperate. Neither option was good.

I rubbed my chin as I mulled this over. This revelation, if – and that is a massive if – there was any truth in it, would be one of the greatest inventions of the 21st century.

I first noticed the sudden movements, before realising that Jean was sobbing.

"I just want my little girl back," she sobbed quietly. Then, gently shaking her head from side to side, she said, "I didn't think it would ever get this far."

"And what do you mean by that, Jean?" I said, walking over. Ruby also looked shocked at these words.

"Jean, what have you done?" Ruby whispered, but loud enough for us all to hear.

Jean sniffed and rubbed a well-manicured hand across her nose. "It's not what you think. I had no choice."

"I think you'd better start from the beginning, Jean," I said. Jean sat up, clutching her hands together, as Ruby and I took a seat.

"It all started a little before Gordon left..." she began.

Chapter Thirty-Five

Jez had never liked heavy accents. At best, they were distracting and amusing, and at worst, they were harsh, hard to understand, and reminded him of a James Bond villain. Jez was under the definite impression that this voice was of the latter, and most certainly with its Eastern European sound, could be a James Bond villain. Unfortunately, Jez was more Johnny English than James Bond, with zero gadgets and zilch firearms. Even if he did have them, nerves had a tendency to get the better of him, and therefore would, more than likely, end up with him being the injured party.

"I zed, 'Who de fvook are you,' fvunny-lookin' man?"

"Who me?" Jez started, but saw the guy step into the light, and stammered out another response. "Christian Society. Let me give you my card," Jez pulled his wallet out and handed over a card that had been mocked up to look real.

"Vot are you doing here?" the guy pressed. There was an essence of a cat throwing a mouse into the air for fun about him.

"I'm recruiting. I heard there were new folks here, and wanted to come and share God's love." He paused momentarily and then added. "Tell me, does God have a place in your heart?"

The guy ignored it. He was a little over six feet tall, with fair hair although not blonde, but slightly covering a cube-shaped head. He looked naturally strong, like he wrestled bears and tackled oak trees down in his spare time.

"You ring zis number," he demanded with a finger that looked like it might actually have bullets in. "And telling zem, I vant to speak. Iv you are lying then ve 'ave big problems."

The number was real, and it went directly to Harry.

Jez nodded as he pulled out his phone. There was no stun-gun app on his phone. There was nothing to freeze time or to produce a poison dart from. No, Jez's phone cost him £10 a month with a free handset. The only real area of danger would be by using the sheer size of the handset and repeatedly hitting this guy in the right spot over three-hundred times. Chances are the guy would have slipped into a boredom-induced coma well before this time.

His fingers seemed bigger than normal, growing and covering the keypad, making it almost impossible to get the correct numbers pressed. Sure, now he wished that he had added the number to his phone book. Hindsight and all of that jazz.

The thing was, the history of this little set up was all to do with some problems that he was having with a gang of blokes. Well, the blokes were of the ages of 16-18, but let's not make out that Jez was scared of a run-in with children now – we have plenty of opportunities for that. Anyway,

Jez, being Jez had responded to jibes by the youths, that he was a little funny-looking by disrespecting a couple of their mothers. Well, who would've thought that these toe-rags were so emotionally moved by Jez's explanation of what he guessed the mother in question's vocation may be, that Jez ended up left on the ground with bruised ribs, one trainer, and his beeper stolen? (Don't ask about the beeper.)

Jez had spoken to Harry about it, who suggested the mock-up of the card. Jez was to ring Harry whenever he felt threatened, and Harry would get someone to him ASAP.

"Hi, Father," he started. "I am at Tulip House, trying to recruit a nice gentleman, but he would like to speak to you before he decides whether or not to join our society."

"Fine, Jeremy, please put him on."

"Hello?" the guy said with an emotion that suggested he expected no one to be there.

"Good afternoon, my son. I understand that you are looking to become one of God's children?"

"Cut ze crap. Who are you?"

"Reverent Harold DuGault, sir. Head of The Christian Society."

After a long beat, the man said, "DeGault? What zort of name iz thiz?"

"A surname is what it is. And to whom am I speaking?"

"Never you mind," he sneered and chucked the phone back to Jez. "No speak," he was commanded.

Jez could feel himself panic. If ever there was a picture with the words 'Bad Situation' on, then this was it. His heart was beating irregularly, seemingly unsure of the normality of rhythm. His ears felt on fire, and he could feel himself begin to drip with sweat.

Even though he felt close to having a cardiac arrest, he hatched a plan. However, this had to wait as he bent over and was violently sick everywhere.

"Vot the!" was the man's response to witnessing Jez's breakfast coming back up at a more lightning speed than it had gone down. Then, "My shoes!" when some vomit splashed onto his previously shiny shoes.

"Sorry," Jez said, wiping his mouth with the back of his hand, and then rubbing the wetness onto his jeans.

As the guy was about to move towards him, Jez looked over the guy's shoulder and with a forced grin boomed out, "Eddie!" As the guy turned around, Jez kicked him as hard as he could between the legs in the most sensitive area of a man....

Two things happened. Firstly, Jez thought that he may've broken a toe, and secondly the guy's neck snapped back around to look at Jez with a glare that could scare a marine.

"S-sorry," Jez started, thinking that this was probably the worst plan in the whole history of bad plans.

"You fvookin' stoopid pig!" he raged, swinging a right fist that clubbed Jez behind the ear and crumbled him to the floor unconscious.

At that point, Jason hurriedly appeared. He stopped and stared at the situation in front of him. "What's going on, Mr Brohenski?"

"Vell, Jason, since you asked, I vill tell." He smoothed his hair, in a way that suggested that he didn't appreciate having to touch up his appearance after having been forced to commit ungentlemanly conduct on a fellow human. "Dis snoopy-man suggested that he was from The Christ-yon Society. And zen he commits quite an unChrist-yon thing of kicking me in ze borwls!"

"Really?"

"Would I make up such stoopidness, I ask?"

Jason was well aware of who Jez was. He was the weirdo neighbour of Eddie's, who hung around *Caper's* drooling over women, because his wife hated him. It was not at all surprising that he was now on the floor, passed out, having tried to kick a Russian gangster in his family jewels. Jason's biggest worry was how he was to tell Mr Brohenski that their hostage had broken free....

"Take me to ze girl," Mr Brohenski demanded.

"Uh, yeah, about that," he began.

Mr Brohenski kicked Jez as hard as he could. "About vot?"

"Well, I've only just arrived a few minutes back-" he started by doing his best to shift liability of the fuck-up elsewhere. "-but I saw her running away, being chased by the other two. The last thing that I saw was her in a boat heading over the lake to Caulfield Hall."

"Excellent."

"It is?"

"Ze mouse is 'eading straight for ze trap!"

"The trap?"

"Ze trap."

"Oh, I see." But of course, he didn't.

Chapter Thirty-Six

A little over seven years ago

Jason wasn't sure what to think as he pulled up into the driveway. The large house that loomed out at him seemed imposing. He could imagine years ago when cars would be lined up as the upper class gathered for another night of fun. He sometimes had visions of the bizarre masquerade party depicted in Kubrick's *Eyes Wide Shut* movie, but that would be an embellishment from stories that his parents had mentioned, and they would know, being the regulars that they were. Things were certainly more PG-13 than that...well, for the most part.

Gordon was an eccentric, but not by look. He never had wild hair, drinking jacket, and a penchant for port, but having been spawned from an incredibly social family tree, he preferred to live the life of a recluse. In the years since his wife had left, Gordon appeared to only use a handful of the rooms in the vast house, with the study being the main one.

Gordon had summoned him here to talk business, and this made Jason feel like a real businessman. For years, he had lived on handouts from his wealthy parents, whilst he played at being a barman. All over the place, he had cloned a *Cruise* in *Cocktail* persona, living the dream of being carefree and available, which of course, meant a small amount of work whilst getting drunk and sleeping with a multitude of barmaids. But '*Capers*' had been doing very well. A number of bands that had previously had weekly slots had gone on to bigger things, but had always managed to fit in a 'free' show into their tour schedule. This meant a number of guaranteed capacity nights and massive food and drink profits, not to mention a new found notoriety spawning sales of merchandise on t-shirts, mugs, and stickers, thanks to some high profile photo shoots, gig reviews, and 'bar-name' dropping. It was now the place to visit for music culture in an area drawing in ever increasing numbers of tourists. Like a tagline or a James Earl Jones voiceover, Jason often would gimmick, "Between the idyllic Cotswold's and the mystical Stonehenge, lies the epicentre for Rock'n'Roll. '*Capers!*': where the music rocks and the good times roll!"

"Jason," Gordon said, stepping forward and offering a hand to shake. Jason accepted, even though it felt a little strange shaking the hand of your best friend's dad. But then, there had always been a strange connection between the families. Jason and Eddie had known each other since they were small, although the two didn't always play together. Eddie had a tendency to go off on his own, whereas Jason wanted to be part of things. Hell, he slept on his own, and he went to the bathroom on his own. This amounted to way too much alone time in his book. At one time, he'd even heard whispers suggesting that Jason and Eddie could be brothers, although the stories never seemed to agree on which two parents had cheated on the other, but talk of swinging was soon hushed away as silly hearsay, the price of coming from wealthy families. Jason never knew what to make of it all. He wasn't that bothered, if he was honest. He loved his parents, and they would always be who he considered to be his mum and dad. The actual stories that people agreed on suggest that at one point the four were close, and they all had the desire for the unusual and showed flashes of odd behaviour. So maybe this was the reason that he felt comfortable sleeping with Jean....

Jason mulled over the line that he had pondered many times before: *you never set out to sleep with your mate's girlfriend, do you?* He had all of the answers to the questions and demands that Eddie would bombard him with, if of course Eddie would ever ask them. But no one sets out to cause that much pain in another human being, especially when the couple have a child together. But sometimes there is this huge attraction between two people, and it could be love; it could just as well be pure animal lust, but the drug-like euphoria of it is much too hard to ignore; the slippery slope that you try to avoid is suddenly impossible to escape from. The realisation that the other person feels the same is half disappointing and half exciting. The chemical reaction of hormones, dancing around in the human chemistry beaker, smoking, bubbling, and ready to explode. The what if's of fantasy and unknown possibility, all these emotions stronger and more prominent than morals, friendship, trust, and loyalty, considered and discarded like a used condom.

Eddie never did confront Jason, and whilst he felt like he dodged a bullet there, from that day forward, their friendship would never again reach previous heights. A few months went by when they did speak, even with the shared business. They both managed with the giant white elephant that followed them both around; ironically, Jean was the go-between, which those who fill their time with gossip were quick to suggest was in fact the original problem.

Gordon didn't seem to be bothered about whether Jason had shagged his son's girlfriend, but then, that was Gordon. He was very focused on things, almost single-minded, and some might add pig-headed about things. So something trivial like a little misunderstanding between two mates and a woman was an age-old problem that the little scamps were able to sort out themselves. Hell, he'd walked in similar shoes as both boys at one time or another, and it wasn't an easy path, but life never was, was it?

They walked into the study and down into the basement. Everywhere you looked were sketches, plans, and mock-ups. Jason never even knew there was a study, not that he thought that there wasn't one. A study, whether here or not, had never come up before in conversation. His mind was wandering aimlessly around now. There was so much to see that he had trouble taking it all in, whilst not knocking anything over.

"Are you ready to make yourself a lot of money?" Gordon asked, as for the first time Jason felt a little uncomfortable. What if there was another reason for him to have been brought here; under a guise of opportunity, a dark-side could well be uncovered? But this line of thought was short lived. Gordon had a gentle way about him that was so unassuming that he probably caused some bother in others annoyed by the passive attitude.

Jason was still looking around at the shelves filled with small electronic mother-boards, and then other boxes of screws, small cogs, and the designs that seemed to marry up the two worlds of old and new into a small box. This was like the popular sub-culture called Steampunk, which brings together the happy marriage of classic motorised parts found in bygone years with a flash of futuristic realism. This appeared to be a workshop all ready to construct a thousand wonderful designs.

"This is a gamble, Gordon?" Jason said, looking at the man in front of him and noticing the sparkle in his eyes and the way he couldn't keep a straight face.

"You only win if you gamble, Jason."

"Gambling is built on an empire of losers in order for a single winner to triumph."

Gordon clapped his hands once to that. "Nicely put. But when you see a demonstration, then you will no longer consider this a gamble."

"I take it that Eddie does not know of this?"

"What? My ingenious revelation, or my business partner choice?"

"Either."

Gordon shook his head. "Eddie is very clever. He is wonderfully eloquent and grand at understanding people, even though he favours not to connect deeply. He is pragmatic and dependable, able to see things from any person's point of view." Jason was about to make a quip about perfection, when Gordon sighed, "But Eddie has a brain that needs to know the answers, and he will not entertain fantastical ideas, follies, or even questions with no answers."

"Whereas...?" Jason pressed.

"You are a business man. A go-getter. You want the girl, so you take the girl-" Jason made a move to state a defence, but Gordon waved it off. "I have no interest in the details, Jason. I need a small bit of collateral in order to finish this off, specifically some rigorous testing, and when this thing sells as big as I expect it to sell, then you will be rich, as will I, and unknowingly will my son."

"Okay, so providing the demonstration is good, then, *Caper's*, the business will give you the money for a 10% stake."

"Excellent, Dragon. I think we have a deal."

"Demonstration pending?"

"As agreed. Come over to this chair here and take a seat." Jason sat down, a wave of nervousness appearing from nowhere.

"Prepare to be amazed!" He had that feeling that he could never go back; this would always be a pivotal moment of his life. If he were to stand up and walk out, then he would always wonder, but if he was to believe Gordon, then this was to be one of the greatest things to witness in his life.

An hour passed almost in a flash, Jason spent a lot of it slack jawed and wide-eyed. Gordon did, indeed, appear to be an absolute Goddamn genius. There is certainly gold in them there hills, and as far as Jason was concerned, either:

1) Gordon was an illusionist. If this was the case then he was incredibly gifted at it;

2) Gordon knew some sort of actual magic or;

3) Gordon has invented something that could be an incredibly defining thing– something that can be used and manipulated into being good and being bad, bringing joy and bringing pain.

"What do you think?" Gordon asked, but from the look on Jason's face and the way that he had been throughout the demonstration, Gordon already knew the answer.

"It's like in the movies when you see the suitcase open and something shines out, the characters are all amazed at something that is so incredibly wonderful that it cannot be put into words-" Jason raised his hands to finish. "My God, Gordon. You have actually created that."

"It's been a long journey."

"You will be known for your dedication once this hits the world."

"There is something, though, and this is going to need an element of trust on your part."

Jason wasn't sure what this was about. "Go on," he encouraged.

"In order to finish this, I need to go someplace for a while, and I may be some time," Gordon started. "I need for you to give this package to Harry. It has a number of things in it, one being a letter to Eddie. It explains things, but knowing him, he will be dismissive of it."

"Sure. How long do you think you will be gone?"

Gordon shrugged. "I honestly don't know. I have something that I need to take care of before I can finish, but I suspect that it will be years-"

"What?!" Jason suddenly said, louder and more forceful than he expected. "You can't show me all of this and then expect me to wait for years before anything happens? No one will believe me."

"And that is the other thing. You cannot tell anyone. Through my research, I have asked some questions of people that may have left me open to others. If the wrong people were to get their hands on this...well, I think that you can probably see the issue. This must remain a secret. If you have a burning desire to tell someone, then it should be either Eddie or Harry, but under no circumstances should it be anyone else. Understood?"

Jason nodded. "As you wish." They shook hands, and Jason walked away, ready to hand over the cash required.

It was ten minutes that Jason sat in his car before he was able to focus on starting the engine. He was still trying to grasp reality again. Suddenly, the window of possibilities had opened wide for his mind to consider many things he thought not possible. He could understand why

Eddie was not told about this. Eddie's mind would go into overdrive trying to calculate how it was at all possible and then escalating the benefits of it to do good.

It's the Devil that always has the new suits, even if the angels are more deserving....

LOST CONNECTIONS

Chapter Thirty-Seven

"It all started just before Gordon left," Jean said, thinking back to those times. Daisy was four and beginning to become quite independent. Eddie was always busy, whether it was tattooing, or overseeing the bar. She couldn't blame him. With tattooing, every single one has to be the best that you can do. There are no off days; the minute you have a bad day and you let something sloppy leave the shop, your reputation is taking a big hit. Eddie has always been big on his reputation and even bigger on perfection. He will charge a customer by the hour, but that will be for the time he thinks it should take, so when he goes over by an hour, because he wants the shading just right, then he will not charge the customer any more. Jean told him once that she thought he should charge them, but his reply was that the customer comes to him because he is professional and is good at what he does. Therefore, they won't leave the shop without being fully satisfied.

Jean carried on. "Eddie had won his second award in a row at the Reading Tattoo Convention, and his schedule had him working his fourth week without a day off. Back then, Eddie always worried that there would be times when he wouldn't have any bookings, and always booked people in, without a thought of rest. Or us. Although, I think back now, and think he was thinking of us when he did those long hours. I feel guilty." Harry nodded.

"It's a killer," Ruby added. "I've had leg tattoos and back pieces that I've been hunched over on for hours, and by the end, I feel like I need to be put on one of those torture racks to iron out the kinks!"

Jean gave a slow nod in agreement. "Yeah, Eddie would come in, play a game with Daisy, read her a story, put her to bed, and then he would be hard at it with a pencil and pad, drawing upcoming tattoos for clients, even ones that weren't booked in yet.

"I'd be saying, 'what's the point, they might not come back?' And he would reply that it didn't matter. If they did then they'd have the best possible tattoo around. And of course, I'd get annoyed."

"You felt left out," Ruby said out loud. She hadn't meant to, but it just slipped out.

"Wouldn't you?" Jean shot back like she was being judged. She was trying to build the story up, but in she comes with her quick diagnosis. Thanks, doctor.

Ruby smiled. "I'm not having a go at you." She paused and looked around, giving them all a moment. "I've never been in that position, so I can't say anything, okay?"

"I've seen the way you look at him, though," Jean mumbled.

Harry laid a paternal arm on Jean's shoulder. "This is not helping. Whether or not Ruby and Eddie are more than friends shouldn't be of our concern. You two are no longer in a relationship."

Jean held up her hands. "Okay. Okay, fine."

"We just want to hear the rest of what you were saying," Ruby said in a hushed voice.

"Jason used to come over once in a while for meals. Sometimes he'd bring whoever he was currently seeing. Well, this one time the shop had an issue with the electricity, so Eddie, being Eddie, told the guy that if he was okay to carry on, then Eddie would stay until the tattoo was finished. So he rang me and told me that he didn't think that he'd be back until 9pm, but Jason and his girlfriend would still be coming over.

"I put Daisy to bed, and at 7pm, I opened the door to find Jason standing on his own. Apparently, he and his girlfriend had just had a talk about the future, and Jason had told her that he mostly saw their future apart. She'd then decided she wasn't hungry, so he'd come on his own."

"I think I see where things are going here," Ruby said. "But sleeping with your partner's best friend is still a way from where we are now."

"Well, if you'd let me finish then it will become more clear!" she snapped.

"I apologise for, er, being insensitive, or whatever, er, sorry. Carry on," Ruby said, and she was sure that even in different circumstances, the two of them would struggle to become friends.

Even Eddie and his dozy neighbour, Jez, had some sort of friendship, as loose as it may be.

"My point," Jean said with a little more than a hint of a glare at Ruby, "Is that I never went looking for someone else. I'm not deaf; I know that's what people say of me. After years of loneliness, I found myself across the table from a man who looked at me with lust in his eyes, not tiredness. Eddie would take my hand and lead me to bed, but he would either collapse asleep with exhaustion, or else he was half listening out for Daisy."

"He thinks the world of her, Jean. You cannot blame him for that?"

"But more than me? How is that possible?"

Ruby found herself rubbing Jean's shoulder, not something that she thought that she would be doing in a million years. "It's normal," she said gentle.

Jean shrugged her off. "And how would you know? You don't have children!"

Ruby nodded, and even conceded the point, but repeated, "It's normal. You're right, I don't have children, but I have a number of friends who do, and they all say that there is love, and there is romance. Romance is the love of a partner, but true deep love is that to which you hold out for a child."

"She's right," Harry added. "I've lost a lot of love in my lifetime, but the biggest loss is through the absence of my son."

Jean looked up at them both, feeling a little picked on. "But maybe you two and your friends just never found that special person that made you think of them ahead of every other living thing in the world?"

"Jean-" Ruby started with a sigh, but Harry could see that these two women could very easily end up winding each other up, rather than understanding what this whole mess was all about. He held his hand up for Ruby to stop. "Jean," he said. "Can you understand how we may see contradiction in what you're saying?" he bothered his beard with his right hand, teasing away at where it went to a point. "You say you loved Eddie more than anything or anyone else in the world, and yet you were tempted, and more to the point, acted upon that temptation with another man."

Jean huffed, but didn't know what to say, so remained silent.

"Okay, I think that I get it. Do you mind if I tell you what I think, Jean? You can tell me to shut up at any stage, okay?" Ruby said. Harry felt a little worried, but was willing to give Ruby the benefit of the doubt.

"I think that you do, or did, indeed, love Eddie. However, there were a couple of things that changed with him, like his longer hours working, the fussing over Daisy, and neglect that you felt." Jean nodded, so Ruby carried on. "Then Jason, who of course, is not a bad looking guy, comes around and he brings these missing pieces to you. He brings his lustful want, he makes time for you, and he's not worried about a child, as he just wants you. So what you are in love with is 60% or 70% of Eddie, and the rest of Jason."

Jean shrugged again and played the innocent child role admirably. "Yep."

"So are you still seeing Jason?" Harry asked.

"I think what Harry really means is when was the last time you slept with him?"

"I don't have to answer that," she said back on the defensive, and Ruby was quick to counter. "No, you don't. But we'd like to know what the Hell-" she turned to Harry. "Sorry Father-" to which he waved it away, "Is going on?"

Jean sat forward with her head in her hands, then slowly her hands combed back through her hair. "Before you go jumping the gun on any of your theories, I had nothing to do with Daisy's disappearance. I knew nothing about it, although I may know who is behind it."

"Go on," Harry pressed.

"Jason got into some debt a while back. He went from not being materialistic to suddenly buying expensive things. Remember the old beat up van he used to drive? And now look at him in his Range Rover. He thinks he's some footballer's wife. He'd go off to London, telling Eddie it was a business trip, and end up partying. Eddie sort of knew he wasn't on business, but as long as it didn't affect him or *Capers*, then he turned a blind eye." She paused for a second and looked up at a picture of herself, Eddie, and Daisy in better times." He sometimes doesn't notice the bad in people. It's infuriating. He doesn't want to cause waves, so he turns the other cheek. I swear he could be like you, Harry!"

"What, incredibly handsome?" Harry added to lighten the mood.

Both women smiled at that before Jean carried on. "Well, this Russian guy was unwilling to ignore anything, especially when he went and rang up a huge bill at his hotel and casino-"

"The idiot," Harry said.

"So a couple of months back, Jason turns up at my flat, and he looks completely shocked, like he's seen a ghost, or somebody close to him had died. I invited him in and he says, 'I'm really in it now. I owe him twenty grand.' So I asked him about his spending, and he said something about a windfall that he was due to get, but now he was unsure as to whether or not he was going to get it."

"What windfall? The kidnap?" Ruby said.

"No, no. At first he said he couldn't tell me and that he was sworn to secrecy, but then later on when we were in bed, he told me. He said that Gordon had invented something that was going to change the world, and he was a shareholder, but he said that Gordon had to go away, and that now he was worried that he would never come back."

"Seven years is a long time to go and tie up a few loose ends," Harry said. "I personally think he went off to do something that ended up killing him instead."

Harry remembered a couple of times that Jason had come to see him in the church for a chat. He'd been vague in detail, but it was clear he'd been involved in something that he was not proud of.

Harry thought it was to do with Jean and the betrayal of Eddie, but now he was not so sure.

Jean wasn't finished. "Anyway, Jason said that whatever Gordon had invented was at Caulfield Hall in the study. So if nothing else, he could sell the idea and the prototype to clear his debt."

Just then, Harry's mobile vibrated. "It's Jez," he frowned.

"Hello," he said into the phone, wondering just what trouble the over-grown fool had got himself into this time. Most likely the Girl Guides were holding him to ransom over non-payment of cookies or the such like.

"Hi, Father," Jez started. "I am at Tulip House, trying to recruit a nice gentleman, but he would like to speak to you before he decides whether or not to join our society." The fact that Jez had given him so much detail was a worry, but why was the klutz at Tulip House? The house where Miss Chambers grew up?

"Fine, Jeremy, please put him on."

"Hello?" the guy said, with an emotion that suggested that he expected no one to be there. Harry could detect an accent straight away, and having just been told about an angry Russian, this was not a good thing.

"Good afternoon, my son. I understand that you are looking to become one of God's children?"

"Cut ze crap. Who are you?"

"Reverend Harold DuGault, sir. Head of The Christian Society." DuGault was the surname he gave himself years ago when trying to pick up women. He had no idea why he'd used it now, he certainly had no intention of trying to pick up a mad Russian, that's for sure.

After a long beat, the man said, "DeGault? What zort of name iz thiz?"

"A surname is what it is. And to whom am I speaking?"

"Never you mind," was the sneered response back, and after a strange sound, heard "No speak," before it was clicked off.

Harry looked at his mobile like the screen might answer whatever question he was posing, then looked up at Jean and Ruby.

"Interesting," he said.

"What was that all about?" Ruby asked.

"Well, that was Jez to start with, but then he handed me over to man with an accent that didn't sound all that dissimilar to Russian."

"What did he say? Does he have Daisy?"

"He didn't really say anything of note, apart from ask me my name-"

"To which you lied," Ruby smiled.

Harry feint a look of fake shock. "That was not a lie. It's a name I called myself years ago when I first met people."

Ruby grinned at Jean. "What he means is it was the name he lied with when trying it on with women," she winked before adding, "And Harry, whilst I think that you already know this, having lied about your name a number of times years ago does not mean that it is any less of a lie now."

"Such a wise one," he said. "Look, the strange thing is that Jez is over at Tulip House. I have no idea why, but he's there, and he's in trouble."

"Let's go then," Ruby said, looking like she was ready to take on the world. Jean remained silent, and it was hard to judge just how things were playing out in her mind.

"Well, this is what I'm thinking," Harry said. "You and Jean go over to Caulfield Hall. I'm sure that Eddie is there now, and everything seems to be pointing there."

"Wait a minute, Harry. You can't go to Tulip House on your own with a crazy Russian bloke there?"

"I won't be going on my own. I'll take Miss Chambers." Even Jean looked up at that.

"Miss Chambers?" Ruby said, slightly perplexed. "The feisty old lady from next door?"

"The very same."

"Well, forgive me for saying this, but I'm not sure that I fancy your chances against some Russian Mafia criminal."

"No one said he was Mafia, or a criminal?" Harry added.

"Well last time I checked, kidnapping was a crime."

"True, but I'm like Clint Eastwood in *Grand Tourino-*"

"And Miss Chambers?"

"Helen Mirren in *Red*."

With a sigh, Ruby shook Harry's hand, "If I don't get a chance to say it again, it's been a pleasure meeting you, Harry. Any request for funeral music?"

"Anything but *Ra-Ra-Rasputin*."

"Deal."

Chapter Thirty-Eight

Daisy

I could've sworn that I'd seen a boy, but now looking down the corridor, there seemed no way that he could've disappeared. For the first time in a long while, I relaxed, and thought that with all of the adrenaline that had been rushing around and with nothing to have eaten or drunk since breakfast, my mind was playing tricks on me.

The problem was I knew I had to find a place to hide, but I still wasn't sure of the full layout of the house. The men would be going around the front of the house, and for some reason, I thought that I should go upstairs. I'd been there earlier with dad, and some of the secret places he showed me seemed perfect.

I think that the corridor would've been used originally as a servants' exit, possibly to put the rubbish out or to go to the ice-house (though I'm not sure whether or not there is one). I passed a couple of doors that had locks on them, like they might be storage and stuff. You can kind of tell that the rest of the house looked old and expensive in that look-at-us kind of way, but down here it looked more business-like, kind of like when I go with Shelly at the back of the shopping centre, when she tries to look cool smoking these foul ciggies, 'cause she knows that a couple of the cute lads that work in Top Man go there for their break. Well, that looks a bit like this.

At the end is a door, I guess to cut off this industrial side of the house from guests. I tentatively open it – it would be just my luck to run into them again.

I look out and nearly jump out of my skin as I see a large mounted deer head, complete with curling antlers, staring back at me with empty eyes. I know that if I go left, that will take me to the front of the house and to the large staircase, but also to the front door. I decide to go right, as I know that there is a second staircase somewhere here.

I jog as best I can along the hallway over the thick carpet that thankfully magics my heavy footfalls into silent tiptoes. I'm dripping too.

I pass a room that goes off to what was probably called a solarium, or some sort of sunroom. Nowadays, we'd have a smaller, boring version called a conservatory. Then I saw the modest small stairway.

There was a part of me that was trying to take everything in – this is my heritage after all – but today had been a day I wish never to have to experience such lows and drama ever again. I turned and tried to run up the stairs, but they were oddly spaced, and before I knew it, I slipped with a big thud and felt the sharp pain of an ankle twist. Bloody typical act of girl-on-the-run!

But worse still was the sudden shout from down the hallway of, "There she is!"

I picked myself up, and despite the flashes of pain, I ran up the stairs as best as I could, watching where my feet went to on every step.

At the top I turned along to the right, following a corridor which ran above where I had come from downstairs. I'd only gone about ten steps before I heard two sets of feet pounding the stairs after me.

Suddenly, I saw the movement of the door, so without thinking, I ran and grabbed it. As soon as I went in, I recognised it and pulled the door shut behind me. As my dad had shown me, I walked four steps up, pushed aside the picture of the cat, and pressed the red button. The flat wooden back came down slowly– almost too slowly.

Just as it stopped, I heard the door on the other side open. I stood there like a statue, still with fear. Pretty much all that was between me and them was a thin piece of plywood.

"What the fuck?" I heard from a voice that had a thick West Country accent. "I tharght she went in ter?"

Then a more foreign sounding response a little higher said, "You fuck-in knob'ead. That a cubord!"

"Well, wur dus ya think she went then, chappie?"

"A nudder room, I say." Then the door closed.

I went slowly up the stairs, and thankfully, my ankle was feeling a lot better.

I heard crashing from below, and again, the danger of it all bit into me like a bullet. I couldn't stay still and headed to the corner, through the door, and up the spiral staircase. I know that this would put me up into an area of no escape, but somehow, the thought of being able to see my surroundings brought me comfort.

I looked out the back and saw the speedboat abandoned, menacingly large against the small row boat that I had paddled over the lake on. As I glanced around, I saw dad's van, and I suddenly had a mixture of fear and relief.

And then I saw the familiar blue VW Beetle pull up, and out got Ruby and Jean. This is, like, totally mad. I would never have thought that I'd see the day when the two of them would travel together in Ruby's car. Things must be bad.

I wanted to shout to them, but I was too far away, and I didn't want to give up my position to the thugs below.

I pulled out my phone and rang my mum.

I saw her fumbling with her mobile and saw her mouth to Ruby before answering. "Daisy, is that you?" she said.

"Yes, it is. Mum, listen-"

"Where are you? Are you okay?"

"Mum! You have to listen. There are two men in the house trying to get me. Watch out."

"What house? Where?"

"Here! Caulfield Hall. I can see you and Ruby..." But at that point I saw another vehicle pull up.

A police car with sirens and flashing lights, full of policemen would have been great, but this was not what I saw. This was a large black-on-black

Range Rover with tinted windows. It stopped, and out got three men.

The phone went off, as I saw the middle man shout at Jean and Ruby, and the other two pulled out guns.

As the guy in the middle looked suddenly at the house, I was sure that I'd been seen, and I ducked down under the window and cried....

LOST CONNECTIONS

Chapter Thirty-Nine

1986 - Harry

"Do you really think that this is the best way to show them?" I asked, pulling up my hood as my simple but effective disguise. She rolled her eyes at me, never once having the second thoughts that were always there to me as an option. I admired this about her. I always thought that I was the strong type— the one who made the decision and stuck to it, happy to '*live by the sword and die by the sword,*' but she was different. She had her morals, and she certainly knew right from wrong, but sometimes, I would look deep into those eyes and wonder just how close to the edge she would go this time.

"They forced themselves upon that poor girl, Harry. What do you think is the best way? Perhaps an hour interview at the police station and a gentle warning would be the right outcome?" she said not so much with sarcasm, but with condescension.

"Of course not."

"Well, that is exactly what they'll get. You know that."

"It seems a little like an eye-for-an-eye stuff."

She scrunched up her face with disgust. "I would never touch those little sods the way they touched that poor child. So it can never be an eye-for-an-eye!"

"Okay. Point taken." I said, and off we went. Part of what she said was right, but the other part was very wrong.

The night was warm, and I was sweating in the dark sweatshirt. It was a little after midnight, and the full moon sat high in the sky, offering a main beam of light all around. On another night, I would've found this quite soothing, offering me a backdrop to contemplation, but tonight, my heart was beating fast with adrenaline. It was beating with fear, it was beating with hope, it was beating with love – but most of all it was beating to the drum called justice.

I saw his ginger hair before anything else. His dark clothing and the pale skin contrasted with the orange colour of his hair grown out into some sort of mop. He wasn't swaying, but you could tell that he'd indulged in the 'devil's water' recently. He was mumbling some *Iron Maiden* song that I only recognised as being so from the tune of the chorus.

He never saw me jump out and hit him with the wooden baseball bat on the back of the head. He went out cold before he hit the ground – and before I stamped on his knee. It wasn't my greatest offering to the human race, but I kept thinking of the poor girl that they'd abused. I was still doing this as the flash of the Polaroid camera went off, making me jump.

With gloved hands, the picture was tossed on top of Terry Ward. Underneath the picture of the broken body were the words 'Justice For Jean.'

The second lad was called Baron, and by witness accounts, was the ringleader of the two. A big-built lad, Baron had shaved the top and sides of his head with some stupid rat's tail thing hanging embarrassingly down the back of his head. He was riding his bike down the path between the church and some houses when the bat smacked him full in the face, smashing his front teeth, before I hit him again on the back of the head to knock him out. He got both knees stamped on and the stupid rat thing pulled out and shoved in his mouth.

We left him with the Polaroid sticking out of the front of his trousers.

In the next few months, we'd go on to bring to justice a dozen or so unruly kids and half a dozen adults, albeit not in the violent way that we did for our first, but then, that was for Jean.

"We've done well," she said one afternoon. "But we cannot keep doing this."

"I know," I said in agreement. I'd been thinking the same thing, but again, my addictive personality was enjoying clearing up the streets. I won't lie, but I felt like a superhero. We had no powers, other than our professional ability to research, plan, and carry out a warning without getting caught. However, there was an inevitability that one day we would grow blasé, and then it would be curtains for us. We talked about getting Terry and Baron again, showing them that we will never stop thinking about them. It would also bring us in full circle, but then it seemed a little over the top, even if we did still worry about the effect that this would have on little Jean.

It was one of the hardest things that I've had to do, and let's remember, I've had a number of demons to battle with over the years. We are middle-aged, and it only takes one smart little sod to spot us and we would find ourselves in a whole heap of trouble. We are not fighting specimens. We surprised each one in an almost cowardly way, so if we were to come up against these animals, they would not stop until we were both dead.

Alice sat me down and had to explain this to me. I was full of excuses about the good job that we were doing, but she pointed out that the only job we were doing was keeping a few nurses in a job at the local hospital. There, hooligans were not learning, nor were they scared like in some deluded moment, we thought that they might be. The danger was that they were just going to evolve and get smarter. We'd had a good run, but it was time to hang up our hoodies and retire gracefully.

And just like that, we stopped. The superheroes gave up the mind-spandex and left the justice to the police. The local paper would run an article on the matter in years to come, asking for us to come back, but I was about to become a vicar, and Miss Chambers? Well, Miss Chambers would most likely do whatever the Hell Miss Chambers wanted to do!

For all I know, she carried on her vigilante-persona without me....

Chapter Forty

"Well, Father Dugan, and what in God's name do you think we are up to?" Miss Chambers said strapping on her seatbelt like it was the final scene in *Thelma & Louise.*

Harry had to smile. On the outside, Miss Chambers always came across as a hard nut to crack. She was wise, but so chilly in her delivery that she should be from Iceland. Harry often mused this to himself. His own little joke.

"I promised a young man that I would look out for him in times of need, and that is exactly what I am doing. I brought you along so as I can show off my manliness and thus overwhelm you into my bedroom. Chambers to my chambers, if you will."

Miss Chambers swiftly slapped him on the arm as they got to his car. "There is no need for that sort of lewd thinking, Father. This isn't some *Carry On* film, and you're no Sid James, and I'm certainly not Barbara Windsor! Anyway, this young and needy man that you speak of, is not much more than an odd-looking half-wit in his forties. He's a living experiment that one day, we will read about that has escaped and managed to interact on a very basic level with a similar species."

"You're always seeing the good in people, Alice. I probably don't say that enough."

"You've never once said those words, nor even vaguely implied them," she countered.

"That's right!" he said as if suddenly remembering an important detail. "That's because I'm a vicar, and as one, 'thou shalt not lie.'"

"Still a comedian, even with the black get-up and dog collar on."

"I love it when you talk dirty to me."

Harry started up his brand new Ford Mondeo and quickly turned the CD Player off as *Mick Jagger* was belting out *'Honky Tonk Woman.'*

"Good Christian music then?" Miss Chambers smiled knowingly.

"There's nothing to say that they are not Christian."

"What about *'Sympathy For The Devil?'* That's a good message that you could bring up in one of your sermons, am I right?"

Within minutes, they were in the countryside and heading towards Tulip House.

"If arguing were an Olympic sport, then you would be a gold medallist," Harry said.

"But if you didn't keep getting details incorrect, then I would not feel the need to correct you, and therefore it is not my superior knowledge, but your own intellectual inadequacy that really frustrates you."

Harry was about to reply with another quip, when suddenly a black Range Rover came hurtling around the corner, sending Harry onto the verge, before he could straighten up back onto the tarmac. "Idiot!" he shouted.

As they got closer, Harry thought that driving right up to the place may not be a great idea, so they decided to drive into the field next door. And this is when they saw Jez's car parked up.

"What's this: a car park or a field?" Miss Chambers said rhetorically.

They jumped out and headed towards the house.

Miss Chambers felt a lot of different things when she saw the house, and not all of it was bad. She'd learnt to be independent and strong. She'd learnt how to cook, clean, and take care of people. She'd learnt to deal with pain and not to rely on other humans. But she'd embraced solitude, welcoming it and treating it like a friend.

She remained fairly pragmatic, considering the things that she had endured, but her cold social output was evident for all to see, and most could not get past that. Harry was different; he understood how she felt by the things she didn't say. She enjoyed the verbal sparring, as he'd seen her enjoy the similar act with Eddie.

"The flowerbeds have been neglected, I see," Miss Chambers said. "It doesn't take much effort to weed occasionally, does it?" and Harry nodded to this, intrigued by how this verbally was the first impression that she had of this place, and knowing that inside she was as much bothered about the blossoming garden as she was on his football trivia.

"What d'you think?" Harry said as they stood behind a bush.

"I'd cut this right back, so as it blooms again in spring," she replied.

"No, I meant the house."

"I know, I was- What is it called?" She tapped her head overdramatically. "Making a joke— jesting!"

"Leave the jokes to me in the future. Saleswoman?"

"Yep. Saleswoman it is."

As Alice began to walk out, Harry called her to get her attention. "You know when the corners of your mouth go up and the sides of your eyes wrinkle, that's called a smile, and people seem to react favourably to it."

"You would not be the first vicar that I have hit, you know?"

"That, I do not doubt."

She strode purposefully up to the door, reached out, and using the large brass knocker, thumped five times.

Harry was beginning to think that nobody was around when the door opened and a shifty blonde guy stood there, looking all around outside past Miss Chambers before finally eyeing her up suspiciously.

"Can I help you?" he mumbled.

"I am sure that you can. Are you the house owner?"

"I don't want to buy anything." He began to shut the door. His accent had a slight hint of European, but was only just able to be detected.

"And I don't want to sell anything."

He furrowed his brow and shook his head. "So what is it that you want – I'm very busy."

Miss Chambers liked to test the waters. "Can I come in?"

"I'd rather you didn't."

"Okay, I respect that. Could I ask you to step outside, though, so as we can talk on a more even level? I understand that this is a slightly unorthodox request, but you would make an old woman happy. It is very important that I speak with you."

Harry shook his head as he watched the events in front of him unfold. How she did it, he would never know, but the fact of the matter is that if he tried doing what she ever suggested, the guy would tell him to get stuffed – or words to that effect.

As the guy stepped out of the door, with one swift movement, Miss Chambers dropped into her palm the police-issue extendable stick, which expanded, and she swung it around, hitting the guy in the back of the head and sending him face down onto the gravel below.

Harry ran out and pulled out his hand-ties, the plastic wrist bands often used instead of handcuffs due to their strength, but light-weight and easy usage and storage.

"Good work again, Cagney!" Harry smiled.

"Maybe I'm Lacey?"

"Maybe you are. Seriously, which is which?"

They walked through the door, not sure exactly what to expect. There was a staircase off to the right and a large room off to the left. They looked into the room and saw a fairly normal looking lounge. There was a twenty-inch television in the corner and a large sofa that had seen many better days. A dirty rug lay on the wooden floor, and the open fireplace looked not to have been used in years.

They came out and walked down the hall. There was a room on the right, and to the left, it opened out into a large kitchen diner.

This was not the same kitchen that Miss Chambers remembered– the one that had a large stove and a backdoor where she sat peeling vegetables, her hands turning blue in the cold water as the breeze off of the lake whipped through, chilling her bones, the same way that it did now.

A number of mugs and beer bottles, plus energy drink cans, littered the sideboard, but this had been refurbished not too long ago, the mahogany replaced by the cool, clean lines of minimalist cream cupboards and dark grey marble worktops.

The other room was dark, with the curtains and blinds pulled shut and was covered with junk. Silently, they backtracked and walked back down the hall.

"Here," Miss Chambers said, grabbing the handle to the cupboard under the stairs. But of course, this wasn't a cupboard, as could be seen by the staircase going down to the cellar below as the light showed them.

"My bedroom was down here," she said, and Harry remembered some of the things that she had previously said.

Some days, I was not allowed out of the cellar.

On one occasion, I was there a week before I saw anyone. Food was passed into the room on a tray.

I thought that I would die down there.

At the bottom of the stairs, they turned left and were met by a door with a large metal catch. Slowly, they opened it.

That is when they heard the muffled yelp.

Left on the bed and hiding his face was Jez, who suddenly looked up. "What do you want from me?" he shouted.

Harry could not suppress the chuckle as he replied. "I'll have a 99, but Miss Chambers would die for a Mini Milk!"

"Thank God!" Jez exclaimed.

"Never a truer phrase spoken, young Jeremy," Harry replied.

"How did you get to be locked up in here, in my old bedroom, Jeremy? Is this some sort of sordid fantasy fulfilled now?" Miss Chambers added, completely deadpan.

"No, I-" Like the majority of people, Jez never knew how to take Miss Chambers. The default was usually with fear.

"Looked like you might be sniffing the linen, there? Am I going to be catching you raiding my laundry basket too?"

"S-sorry, I-I – Look I'm just glad to see you both! There is some crazy shit going down, I mean, the fuck is this all about?" Jez was spinning around slightly, trying to put thoughts in the correct boxes and failing spectacularly.

"Where's the flush on your potty mouth, Jeremy?" Miss Chambers said, straight to the point. She was never one to let people off at times when their emotions may well be to blame for such talk.

"S-Sorry!"

Harry waved off the apologies, knowing that Miss Chambers could carry on this charade for days, whereas he was more of a mover. "How many are here?"

Jez shrugged. "Dunno? I saw two guys earlier, oh, and Jason too!"

"Jason, eh?" Then after a moment's thought, "Any of the guys about 5'11", blonde hair, with only a slight accent?"

"Nope."

"Interesting. What about cars outside?"

Jez smiled like they had just hit onto his specialist subject. "Yeah, a white van and two Range Rovers – one of them being Jason's"

"You know what that means?" Miss Chambers said in a hushed voice.

"They are probably already at Caulfield Hall."

Jez slapped his forehead. "Yeah, Jason and some guys were running and shouting something about, 'she got away' – which I reckon is Daisy. They headed off down along the bank of the lake.

"Right," Harry said, "Let's check out the rest of this house and then make our way over there."

Miss Chambers looked around the room again, filled to the brim with nostalgia. She cared not if she never saw this room again. "I'm about ready to leave now, if truth be told," she said.

"I quite understand that. Why don't you and Jez here head back to the cars. I want to quickly check out that no one else is here."

Jez was nodding to this. "Should we not ring the police?" Harry looked to Miss Chambers, who shrugged. "I cannot decide whether that is a very good idea or a completely stupid idea."

Harry was also unsure. The right thing to do was to call the police, but the facts were that they could not be entirely sure what the motivation behind the kidnapping was. Of course. they had rumours and a whole host of ideas, but as the old saying goes 'ain't nothing stranger than folk.' He also had a number of unanswered questions running through his mind: What if they caught her? Would they hear sirens, cut their losses, and kill her? What if this invention didn't actually work? Or they couldn't find it? There is a lot riding on something that was demoed a long time ago, and what if it was just an illusion? History does not tell stories of Russian gangsters and illusionists skipping happily down the road together, chuckling at how they've been fooled by another man's cleverness.

Harry tugged his beard again, showing another of his thinking traits. "How about we ring them when we get to Caulfield Hall?"

"What, like as soon as we arrive?" Jez said, always keen on the exact details.

"Either that, or we check out what's happening."

Jez then smiled again like he had just finished breaking wind. "I've got it! When we get there, I'll wait in the car, and then if you don't come back out or signal to me, then I will ring the police."

"A poultry plan. That's what I'd call that," Miss Chambers chuckled, emitting a sound that suggested more sarcasm than real thigh-slapping humour.

"I don't get it?" Jez frowned.

Harry laid a fatherly hand on Jez's shoulder, although he did have to reach somewhat to do this. "I think that Miss Chambers may well be having a small laugh at your expense, lad. The suggestion would be that you are perhaps a little worried about leaving the car when we get there, and so could be seen as acting a little chicken."

"Damn straight, father. I'm four-parts shit scared. They bashed me on the head and locked me down here. What the fuck am I going to do if they do that again? I may already have brain damage."

"I think that is a certainty, Jeremy, although the duration of its manifestation may well be in question," Miss Chambers quickly added.

"Amusing," Jez retorted. Then when they reached the top of the cellar stairs, he and Miss Chambers tentatively made their way back to where their cars were.

Harry carried on up the stairs to the next floor. He came across a nice sizeable family bathroom and three bedrooms. Two were a fair size, and the other was slightly smaller, but all were set up with beds and looked to have been slept in recently. Then Harry found a fourth room, which was the biggest. In here was a large map of the area. Then upon one of the walls were pictures of Gordon, Eddie, and Daisy. It looked like a police incident room set up with the visual leads and thought process. This was another jigsaw falling into place. It was like he had worked out the missing pieces, but still needed to locate them, and now all that was left were a small handful.

Apart from the guy outside, the place appeared to be empty.

So this must mean that they are all over at Caulfield Hall. Suddenly, Harry felt tension in his head and a heaviness in his heart, as he could only imagine what was currently happening there.

He pulled his phone out and snapped a few quick pictures. He hovered again over the '9' button, wondering whether or not he should press it three times.

He shoved the phone back into his pocket and made his way out of the house, pausing momentarily as he heard the sudden groans of the guy on the floor.

LOST CONNECTIONS

Chapter Forty-One

The secret stairs in the cellar wound down, and then what opened up in front of me was a large room, predominantly stoned-walled there were shelves packed with electrical items and plastic casings. The wall held a couple of large detailed blue-prints of something that looked like a walkie-talkie. Again, it seemed a bit like a sick joke. What if these people had been told that there was something amazing here, and all that turned out to be here was a modified walkie-talkie?

There was a leather couch and a chair with one of those globes that I was sure would fold back to reveal a drinks cabinet, and in the corner was a very large double-doored mahogany cupboard/wardrobe. In the corner sat a large mousetrap, still pulled back and set ready to snap on any unsuspecting rodent. Next to it was a large grandfather clock.

Behind the clock...

I walked up to the clock, noting that the time seemed right. This was a little odd, as these clocks needed winding almost every day, I thought. But I concluded that my dad, being my dad, had this running off of some long-life battery someplace or a solar panel that keeps it ticking.

I ran my hands down both sides of the clock and instantly noted that on the right-hand side there were three sets of hinges. I pulled the clock that way, but as expected, there was a trigger someplace on the clock. I prodded, pushed, and twisted things, but nothing seemed to work. With my inquisitive mind, I opened up the clock and pulled the chain that winds the clock. I heard a click sound and so pulled the whole clock towards me.

It opened up, and behind it was a small safe.

There were eight numbers required. Without any thought I pressed 02101966 – my brother's date of birth. As I heard the click, and the door began to open, I smiled– half with resignation and half with triumph.

There were three things in the safe: a handbook or manual, a handset, and a CD.

The manual had been put together by my father, and seemed to tell me the whole workings of the handset. I stumbled over to the sofa, and plonk myself down, drinking up the revelation in front of me. I looked at the handset, turning it around in my hand and wondering whether this is all some elaborate trick.

I'm not sure how long I sat there looking over this manual, but my mind was unable to fathom exactly what these claims meant. I'd re-read a few of the chapters again and again, but it definitely seemed to claim that with this handset, I could speak essentially to the dead. Or more to the point, I could ring into the past and speak to somebody who is dead now, but who was alive back then.

I wonder whether this is just a delusion that my father has got caught up in. He wanted to see and speak to Ben again so desperately that he has made up this fantasy, suggesting to himself that he has designed and built something that could speak to his dead son – his favourite son– again.

And with this whole unfortunate episode, he has also dragged a lot of people in with it, and ironically, the catalyst of him losing his most important person, could eventually result in me losing mine. His obsession and creativity invented, not a life changing telecommunication breakthrough, but a world where the lines of fantasy and reality blurred to the point whereby nobody knew what was going on. Even Jason was sucked into thinking that he was investing into history, whilst funding my father's psychological breakdown. At some point, something must've happened, and that's why my father disappeared. If you've invented something as amazing as this, then why would you disappear for over seven years?

I hate to say this, but my father is nothing but a great big fraud— a charlatan of the highest order.

I wanted to take no chances, so I picked up one of the walkie-talkies from a box on the side, that I presumed my father was going to use to 'transform' into his invention, and put it into the safe. Underneath, I picked up some paperwork, and underneath that, I carefully picked up the mouse trap, and with the gentle touch of a bomb-disposal expert, I turned it over and placed it under the paperwork upside down. I then shut the door. I returned the clock to its original position and placed the real invention, manual, and CD on the side with the other walkie-talkie, booklets, and CDs. Buried in plain view. I walked back up into the study.

My legs felt like I was wearing lead boots, and there was a pressure building up inside. I wondered what was going to happen when they found out that whatever rumours they have heard, the handset is nothing more than a useless oversized mobile from 1988?

And then the world takes another turn.

I hear a bang and a crash from upstairs, followed by shouting.

And then my mobile kicks into action with voicemails and text messages. Whilst I have been caught up in this, a whole host of things have happened almost all around me....

Chapter Forty-Two

"Mum! You have to listen. There are two men in the house trying to get me. Watch out."

"What house? Where?"

"Here! At Caulfield Hall. I can see you and Ruby..." Just then, a large black Range Rover appeared.

"Run!" Ruby shouted, pulling Jean along with her. Jean had not run for a number of years, but pumped her legs like she was in the Olympics with the chance of a medal.

As they burst through the front door of the house, they could hear the sound of car doors opening and feet on gravel behind them.

They ran past the study, ignored the open door to the drawing room, and went straight up the stairs, taking two at a time. There was something about being on another floor that gave them hope. Ruby took the lead, running into a bedroom and with relief, seeing an en suite bathroom. They ran in, and Ruby shut the door as quickly and as quietly as possible. She locked it and sat down on the floor, listening as the pounding feet got louder.

"Don't be fookin' stoopid!" the heavily accented voice shouted. "Carme out now and nobody will get hurt."

Jean and Ruby looked at each other both frozen with fear. Whilst they had found a place to hide with a lock, the reality was that a lock would not stop the person behind that voice. In hindsight, one of those 'double-back' manoeuvres would've been best, but what can you do? Fly or fight, they say, and it was the former that both women thought was the best outcome. But here, they were cornered like prey, with the predator waiting to pounce.

"We know you're in there," another voice said. "So before we smash the door down, why don't you just come out?"

"We've called the police!" Jean shouted, bordering on hysterical.

"I'm sure you have," the voice replied. "And if that is the case then they'll find two dead females in a bathroom, and another little girl skinned alive!" Ruby cancelled her mobile upon hearing that, just as the first ring of 999 could be heard. Jean was frantically shaking her head, although it was unclear to Ruby whether or not this was to her ringing the police or cancelling the call to the police.

"I give five seconds," the heavily accented voice demanded. "And then we come in!"

Ruby grabbed the toilet brush, which thankfully was metal, rather than the normal plastic ones that can be bought. That said, it seemed a pretty poor weapon, although slightly better than Jean's, which was a bar of soap. You had to wonder how many times in history *'Imperial Leather'* soap had been ready as a weapon to the death.

"Five!" he started.

"Four!" Both Ruby and Jean looked at each other with their hearts beating fast.

"Three!" They slowly got to their feet.

"Two!" Thinking back to any possible film that they had ever seen, they stood strong in a stance ready for action, both unsure exactly what you are meant to do in this situation.

"One!" The door exploded off of its hinges, reducing the strong stances to back on their heels. Jean threw her soap, which hit the taller of the two on the top of his head, but failed to slow him down. And Ruby ran at the other guy with the toilet brush, but as she swung it, she felt something smash against her face like a breeze block. A bright white light flashed, and then everything went black. The hysterical shouting from Jean faded out as she lost consciousness. Her last thought was, *At least I died fighting....*

LOST CONNECTIONS

Chapter Forty-Three

Jason opened up the door of the boathouse and walked in. As the door closed behind him, he slid down onto the floor with his head in his hands.

Oh bloody-shittin'-heck, how the fuck do I get out of this? he thought. *How did this all go so horribly wrong?* The summary sounded bad, so he went over it again in his mind. Gordon came to *him* with an investment opportunity. Granted, he didn't run it past Eddie, but shit, it was his own old man. The investment seemed so good that it would bring a lot of money to *Capers*. Again, how could that *not* be a good decision? Okay, so from there, things did get decidedly ropey. Perhaps the champagne, women, and weekend benders in London was a bit over the top, but the investment seemed watertight. There seemed no question of '*ifs,*' but it was all about the '*when.*' The gift-horse was there strong and frisky with unbeatable odds. He was just waiting for the race to start.

He thought about some of those nights, dressed up in a newly bought three-piece suit for the first time in his whole God-damn life. One that cost as much as his first car, and drinking whatever-the-fuck he wanted. Having woman leagues above him thinking he was something special. They were walking up to him! *Un-fuckin-believable!*

This was not inheritance money or an afterthought allowance slipped to him whilst mummy and daddy went to the Caribbean for a month. This was money he'd earned through hard work and good business. Fine, he'd overspent, but this was nothing more to him than the money he was going to get back. Money he was owed.

The feeling that he got flipping through notes like he was some king was amazing. But his money didn't keep him in this persona for too long, and his Russian Fairy-God-Father went from bearing gifts of credit to demanding payment, too quickly shattering any idea of a fairy-tale ending. He was scammed, but in a completely transparent way. He knew the credit would only last so long, but he decided upon the tactic of ignorance.

His own father had said to him, "Son, try not to ever piss anyone off, but if you happen to, never let them be Russian, or you may as well book yourself in with an undertaker!" Jason had laughed at this line many-a-time when growing up. This line ceased to have the same humour attached to it now, even if the man in question was not even Russian.

Two weeks ago, Jason had been closing up the bar when two men jumped him and bundled him into a car. At first, Jason thought that this was it, he was going to end up like some victim of Mafia crime like he had seen in a number of Hollywood movies. However, they stopped the car and sat him up.

They were outside the beautiful house of his parents. Whilst there was a bush and a couple of trees, he could see both of his parents in the conservatory. His dad was sat drinking from a mug, and his mother was laughing at something that he had said. A beautiful couple happy and content with the world.

"If I don't get what you owe me, then I will kill them both." The guy grabbed Jason's face with his hand with a vice-like grip around his chin, with his fingers touching one cheek, and his thumb buried deep in the other. "And I don't mean quickly!"

It was all too much for Jason, who completely broke down. And with the flashes of his parents happily unaware of what was going on a stone's throw away, Jason spilled out the invention that Gordon had shown him. Satisfied for now, they kicked him out into the road there and then.

A week later, Jason was trying to break into the study, but to no avail. He was beginning to get desperate. He'd tried everything, even trying to smash the windows with rocks, but of course old Gordy had thought of that, and at some point, had replaced them with reinforced glass. It was of no amusement to think that technically, Jason and Eddie had probably unknowingly financed this. There was an air of Morrisette about this whole thing.

It was one of the worst calls of Jason's life when he had to ring the guy and explain that he couldn't retrieve what he needed to. He ended up with the following response: "Stoopid fookin' Ingliss! Luckily, I've been doing my research, and I think I may have found a weakness. We will be in touch." And of course, they were. Last night at the club, the men arrived, pressurising him into getting Eddie to come over. He couldn't do it. He kept telling them that he was trying, but Eddie was there to have fun and a few drinks. And of course, they waited for him outside, where they were meant to put him in their car and take him to the Russian. Then they would go to his house, get rid of the vicar, and kidnap the daughter until Daddy got them into the Caulfield Hall study. But Eddie has never minded a fight, and never more so than if he's jumped upon. His morals tell him never to start a fight, but if someone else is brain-dead enough to start on him, then he will do all in his power to finish it. By the sounds of it, that's exactly what he did, as both guys were unable to join in with today's adventure, instead resting up, having spent the night requiring medical attention.

Jason had this doomed sense that he had somehow started off this spinning top that had careered out of control, destroying things in its path, and he was ultimately the one to blame. Someone with an inflated ego may well have felt proud of this and full of power, but Jason felt nothing but sick in the stomach.

He also thought about his talk with Harry. Of course, he had not gone into details, and for the most part his mumbling for forgiveness, admitting to making the wrong choices, and feeding a greedy habit could well have been attributed to his not-so-secret liaisons with Jean. This was clearly the assumption that the vicar had made, and he, for one, was not going to put him straight. That said, though, whilst you could argue amongst yourselves as to which two actions were deemed the most severe, Harry had offered him a simple pragmatic response: *Blame is a creature that can easily grow out of control. Forgiveness is strong, but short lived if not coupled with actions. Move forward and look to put right your wrongs.*

Harry was a good vicar. He had, for the most part, been a good man beforehand, and had offered advice with a more sports-related stance, rather than ecclesiastically. He was often heard waxing motivational gems like '*If you believe, then you achieve*' and '*It does not matter how slow you go, as long as you do not stop*' or '*Our greatest weakness lies in giving up,*' all taken from the likes of Einstein, Edison, and even Walt Disney ('*If you dream it, then you can do it.*')

So here he was sitting down, hiding from the world, whilst his friend's daughter is running for her life. Crazy people are angry and desperate and he is sitting- *He shot his head to the side; he could have sworn that something large was swinging in his peripheral vision. However, when he looked, there was nothing there.*

He picked up his mobile and called Eddie. He wasn't sure why, but it just felt like the right thing to do.

It rang once before being answered. "Jason? What's going on? Where are you?"

"Eddie-mate," he said. "I'm so sorry man. I never wanted this!" Jason's voice began to crack.

"What are you talking about? Are you in London?"

"No, I'm-" His throat was so dry, the words lodged there. "I'm at Caulfield Hall."

"Caulfield Hall? Whereabouts? That's where I am."

"I'm in the boathouse." *He swung a glance over his shoulder again.* "Uh, s-sorry, I keep thinking that I am seeing something out of the corner of my eye."

"Large and swinging?"

"How d'ya know?" Jason heard Eddie sigh. "I've seen her too" Eddie said. "Come out in the open. That place gives me the willies."

Jason didn't need to be told twice. He'd begun to see his own breath, even though it was warm enough outside to be wearing a t-shirt. He got up and walked rather more quickly out of the door.

LOST CONNECTIONS

Chapter Forty-Four

I'd probably been in here an hour by the looks of things, and outside of these walls, a whole load of shit was going down. This once again proved that the study was certainly an enclosed room within the Hall. You felt a million miles from anywhere else when you were down there. I'd been checking my phone when the call from Jason came in.

I scanned the rest of them as I walked across the room. The best call I had was from Daisy saying that she was okay, even if it was in a hushed voice. Then she sent me a text:

Dad – Am in the cool place u showed me earlier ☺ Will w8 here. B care4l, Sum men here 2 lookin 4 u. ☹ Got away from them ☺ D x

I smiled and texted her back:

Sorry, have been in the study. Found a cellar. Stay where you are. Jason is at the boathouse. Am going to meet him first.

I sent it and then looked at the other messages that I had. There was one from Jean:

Me and Ruby are on our way over to Caulfield Hall. Hope to see you there. Jean

She used to sign out with a kiss at the end of her messages, but I guess things are different now. For some reason I felt a bit sad about that. And then I suddenly grasped what was happening.

Daisy and Jason were here, Ruby and Jean were probably here by now, and there are two men wandering around looking for me.

Then I received another text from Daisy:

Ruby + Jean R here! Another car came 2 with 2 men in, they chased them into the house! Help them Dad! I'll stay here x

My mind was drained with the overload of feelings. I wanted to be with Daisy, but she was at the furthest part of the house away from me – and most likely the safest person. I needed to find out from Jason what was going on, and it didn't take a genius to work out that along with the invoices, his lying about being away on business, getting jumped at the club last night, and him hiding away in the boathouse, that he knew more about the kidnapping than anyone. And then I had the two ladies that both have a piece of my heart. Things are complicated. And anyway, my heart is with the girl in the tower.

I rang Jason back. "Hello," he said.

"Jason, what the hell is going on here? I'm told that there are four men around the house looking for me, and someplace Jean and Ruby are here too!" I missed out the detail on Daisy. My trust for Jason was currently on holiday, as it would be until I got the truth and a massive apology.

"Shit," he said. "I'll see you in there. Where shall I meet you?"

"Head towards the back of the house. There's a backdoor. It used to be like a service door. I'll meet you there."

"Okay." Then there was a beat before Jason said solemnly, "I'm sorry, Ed."

"I guess you are."

Chapter Forty-Five

"You got any music?" Jez asked from the backseat. Harry smiled to himself as Miss Chambers answered, "No, we do not. Jeremy, you may think that we are on some pleasant drive in the country, but us adults have more pressing matters to attend to than satisfying your every need!"

"I was just asking, is all," Jez replied, stung.

"Next you'll be asking, '*Are we nearly there yet?*' or whining '*I need the toilet.*' Really!"

Jez felt like sulking, and muttered back, "How old do you think I am?" Then (not rhetorically) answering, "Forty-four! I am forty-four!"

"Calm down in the back, Junior," Harry grinned, looking at Jez in the rear-view mirror and winking, just before Miss Chambers had the last word. "Yes, Mum and Dad are trying to concentrate up front."

Jez felt his fists tighten. That old biddy really got his goat. She seemed to always feel the need to make you feel vulnerable; it was her MO, or whatever they say on CSI. That Latin abbreviation thing. He knew that the whole of this deal was pretty crazy, and yes, he couldn't help but think how he would tell his followers about it in his online blog, but the thing is, *she* will not be getting a mention, that's for sure! No way, lady! *You can go write your own blog*, he thought to himself with a little half-smile. But at that point, she turned around.

"What is that stupid smile all about? Have you got wind?" Jez rolled his eyes up to Heaven. "I'm not sure that the good Lord is a lover of your bodily-extractions. What's your take on it, Father?"

Harry was amused by how Miss Chambers worked. She liked to make others think that she was incredibly religious, almost to the point of being God-fearing, but the flat-out truth was that she wasn't that religious at all. She liked everyone to think that she was wholesome, and with Harry being a vicar, she kept up appearances to somehow support him, but Harry knew that when she threw a question of divinity at him through a flippant remark, he was being tested, and therefore, his response held all the more weight, and thus more pressure.

"God understands all that is natural as equally as he appreciates politeness and self-control," Harry said in his usual controlled manner.

"Of course, what the good father is saying is that it would be advantageous to your welfare if you were to exercise some self-restraint by means of clenching the gluteus-maximus muscles until such a time as the feeling passes, or we are out in the open fresh air. Is that not right, Father?"

"I cannot disagree with that statement at all."

These two are a bloody double act, thought Jez. A geriatric Terry & June. Or a mixed-sex version of *The Two Ronnies*. And with that, he whipped his phone out and cobbled together a statement to amuse his followers on *Twitter*.

Harry pulled up just past the turning to the driveway of Caulfield Hall. "We can't pull in there. There is no quiet way to pull up to the house, so we may as well turn up beeping the horn."

Suddenly, Jez sat up straight and looked like he was about to combust. "Ah ha!" he said. "The old bonnet up and triangular warning sign behind the car routine, eh?"

Miss Chambers shook her head of grey hair, a movement which swung her pearl earrings back and forth, and tried not to use the Lord's name in vain. "Not quite," Harry replied. "I was thinking of just leaving it here. That way it would be quicker to getaway than having to put the bonnet down first.

"Fair point," Jez conceded, although he did think that he would still give off the impression that the car had broken down. It was in too many films for it to be a bad idea.

Harry and Miss Chambers got out, and when Jez failed to move, Harry opened the backdoor for him. "Look, if you are not coming, then why don't you stay in the driver's seat with the keys? That way, if you need to get away then you can, rather than being left in the backseat like some unsatisfied date."

"And how would you know about unsatisfied dates, Father?" Miss Chambers enquired with that playful chuckle that put Jez on edge.

"Miss Chambers, I know nothing of unsatisfied dates. Every single one of my dates has been thoroughly satisfied."

"Is that right?"

"The God's honest truth." Their voices got quieter as they carried on their banter walking away from the car. Jez sat there in the driver's seat with his mobile in his hand unsure what to do now. Maybe he could update his *Facebook* page.

Harry and Miss Chambers walked up the driveway. There really weren't many places that you could arrive in a stealthily fashion on a driveway dotted with the occasional tree and flat fields either side.

"It's a beautiful house," Miss Chambers said. "Slightly too grand, but the Gothic-touch is subtle enough to not make it too haunting, don't you think?"

Harry stopped a second and looked at the array of windows. "Indeed. We've experienced a few good nights here many moons ago."

For a moment their hands brushed together, finally stopping in a gentle clasp, both floating back to a time of jazz-playing hired-bands, a little too much sherry, and stories of escaping native tribes in Africa or South America. The driveway was lined with cars, and the guests were decked out in their best clothes. The happy, and the-pretending-to-be-happy, affluent high-society kissing cheeks and hands, with men smoking cigars and women daintily puffing on thin French cigarettes in holders like they were Audrey Hepburn.

"You're still a beautiful woman, Miss Chambers," Harry commented.

"And you're still a senile old man, Harry Dugan. Or perhaps just a little bit too sentimental."

"You always knew how to under compliment," Harry grinned with a wink.

"And you always have known how I felt." And of course, he did. Then just when he thought that his heart was done beating, he noticed a figure up in the tower– a waving figure that looked remarkably like Daisy.

"The tower," he said. And as Miss Chambers saw her, she mumbled. "My word, that child is a bloody miracle."

They quickened their pace as the got to the cars and debated just where they should go now.

"We should've brought that big lummox with us, Harry," Miss Chambers said.

"What, for protection?"

"No, he's a big target. They are sure to go after him first. We would have a chance to get away."

"You are a wicked woman!"

As they walked through the front door, they were met by a thump and a muffled scream, but it was coming from another floor. They couldn't help both stiffening up. What were they getting themselves into here?

Harry had been in some tough situations. In his younger years, he'd been caught in the middle of a football riot. Well, caught was perhaps not the right way of putting it; it wasn't like he was in the wrong place at the wrong time, but he was with his friends who were regulars in the London area, and he had gone there for the weekend, knowing full well that they liked to get a little more physical of an afternoon than just a couple of pints down the local and then off to the football. It wasn't totally his scene, but the adrenaline rush of no-holds-barred fighting outweighed the strict and disciplined amateur boxing that he was involved in.

Miss Chambers was no slouch either. She was seen as a tough feminist, quick-mouthed and sharp minded. She stood her ground against anybody, but that really just meant that men were scared of her.

However, the two had peaked in life a while ago, and that is perhaps why they never noticed the two men behind them until it was too late. Both men had handkerchiefs with chloroform on, and with a quick lunge, they had wrapped their arms around the front of their victims and smothered their noses and mouths with the rag. Harry bucked his assailant as best he could, but within five seconds, his arms and legs turned to lead, then melted to jelly, whilst his head became fuzzy, and eventually everything turned to black.

Chapter Forty-Six

I placed my finger over my mouth as Jason joined me at the backdoor, the universal sign language of '*be quiet.*' He looked almost defeated, and his eyes jumped around, unable to return my eye contact.

"What the hell is going on, mate?" I said in a hushed voice, but I wasn't looking for an explanation. It was just a comment that slipped out.

"I'm so sorry, Ed. I didn't know that it was going to get like this. I was in debt, and they found out about your dad's thing."

"The walkie-talkie?"

"Uh, yeah." We started to walk back along the corridor. "I didn't know that they were going to go after Daisy."

"Look, we have to find the girls now. We'll have plenty of time to talk later."

"Okay." He then added, "I'll put things right."

I stopped and put my hand on his shoulder. "*We'll* put things right," I corrected. "The only way that we can do this is by working together, okay?"

"Okay," he nodded.

We turned into the main corridor that eventually would join up with the main staircase and the study.

It was then that I saw them – and they saw us!

"Hey!" they shouted and broke into a run.

I grabbed Jason, and we sprinted in the opposite direction towards the back stairs.

It was a strange feeling running through this house. Suddenly everything seemed to slow down. I was transported to the many times as a child I had run around these corridors and up the stairs. I had mapped out escape routes in my brain. I am not going to try and sell you a line that all of those hours of my childhood were preparation for this moment now, as I don't believe this to be true. It was just a means to an end– a way to alleviate the boredom, but injecting a little excitement.

With each step, I felt the familiar lump in the carpet, the slight decline before the stairs that you would never normally notice. The strange spacing of the stairs and the places on the handrail that were the strongest. Half of me was running for my life, and the other half was an excited child again, running away from the made-up bogeyman. Muscle memory in full effect.

At the top of the stairs we ran to the second door on the left. This took us into the spare room. In front of us after entering the room, were two doors.

"Through there," I hissed to Jason, pointing to the one on the left. "I'll meet you the other side." I opened the one on the right, which went into a large, dark cupboard, leant to find the bar mounted onto the side, and took a big step to the left onto a ledge. From there, I leant over and pulled the door shut slowly, just as I heard the feet enter the room.

I slid the wall behind me to the right, allowing me to go through into a crawl space, and slid it back as I heard the door open. I moved to the side and slid another panel open, spotting Jason. I beckoned him in. And that's when we heard it.

"Uh, ahhhh!" was the sound with scraping, followed by a large thud. The cupboard that I'd just been in had no floor, but a large drop. The bottom was in a cupboard downstairs just off of the kitchen, and God knows what could be at the bottom.

"Open in two seconds," I whispered to Jason, just as a voice called out. "Victor? You okay, man?"

I went back the way that Jason had come, and waited for a split second for him to start to slide the door open.

I slowly opened the door to the bedroom and saw the guy bent over the hole. A flash in my mind of Daisy was all that I needed as I charged him. For a split second, I thought that I was going down the hole too, but a combination of the rail and Jason grabbing me stopped me following him down. The "Hoof" sound from below sounded like one had hit the other.

"Jesus, that was bloody stupid," Jason said. "Fuckin' cool! But stupid nevertheless."

"Wankers thought they could waltz in here," I said, adrenaline not so much running through my veins as strongly pulsating. I suddenly felt invincible, which can be a dangerous feeling.

We grinned at each other, and it was suddenly like the old days when we would drink and end up doing crazy things together. We walked out of the door full of bravado. Two down and two fuckers to go!

"Vat hav vee here?" a guy that I'm guessing does not hold a British passport said, waving what looked like either a very impressive water-pistol, or a true-life gun.

I'd never come into contact with a gun before, other than a rifle when clay pigeon shooting, and I could feel the blood and bravado drain from me in seconds.

"Where's my daughter?" I said through gritted teeth, but I was a long way from being Chuck Norris or even Jason Stratham.

"All in good time, Edvard," he said, but I hoped to God that this was a bluff, and Daisy was still safe in the tower.

There was another large guy standing next to him – but then, there would be, wouldn't there? It was almost like bad-guy 101. This was the bodyguard of the leader, and the other two that had disappeared into my version of Narnia were just foot-soldiers.

"Guess vere ve are going?" the guy demanded. I really wanted to reply with *'Costa Coffee,'* but I'm no action hero. Instead, I shrugged.

"The study. I believe that there is something for me there, no?" And then he nodded to his large friend and then nodded to Jason. The guy stepped forward and punched Jason square in the face, sending him flat on his back.

I jumped in. "Hey!" I shouted. "Leave him alone, or you're not getting anything."

"Interesting..." the guy said. "He double crosses you, and yet you still stand by him." I held up my hands in a 'Well?' kind of way, but I think that it came across more as an act of surrender. In any case, it did the trick.

"Fine," he said, and off we walked. All the while, I wondered whether I could fight the big man and win. It seemed like it would take something out of an action movie to kick the gun away and then beat up the weight-lifter, and I just wasn't ready for the challenge yet.

The walk towards the study felt a little like The Green Mile. Once they had my father's invention, then what use was I to them?

My mind flashed a hundred ways of escape, but whilst I thought that I could get away, there was Jason, then there was Ruby and Jean, and above all else, I had to somehow get to Daisy. I was closer to her now than I'd been in a long time, but suddenly we were walking, and the gap between us again began to grow....

LOST CONNECTIONS

Chapter Forty-Seven

Jez sat staring out of the window and glanced at his watch. And then at his mobile. And again at his watch. Time was moving slowly, and nobody was sending him a text or ringing him. He thought about ringing his wife.

Now, there was a thing. It was perhaps true to say they had a relationship that was up and down. It wasn't that they fought a lot; it was just that they had large bouts of distance from each other, and then, like last night, they would end up in the throes of deep passion. Jez smiled to himself as he slipped some REM into the CD player. He'd been beckoned by his wife, who had decided to come all the way out and pick him up from a drunken night out. She was full of surprises.

His memory was almost there as he remembered small talk, and she seemed genuinely interested in what he'd been up to. She'd helped him into the house and then had instigated undressing, whereby she kissed him from head to toe. The tiredness that Jez had felt earlier disappeared in an instant, and he even felt himself sober up a bit as he fell in love all over again. It was true, he enjoyed telling others that his old lady was tough. In some ways, he played on the sympathy, but deep down, he did love her. He couldn't be sure whether he would still love her in ten years' time or even next week, but at the moment, he was more than happy with the situation.

He hummed along to the music and wondered what sort of a place you would have to be in to be surrounded by 'shiny happy people laughing.' Most likely a cult, he thought, or a gym. "Sweaty, flabby people farting" he sung, changing the lyrics and laughing to himself.

He decided to send a text to his wife anyway. It was a little out of the ordinary for them, but hey, this was him being a little spontaneous.

He smiled again to himself as he typed:

Just thinking about u and the blistering sex. I think that I can still smell you. x Ironman

That, he thought, is a nice gesture.

He looked through some of the other CD's as he let the time go on a bit. The Rolling Stones was here a couple of times, Jethro Tull, The Doors, U2, and Guns'N'Roses. Jez wasn't sure exactly what music the local vicar should favour, but Axl Rose screaming about drink, drugs, fighting, and loose women through a mixture of similes, nouns, adjectives, and a spit-full of profanities was not an answer he would go for on an episode of *Family Fortunes*. He would think that 100 people would suggest something classical like Beethoven or Wagner, or perhaps squeaky-clean Sir Cliff Richard, or some show-tune soundtrack by Andrew Lloyd Webber− not Slash's beautiful riffs, backed with Izzy's rhythm guitar, and the deep pulsing bass from Duff, whilst− depending on the era – either Steven Adler's perfectly simple drum beat, or Matt Sorum's slightly more percussionist's flare pounded the tempo.

Jez looked at his phone again as he saw he had a reply from his wife:

Ironman – Cass left her phone here. I will pass on your message. Cass's mum.

Shit! Jez thought, he was in deep doo doo. Cass's mum was completely uptight, and as far as he was aware, in the fifteen years that he had known her, there had been no evidence that she owned, or had ever come into contact with a sense of humour.

Jez started to reply, focusing in on easing her mind that by blistering, he didn't mean that either of them were left with welts or sores, but then quickly realised that perhaps the best course of action was to ignore that he'd seen the reply completely. If ever there was a time to procrastinate on phone usage, then this was it.

He looked at the time. They'd been gone a good half an hour now. Just what in the hell were they up to? And then the thought hit him.

What if they were all dead? It would be like one of those horror movies when everything had already happened. This would be the last scene as he walked slowly up to the house. The music would be all nice and serene, the camera work focusing on the birds in the trees, the sun shining brightly. The horror is over, and this is to calm down your heart rate again. He might even whistle a jolly little tune as he pushed open the door. The music would be replaced by haunting strings as he sees bloody hand prints and the evidence of a lost battle. Slowly, he is drawn deeper into the house, where he is met by broken limbs and bodies in pieces like a crazy-person's idea of a human jigsaw puzzle.

His hand would cover his mouth from the smell of death, and then he would hear a sound behind him.

He would turn, but it would be too late as the stranger brings down the axe handle for the fatal blows, and he is another victim decorating the house with his blood.

The screen goes black, and we demand a sequel. Roll credits.

That's it, he thinks, *let someone else be the hero*, and he turns down the music and rings the police.

Chapter Forty-Eight

I pushed open the door to the study and almost felt the pain of every inch that came into view. It was now so easy to open, which seemed such a disappointment, considering all of the trouble that my father had gone to in order to stop people from getting into this room. The plus side was that I knew that whatever happened to me, Daisy should be fine, and perhaps if I really thought that giving these people my father's life's works was a direct swap for Daisy, then I wouldn't have an issue doing so. But there are few things in life that wind me up, and one of those would be people expecting to take something for nothing.

"What is it that you're expecting?" I said, more as something to say.

"I sink you know," he replied.

We walked in, and we all stopped. The study was, indeed, a room that radiates knowledge, hard work, and deep thought.

"A lot of crap," the bodyguard muttered in a deep tone.

"My father worked for many years, and you want to come in and take it all?" I said. I couldn't help it; the pressure was building up. I felt a little bit like I did years ago in my fighting days. I used to get worked up with adrenaline for most fights, but there had been one against a Scottish guy, Declan Mckay, who had taken it upon himself to make fun of my family and get amateurish t-shirts made up with derogatory slogans on. He managed to unleash an ugly Neanderthal side to me that I wasn't aware of. And this is ultimately what finished my career.

From the first bell, he came out swinging wildly, looking for the big knockout punch. I made sure that I had good head movement and used my legs to weave my body from side to side, helping to evade the punches. My defence was tight as I took shots to the arms as my elbows protected the danger spot under my ribs. After the first minute, he'd almost punched himself out, whereas I'd only tapped out a few jabs, mostly as feelers and range finders. Having felt his best shots without too much pain, I was full of confidence. Pictures of him laughing at me flashed in my eyes, and for a moment, I didn't even feel like I was in that ring anymore. I jabbed him once with a right, then brought a solid left crossover to his jaw. As he rocked, I bent down, planting my feet firmly, and fired a hard shot under his ribs and then sprung with everything I had in an uppercut. A couple of his punches grazed my jaw and then my ear, but he was missing wildly. I went in for the body on his left and then right side, and I felt him sag. The uppercut snapped his head back, and his eyes were already rolling up as he began to topple, but the aggression led me to land another hard haymaker to the side of his head. He hit the canvas sideways and laid there like a crumpled toy. I saw the ref already waving it off before he had got to counting past three.

I was so fired up, Harry had to grab me. I was thinking about kicking the man whilst he was laid half out on the floor of the ring. How messed up is that? I remember Harry shouting at me, "It's over, Ed. It's over." But there was part of me that was still raw with the words that had been spoken, and this still didn't seem like enough.

A few days later, I was to be hyped up for a big amateur fight. A week later, under Harry's guidance, I'd retired.

I wasn't going to be silly here, but this guy brought it all flooding back. He was dismissing the ingenuity and hard work that had gone into this, whether or not it actually worked. I had a hard time here.

"When do I see my daughter?" I said through gritted teeth.

"You seem to lack priorities, Edvard." he said to me. "Your daughter should not be of your concern anymore. The area that you need to focus on is how much you value your own life. Be aware, we *will* kill you!"

"And how do I know that you will not kill us anyway?" I pressed.

"You don't." He grinned. I really hope that he was bullied as a child.

"And what about Ruby and Jean?"

He smiled at this. "A lot of people seem to be in on this, no? Perhaps it was not such a good idea to tell them all now, huh?"

"What is your problem?" I shouted. I don't know why. It was not even something that I would normally say.

"I will not lie to you, there was blood with them. Are they dead? This I cannot answer. Are they alive? Maybe." He held the grin, then let it slide ever so slowly into an angry sneer. "You need to focus on this. Now where is it?" he shouted.

I walked to the bookcase and opened it up, revealing the staircase down below. I flipped the switch for the lights, and we slowly descended to the place that could very well become my last resting place.

Again, there was much to take in, but I walked over to the clock, opened it up, and then put in the code for the safe. I opened it and stood back.

"In there," I pointed, as he barrelled past me, lowering the gun and reaching inside. Then the next second, I heard the snap of the mousetrap. I slapped the gun out of his hand. At the same time, both Jason and the bodyguard came together.

I punched the guy hard in the face, which after the fight last night, was not the best thing that I could've done, but he toppled. I guess that he was used to hiding behind guns and having his bodyguard do the dirty work. I kicked him hard in the face and I reached for the gun, but when I had it, there was an awkwardness to it that I wasn't expecting. I swung it around to hit the bodyguard with it (like I had seen in movies), but ended up brushing his neck with my own hand, which sent a lightning bolt of pain up my wrist and arm. The bodyguard was in the process of squeezing the life out of Jason when I screamed "I will shoot your fuckin' head off! Let him go!" The guy suddenly swung a fast punch that I had to dodge before I tried the gun-handle-to-the-head routine again – but again would have done more damage with a can of beans. He kicked out and took my legs away, and I fell to the floor, dropping the gun. Jason made a move for it, but the guy used his force to push Jason the minute he was off balance. He then shoulder-charged me as I went to retrieve the gun.

He grinned as he grabbed the gun and stood over me.

This was it. My last moments here.

"STOP! POLICE! PUT DOWN THE WEAPON!"

Chapter Forty-Nine

The police burst in as the place exploded into chaos. We were all told to get down and keep our hands where they could be seen, and momentarily, I genuinely feared for my life. Then in came Jez, who was cowering and looking about as out of place as a Girl Guide in a Gentleman's Club. His hands were half raised, like he was sure he was going to be shot at any stage, and I wasn't sure just how good his defence would be. Like a modern day footballer, he was ready to hit the deck with any slight contact or confrontation.

"Which one of you is Edward?" a silhouette behind a bright torch said.

I pointed a finger as I raised my hand. "Me," I said. "There are others held here. Two women. Can you find them? And my daughter." I was babbling now, and noticed there were suddenly many police officers ready for action.

"Okay, okay, sir. Let's take things one at a time."

I was helped to my feet, when another officer came down the stairs. "Guv," he said. "I have two people tied up in a room down the hall. I've called an ambulance, as they don't appear to be conscious."

"Two woman?" I asked, but the officer was already shaking his head. "No, a man and woman of a more mature age. One appears to be a vicar."

The inspector then motioned over to the guy of Eastern decent and his bodyguard, and two policemen quickly put them in cuffs. "Well, well, well, if it isn't my favourite Croatian, Tomislav Matich. You're a very popular man, so I am led to believe. There are a lot of people from many different countries looking for you!"

Tomislav looked up, defeated, but defiant. "You look at what these people have here," he said, nodding down to the walkie-talkie. "That thing might be of interest to your national security."

"Is that right? What is it? A nuclear warhead?" the Inspector dismissed.

"That thing can talk to the past."

"The past? What like a telephone back to your birth in 1961, whereby I could stop the doctors keeping you alive?" he chuckled.

"That is exactly what I'm saying. Think of the power it would hold if it was in the wrong hands."

The inspector raised his eyebrows, "And of course that was your main concern when you kidnapped this man's daughter? For the good of Great Britain's national security?"

"I didn't kidnap anyone," he said. "That was nothing to do with me."

"Is that right, Tomislav? So you would know nothing about Tulip House then?" Tomislav remained blank-faced, giving nothing away, but I saw the fingers behind his back twitch in a slight admission of guilt. I agree that this is not something that would mean a lot in a court of law, but sometimes it is these little tells that can help us to know that we are on the right track. Of course, I know that the evil man is as guilty as sin, but the police may not know this.

"I had a phone call a while back that led one of my men to the aforementioned property, and would you believe that not only did they find a room with all of your plans nicely laid out – which I thank you for, by the way – but also the short-lease of the property is in the name of a known associate of yours. About now, there is a crime scene currently being dusted for prints that I would bet my beautiful wife on, is full of your grubby little digits!" He then picked up the walkie-talkie. He pressed the button and said, "Hello, hello? Is anybody there?" We all waited a few seconds, but of course, nothing happened. "Hmm, nothing there? That's a big surprise."

Tomislav threw me a deadly look. "That's all that I know," I said. "You wanted what my dad had in his safe, and that is it. I had no idea what it was or what it allegedly did." Tomislav then looked at Jason, who was looking incredibly uncomfortable.

"I saw what it did. But that was over seven years ago. It could well have been a joke. Gordon was a little bit, er, eccentric – no offence, Ed."

I nodded. "No need. My father disappeared without word seven years ago. He told me nothing of this *'so-called-revelation'* that he'd been working on. If you ask me, he believed that he'd invented something, and talked a few people into believing him that he was about to unleash something to the world that would change the face of history forever. I agree that if his claims had been true, then it would be a truly powerful thing, but come on? A phone that talks to people in the past? However would that even be possible?"

The inspector grinned at that. "Beautiful justice here. Tomislav, a little advice to you – should you ever have another free day in your life – if a deal is unbelievable, then guess what? It usually is impossible." He turned to his men. "Get them out of here!"

Then another policeman came in with Jean. I felt myself feel relieved, but instantly wondered about Ruby.

"Guv," the policeman said. "I have this lady here and another lady being treated for concussion. There is one ambulance about two minutes away and another about ten minutes away."

"Um," I started. "Another ambulance might be needed. A couple of his men sort of fell down a hole from upstairs."

The inspector raised his eyebrows again. "An accident, you say?"

"An accident," I agreed, looking at the floor and with not a lot of conviction. The inspector turned to one of his men with a grin and then turned back. "You don't have CCTV cameras here anywhere, do you?"

"No, sir, I do not," I replied as I put my arms around Jean.

"Oh, well. It would've been nice to have seen exactly what went on here!"

And then the most wonderful sight filled the room. Daisy appeared like an angel and ran to me.

"Dad!" she cried out with tears streaming, and I filled up with so much emotion that it poured out too.

"Daisy!" I said with a huge lump in my throat. I held her so tight that my arms ached. It was the best feeling in the world.

The inspector was clearly trying to join the dots as he said, "The kidnapped daughter?"

"Yes," Jean managed. "My beautiful daughter."

"I escaped, Dad!" she said proudly. "I ran so hard and then jumped in a boat and rowed across the lake! They were following me in a speedboat! They nearly had me, but I ran up here and up to the room where you showed me earlier! This house saved my life, Dad!"

"Right," the inspector said. "I know that you have been through a lot, but I am going to need you to come down to the station to tell me exactly what has been going on here. I need to somehow timeline this whole thing, so as we can get the details straight, should it go to court.

"What?" I said, "This might not go to court?"

The inspector held up his hands. "No, it's not what you are thinking. Our friend out there is wanted by so many authorities that, with no disrespect to this horrible crime that you've been put through, believe it or not, he's done worse, and therefore it will most likely be those crimes that he will be tried for. This will be taken into consideration, but if you think that kidnapping, attempted murder, use of a deadly weapon, blackmailing— to name but a few things— are still not considered as bad as his other crimes, then you can understand that it's unlikely that he will ever be a free man again."

I nodded my head, and then all of us made our way out of the cellar. I glanced back at the real walkie-talkie, and part of me wondered if there was anything more there than a handset— one that you could speak to someone else with its twin at up to 300 feet away, but the possibility of this was too great. I chuckled again at how my father had tricked a number of people, including a hardened international criminal. Well done, Dad!

Still holding Daisy's hand, I walked up to the ambulance where Ruby sat with a large lump on her head. Jez was bouncing around like a human version of Tigger.

"How are you doing?" I asked her.

She smiled, the stud in her pierced tongue glinting in the sunlight. "I've been better! How about you?"

"I think I could sleep for days!"

Ruby then looked past me. "Hey, thanks, Jean, for looking after me."

"You're welcome," she said. I then noticed that Jason was hovering around behind us.

"Jason, get your ass over here!"

"Language, Dad!" Daisy smirked.

"I'm sorry. All of you. I'm just so sorry," he said, and I saw the tears in his eyes, which was certainly something I never expected. He looked like a defeated man.

"Uncool, man," Jez said. "Look at the old folks!" Harry and Miss Chambers were both sitting up, and suddenly looked up at that.

"I'm going to ask that you have a lobotomy, Jeremy," Miss Chambers said. "Have you thought about moving house?"

"Good one, Miss C!" He grinned.

"Foolish lad," was all she replied with, and Harry was grinning again.

I then looked back to Jason. "Jase, look, we have a lot to talk about. I think we also need to look at our whole business relationship." Jason hung his head. "Look, what I'm saying is that we can't sell this place." I gestured with my hands at this large house. "We need to branch out and look at how we can turn this place into money. Wedding receptions and movie sets, just a number of ideas that I have thought about. Catering by *Capers* too!"

"Really? I thought you we going to buy me out?"

"Kick your backside is what I should do, but no. We are good business partners – well, when you're not investing in my father's tricks."

"You know about that?" he said, shocked.

"I know all about that, Jase." I then looked at Jean. "And whilst we are at it, if you two are an item, then be an item, but let's stop the sneaking around."

Jean looked at Jason and then at me. "Well, I'm not sure-"

Jason then jumped in. "I've caused a lot of shit, so-" I stopped him there. "Look, whatever you are is whatever you are. I think that one thing that we should all be able to take from this is that we need to be open with each other." I stopped for a second, and my eyes started to well up as I put my arm around Daisy. "I'm not going to blame anyone. There are so many things that have snowballed from a lot of bad decisions. We're an unlikely bunch that are unable to fully function socially with each other. I'm as much to blame – even indirectly – as anyone. We are connected, but not connected-"

"We're lost connections," Daisy said, and we all stood there for a moment taking this in. The sun was beginning to set, but the birds still chirped around. There was a smell of cut grass from a farmer close by, who was unaware of the drama being caused an acre or two away.

"Dad?" Daisy then said.

"Yes, my girl?"

"So what about you two?" she said, looking between myself and Ruby.

Ruby looked slightly embarrassed, but flashed me a beautiful smile as our eyes met, then managed to say. "Well? What do you think about there being an us?"

"Well," I said. "I guess that is another question that I've been giving a lot of thought to." I bent down, and we shared an awkward kiss. "Let's see how things go?" I said.

"I'd like that," she replied. "I may need someone to look after me with this concussion though."

"Yes, you had better come back to ours then," I grinned.

Miss Chambers piped up with her usual tact. "Don't keep me up all night with all of that raunchy fornication."

"Gross!" Daisy said, and Ruby's face turned the colour of her name.

After a little more small talk, Jean, Daisy, Ruby, Jez, and I headed off to the station, where we gave a rough outline of the events as they unfolded. Jez kept trying to jump in and make things either sound more exciting or bringing it back to anything that he felt he had added to the day. The inspector grew tired of this and gave each of us slots to return within the next few days.

We got back a little after 7pm, whereby we ordered pizzas, but the truth was we were all physically and emotionally tired out, and our appetites not quite what we thought them to be. We tried hard to get back into normality, but it had been a long and stressful day. My head hurt with tension, and a thousand thoughts spun around my head.

Ruby did, indeed, sleep in my bed, but I slept on the floor of Daisy's room. I laid watching her for an hour or so, too tired to sleep, with my body still trying to regulate to something that might be close to normal. I could hear Harry speaking to me about lessons learnt in life over the past 48 hours, and any other type of religious spin that he could turn this ordeal into a good situation. I'd let him have that– certainly there could well be a small bit of truth in it; that much I was willing to concede.

And of course, being a man, I confess to popping my head around the door of my room when I got up to go to the toilet, and I thought to myself how I was standing there between two very important women in my life.

"Are you just going to stand there?" Ruby said as she opened her eyes.

For a second, I felt like I had been caught in the act. "I hadn't really thought that far."

"Liar," she said, sleepily throwing back a corner of duvet by way of an invite.

This was a feeling that I was not used to. I slipped under the covers, and immediately we embraced with only underwear between us. I felt like I was seventeen again.

"Hello," she whispered.

"Hello," I replied, and we kissed. Our hands that usually gripped tattoo machines now glided over the contours of our bodies. Words were lost in kisses, and our breaths irregular. After a time, we did the sort of things that lovers do. And being true perfectionists for an attention to detail, we did it again.

The sun was nearly up when I slipped back into the sleeping bag on Daisy's floor, complete with a smile that was broader than Broadway.

Epilogue

It was only a couple of days before the police allowed us full access again to Caulfield Hall. The two men who had 'fallen' down the hole in the closet were not dead, although may well have hoped they were, when faced with the charges against them. All of them were arrested, along with another couple, which included the two men who did the kidnapping and the recovering brawlers that I'd fought at outside of *Capers*.

Tulip House is still a crime scene, although another turn up for the books was that Harry turned out to be the owner. He'd purchased it many years ago with a combination of savings, investments, and a little money my granddad had left him. The romantic old sod had wanted it done up before giving it to Miss Chambers. However, whilst awaiting the refurbishments, he'd left it in the hands of an agent to get someone in, so as to build up some cash. The last tenant had left a few months back, and his agent had failed to advise him of the new tenant – one that would surely have not passed any sort of background check. Tomorrow, Harry was going in to advise them of their breach of contract. He hoped they enjoyed the under-the-table hush money, and was still deciding whether or not he needed to take it any further. I think he was going to ask God just how much forgiveness is warranted in this situation.

So here we are in the cellar looking around. We're trying to understand what my father's motivation was for in regards to this big charade. And just what the Hell Jason saw all of those years ago.

I'm here with Harry and Jason. Daisy is at school, and Ruby is back knocking out some killer tattoos, although she's coming around for a meal tonight. In fact, she's barely left, if I am honest, which is just damn fine with me!

Jez is, no doubt, telling everyone around the coffee machine about his eventful weekend, with a huge emphasis on him in a James Bond lead role. Jean is cooking something for Jason in preparation for them having a big talk, so that could go one of many ways. And Miss Chambers is no doubt wiping off the voodoo doll of me, ready to go back to the normality of sticking pins in every which way she can. Bless her.

"It seems almost too easy and obvious," Jason said, having read the manual twice. Harry was looking over the walkie-talkie a couple times in his hands. "This is a little different from the prototype, but the thing I don't get is the large box it gets plugged into?"

I looked around the room. There was nothing that either looked that big, or that could carry the sort of energy required. And then I saw it.

The large two-door cupboard looking like some sort of wardrobe. It was so big that you actually didn't see it for looking. Hidden out in plain view, which couldn't be any more typical of my father.

Jason saw me looking. "Yes!" he said, "that was it; the cupboard was open!" He went over and opened up the doors. Inside, it looked a bit like a small elevator with a large control panel, a keyboard, a chair, and a large screen. Cutting edge for seven or more years ago. "There's where your money went, boys!" Harry laughed.

"Yeah, a fancy man-cave for my father to sit and watch Super Sunday Football!" Jason grinned at this. "Money well spent, I'd say!"

"What's this?" Harry said, pointing to a folder.

"Another manual," I said.

"Not just a manual," Harry said as he flicked through. We went silent as he was looking. "I'm, er, I'm not sure what I am looking at here. Ed, tell me what you see?"

I looked and saw a bunch of pictures. And then I realised just what it was that I was seeing.

"That's my dad and my brother," I said. "But my dad looks too old for it to have been at that time when my brother was alive."

"Maybe he was just not his best that day," Jason added.

"Look at the paper," Harry added, shaking his head. My father was holding a paper and smiling. It was a copy of the local newspaper *The Evening Advertiser*; I could just make out the date, although I didn't need to. The picture, type setting, and adverts told me that it was within the last few years, and my brother had been dead for over 25 years. The strength went from my legs, and I slumped down onto the chair.

"What?" Jason said.

"Gordon is holding a recent newspaper and stands smiling with Ed's dead brother."

"Photoshopped?" Jason said.

"It's possible," I agreed. "But we also have to think that with everything that we know, there is also another scary scenario." Harry was with me there. He looked at the wardrobe-turned-elevator-turned-control centre and said, "We cannot overlook the possibility that your dad has built a time machine."

"Get the fuck out of here," Jason eloquently replied, but the cogs in his brain were turning. "How can you- I mean, how is it possible to- Shit!"

"I'm not going to jump to any conclusions," I said. "But if – and that is a big if – if the walkie-talkies work, then we have to understand that there is a possibility that he did manage to design and create a time machine. Professor Stephen Hawking has not dismissed the possibility of time travel, and has talked in great detail about it."

"Yes, but that is about wormholes and the such like, not an actual time capsule machine," Harry said. "I believe in God and the such like, but this is all getting a bit too much, even for me."

So we connected up the walkie-talkie and followed the instructions, adding codes, pressing buttons, waiting for the small electronic room to power up. Then finally having added a date from back in 1985, I dubiously typed in the telephone to this very house. Part of me expected to hear the telephone ring from above me, but it did not. However, on the other end of the walkie-talkie, we could all hear the phone ring.

And then it was answered.

A small voice full of beans said, "Good afternoon. Welcome to the circus. I am the ringmaster!"

That voice caught me completely by surprise. "Hello? Who is this?" I then lost my grip and dropped the handset with a clang as it hit the control panel. I picked it up just in time to hear the response:

"Edward," he said. "Who are you?" Jason and Harry both looked at each other in complete shock at what they were hearing.

"A friend," was all that I could think to say, and then I quickly added. "Is Ben there?" And at that point, the same conversation came flooding back as it had when I was a boy.

"Nope. He's off with some girl. He should be back either later *or tomorrow-*"

"*If he got lucky*," I said at the same time as he did. Then, "Jinx!" Exactly as the other person had done to me all of those years ago. There was a pause again, and then he was gone.

"Bloody Hell!" I said, completely confused. "I just spoke to myself! My nine-year-old self!"

"It turns out that your old man is a genius," Jason said.

"So where the fuck is he, then?" And that was the burning question that would most likely go with me to my grave.

And then the walkie-talkie crackled, and an orange light on top flashed a couple of times before we suddenly heard static, which turned into a voice.

"Ed? That you?" the voice of my father said.

"Dad?" I replied. Jason and Harry were once again exchanging puzzled looks.

"Took you a while to finally use this thing, huh?" I nodded, and then realised that he couldn't see me nodding like an idiot.

"Uh, yeah. I think I might've just spoken to myself in the past." He gave a loud roar of laughter that rolled back the years. My father didn't laugh very often, but when he did, the sound that came out suggested that he really enjoyed it.

"Yep, more than likely, son. I've been waiting for my machine here to tell me when you used it, and here we are! I have to say, though, I'm struggling to get through on mobile phones though. Not quite got there yet."

"This is a lot to take in," I said.

"Thought it might be." And then there was silence.

"Dad?" I said, but there was nothing.

And then the doors of the wardrobe slowly shut like they were on some mechanism. A noise like a server working overtime started up, and I pictured a bank of small computer fans busy trying to stop the machine from overheating. Then there was the sound of a crackle.

And then silence. I might've expected smoke, but there was none.

The three of us stood there with jaws dropping towards the floor as the wardrobe was opened by someone from the inside....

Acknowledgements

A big thank you to my wife and children who know sometimes I am extremely focused on writing. And forget about them. Sorry about that.

A huge thanks to the members of *Jim Ody's Spooky Circus* - my street team, and specifically my group of advisors Simon, Angela, AJ, Cheryl, Dee, Terry and Ellie who listen to all my crazy ideas and advise me whether or not they are worth pursuing!

Thank you to Caroline, David and Jason for your continued support. Also, to Andy Barrett, Maggie James, Caitlin, Sarah Hardy, Valerie, Bella James, and Kerry who also try to steer me in the right direction. Or try.

A special mention to Emmy Ellis @ studioenp for her wonderful design direction.

As ever a huge thank you to all of the editors working tirelessly to make my meanderings be able to be enjoyed. Especially to Shelagh who is also another personal advisor. I don't always listen, but she is still there shaking her head at me, ready for my next maverick idea.

And finally thank you to you, the readers. For reading, for enjoying, and for getting behind me. Without you there would really be no point!

ABOUT THE AUTHOR

Jim writes dark psychological/thrillers that have endings you won't see coming, and favours stories packed with wit. He has written eight novels and over a dozen short-stories spanning many genres.

Jim has a very strange sense of humour and is often considered a little odd. When not writing he will be found playing the drums, watching football and eating chocolate. He lives with his long-suffering wife, three beautiful children and two indignant cats in Swindon, Wiltshire UK.

Connect with Jim Ody here:

Facebook: www.facebook.com/JimOdyAuthor

Jim Ody's Spooky Circus Street Team: https://www.facebook.com/groups/1372500609494122/

Amazon Author Link: https://www.amazon.co.uk/Jim-Ody/e/B019A6AMSY/

Email: jim.ody@hotmail.co.uk

Twitter: @Jim_Ody_Author

Instagram: @jimodyauthor

Pintrest: https://www.pinterest.co.uk/jimodyauthor/

Bookbub: https://www.bookbub.com/profile/jim-ody

Want to read more books by this author?

Here are details of three more books for you to get your hands on!

The Place That Never Existed

For Paul and Debbie it was meant to be the happiest time of their lives.

A small village wedding in front of their family and friends, followed by a quiet honeymoon in Devon. Not everyone had been happy to see them together. A woman from their past refused to accept it. Her actions over the previous year had ended in tragedy, and had almost broken the happy couple apart.

Now, away from it all in a picturesque log cabin, Paul and Debbie look forward to time spent alone together... But she has found out where they are, and she will stop at nothing to make sure that the marriage is over... forever.

But Huntswood Cove isn't just a beautiful Devonshire fishing town, it has its own secret. Recently, people have begun to disappear, only to turn up dead in suspicious circumstances. The locals begin to question what is going on. Soon everything strange points to the abandoned house in the woods.

The house that nobody wants to talk about. To them, it is the place that never existed.

?

Question Mark Press

Beneath The Whispers

Scotty Dean didn't expect to run into his childhood sweetheart deep in the woods. Especially having just been dumped by a woman well out of his league.

But Mary-Ann needs him to get back a USB stick that has fallen into the wrong hands. He knows he shouldn't get involved, but as old feelings resurface, so do the hidden secrets.

His past collides with the present and Scotty is surrounded by whispering voices – but what is it they're trying to say?

?

Question Mark Press

A Cold Retreat

As a child, Penny dreams of being a princess. She knows life isn't exactly like fairy tales, but she hopes it can be similar.

The future isn't so kind to Penny. The princess in her reality turn out to be evil. Battered and bruised she hits rock bottom.

Years have passed but the past cannot be forgotten. Now someone is intent on making the men pay for what they have done.

This is a chilling tale of revenge that explores the impact of not being able to say no.

?

Question Mark Press

Printed in Poland
by Amazon Fulfillment
Poland Sp. z o.o., Wrocław